Dedalus Original Fiction in Paperback

PLEADING GUILTY

Paul Genney, after leaving Bristol University, worked as a
dentist for six years before becoming a potato merchant. He
stood unsuccessfully twice for parliament in the 1980s before
becoming a criminal barrister.

He now divides his time between his homes in Grimsby and
London and his chambers in Hull.

Pleading Guilty is his first novel.

Paul Genney

Pleading Guilty

Dedalus

Published in the UK by Dedalus Ltd,
24–26, St Judith's Lane, Sawtry, Cambs, PE28 5XE
email: info@dedalusbooks.com
www.dedalusbooks.com

ISBN 978 1 903517 57 4

Dedalus is distributed in the USA by SCB Distributors,
15608 South New Century Drive, Gardena, CA 90248
email: info@scbdistributors.com   web: www.scbdistributors.com

Dedalus is distributed in Australia by Peribo Pty Ltd.
58, Beaumont Road, Mount Kuring-gai, N.S.W. 2080
email: info@peribo.com.au

Dedalus is distributed in Canada by Disticor Direct-Book Division
695, Westney Road South, Suite 14, Ajax, Ontario, LI6 6M9
email: ndalton@disticor.com   web: www.disticordirect.com

First published by Dedalus in 2007
Pleading Guilty copyright © Paul Genney 2007

Typeset by RefineCatch Limited, Bungay, Suffolk
Printed in Finland by WS Bookwell

A C.I.P. listing for this book is available on request.

For Paula. The Light of my Life

Chapter 1

I stood watching our cleaner shining up the brass plate outside the door. He was working his way down the long list of names using a yellow duster which he occasionally moistened with his lips.

It must have been something in the saliva – the brass danced like gold as it caught the morning sun.

"Come on, come on . . ." I put an arm around his shoulder and squeezed him closer. "I know you did it only last week, but nothing lasts forever – and there's an awful lot of bottles on the floor . . ."

He turned to me and began scratching at the elastic bands he wore round the sleeves of his shirt. "Anything for you Mr Wallace. Just as soon as I've finished this."

"Don't bother with the environment," I told him. "Just chuck everything in the bin." I swung my red bag over my shoulder. "Oh . . . and I don't suppose you could polish my car as well?"

I like being neat and tidy. Gives a good impression. Clean white shirt, immaculate stiff collar, shiny shoes, starched and fluttering bands. And now a gleaming car.

I strode into chambers and gave Doreen, our receptionist, an affectionate pat on the head. "Morning Doreen. No messages; no appointments; no visits to prison. Nothing. After court I'm off for an early lunch." I lit up another cigarette as she winced and looked away.

"And where's Giles? He said he had something to say."

"He's in his room," she told me, "with Mr Jackson. I think they're having a row."

Not again. There's always something. Giles, our newly elected head of chambers, trying to enforce what he sees as discipline. Our senior clerk, Jackson, sticking up for what he thinks is right.

I ran up the stairs and threw open Giles's door.

"What do you want? We're having a meeting."

Giles seemed exasperated. He stood in the middle of his room, bursting out of his waistcoat, wagging a finger and trying to control his blood pressure.

"For Christ's sake. Do you have to smoke? I think we should bring in a rule."

"Not another one we don't. We've got enough as it is." I looked across at Jackson who was lolling indolently, half-sitting on the edge of Giles's desk. He winked back and produced a cigar.

"We're having a discussion . . ." he remarked, "about my expense account. Mr Baring here seems to think I spend too much."

"No . . . no Giles . . . no . . . . Let's not be hasty . . . Jackson has to entertain to bring in work."

"Entertain! You call this entertaining?" He reached into the pocket of his well-filled trousers and struggled to produce a slip of paper. "A thousand pounds in under a month!"

"Add it up," I suggested, "that makes, let me see, twelve thousand pounds a year. Chickenfeed! Count the numbers in these chambers. Fifteen doing crime. Half a dozen in family. One or two pretending to do civil. McIntosh a specialist in drains. That makes . . ."

"Twenty four." Jackson told me.

"Yes. Divide that into twelve thousand. Comes to . . ."

"Call it £500?" said Jackson.

"Yes. Now take off tax. I assume at 40%. That makes . . ."

Jackson spread his hands and smiled."About £300. Works out at about a 'fiver' a week. Oddly enough the approximate price of a packet of cigarettes. And what are you getting? Lots of lovely work. Which in my opinion wouldn't other-wise come in. I have to take out people, and I have to treat them when I do. Runners, solicitors, the odd shandy for the C.P.S. It's called entertaining – getting to know our clients and making them our friends. And now. If you've finally finished . . ." He carefully buttoned up his jacket and brushed down the lapels. ". . . If you'll excuse me. I've got an appointment at ten."

He walked off down the passage and whistled as he went down the stairs. We waited as he paused to bark at Doreen – deliberately loudly so we could hear.

"I'll be back at four."

"This is insufferable." Giles turned his moonface round to me. "Oh for God's sake, don't light another one . . . I'm bloody head of chambers, not him. I should be taking out solicitors and clients . . ." He wafted his podgy hands at the smoke. "I should have a special account." A thought struck him. "And how do we know what he is spending our money on? Does he ever put in a list of expenses? I can tell you. No he does not. Probably spends it on himself."

"No . . . No Giles . . . no." I was getting tired of saying this. I tried to soothe him. ". . . Wait till chambers meeting. Think about a special fund for you."

I looked round at his tawdry surroundings. The peeling paint, his overflowing wastepaper basket, the piles of correspondence, his soiled shirts and collars thrown in a corner, the one solitary brief cringing on his blotter. Rows of dusty books stacked on woodchip shelves that stretched from ceiling to floor. Halsbury's Statutes; The All England Reports; Atkins Precedents on Pleadings; Current Law. Did he read all this stuff? Where did he find the time? And what was the point if he did?

"Come on Giles." He was sat now, slumped at his desk. "Come on. You won't be long in court. Why not take me to lunch?"

Why not? What else was there to do? Come back from court and go to my room – my now immaculate room – and sit looking at a brief? Finally take off the ribbon and try to read the case. Make a few desultory notes. Nod off to sleep. Put in a bill for my work. Go downstairs and try to chat up Doreen. Listen to her boring bloody tales, all the time looking at the big black clock ticking away on the wall with its Roman numerals and filigree hands (I could describe it in detail). Finally giving in and going outside into the winding cobbled lane and pretending to be about some business or other striding purposefully away until, at the last minute, ducking into a passage and cutting through to the Stag at Bay to find Jackson – now at least four pints ahead of me – conducting his own bloody court.

And up on the bar pints and empty bottles, dirty plates stacked on a chair, a packet of cigars in his breast pocket, his arm round my shoulders, the barmaid leaning over ready to top up his glass.

No. I don't think we need a list of 'expenses'. I think we know where they went. With me, and McIntosh, and occasionally another chum Humphrey whiling away happy hours laughing at the generosity of the rest – until Jackson red-faced and tottering finally decided to go back to chambers, and having struggled out of his jacket, and found his half-moon glasses, would look up the court lists and dole out the work.

"Lunch?" Giles looked up miserably. "Why should I take you to lunch?" He recovered his lonely brief and felt the weight in his hands. "This job's fucked," he muttered. It's what we always say. Perhaps this time we're right.

I remembered when the previous head of chambers had finally retired, and the competition to step in his shoes. Giles had promised 'efficiency' a 'cap on expenditure', a 'thorough audit of the books'. It had an ominous ring. But chambers went for it. Members saw expenses reducing, and less for them to pay. Giles won in a landslide and set about his task. He stopped smoking and has grown fatter and more useless ever since – delving into things that don't concern him, forever rocking chambers' boat. I don't like it. I don't believe in it. Why change a system that was working – to bring in something else? But it's done now. And Giles keeps telling anyone who'll listen he is 'bound by his manifesto commitments' to set everything to rights.

"Come on Giles . . . come on."

But the intercom interrupted with Doreen's unmistakable whine, "I've got Mrs Baring on the line . . ."

"Oh for Christ's sake . . ." everything seemed to irritate him, ". . . tell her I'm out. Tell her I've already left for court." He prised himself out of his chair. "Let's get out of here before I choke."

He threw his brief into one of those stupid shopping trolleys that people seem to use these days and staggered down the stairs into reception where Doreen was still talking to his wife and, (seeming to forget that he was supposed to have already left) announced, "Mrs Baring says she won't be home till six."

"Oh for Christ's sake." He pushed open our heavy oak door and we realised for the first time that McIntosh was waiting for us in the street.

Tall, elegant, and enviably slim he was leaning against the wall with some briefs bound up in the cord of his robing bag. I quickly counted five. Although we belong to the same chambers we are all independent; driven to actively compete. We share expenses – the rent; rates; the staff. The money I make I keep. But don't think work comes to me for excellence; the way I perform in court. It doesn't. It comes in, if it does come in, because of our head clerk, Jackson, and the way he pushes it, if he does push it, sometimes my way sometimes not. Or is it the way I ingratiate myself with solicitors or their runners or the way I get on with punters or the general luck of the draw?

There's really no way of telling. I wonder why I try.

"Ready are we?" McIntosh looked around him at the fresh summer day and the angled sunlight already beginning to warm our narrow cobbled lane. "I've got a busy day."

And with that we were off – McIntosh and I swinging our bags, and Giles pulling his trolley behind. We turned into Town Hall Square to the usual bunch of demonstrators – were they the same as last week? – clustered at the foot of the Town Hall steps waving their placards at the sky.

A man was pacing backwards and forwards at the front shouting into a megaphone, "What do we want? What do we want?"

"What do we want? What do we want?" his supporters chorused back. A lorry accelerating away from the lights drowned out the reply. Nothing special I supposed. More money and a little respect.

McIntosh sauntered across.

"What do we want? What do we want?" they started the old refrain.

He leant down towards the man with the megaphone confidentially. As if trying to be helpful, his voice in that penetrating way of his carried across the square.

"New anoraks would be nice."

He turned to laugh with Giles as I hurried to catch them up. I could hear their voices wafting back. Confident, slightly affected, voices. Voices used to cross-examine a witness, persuade a jury, swing a judge. Seduce another man's wife. Barristers. Trial Counsels. Gladiators in the arena but not their blood in the sand.

They waited for me at the flight of steps leading up to court. Our court. The Combined Court Centre. A new building to replace the Old Quarter Sessions with its ancient oak panelling and pointed metal railing round the dock.

'A new court for a new millennium' according to the fool who opened it; with its open plan courtrooms and cheap furniture; its limited use of stone facing and one – out of proportion – dome, sitting almost floating, semi-detached on the top.

"Harry. Listen to this." Giles seemed to be cheering up. Waiting by the invalid ramp, he wanted to get in on the act. "Have you heard the one about the old lag?"

Had I heard it? Of course I had. Everybody had. Many many times. I squinted up into the sun.

"This old lag. Must have been seventy if he was a day. Up before Irvine in York. Done another string of burglaries. Judge gave him fourteen years."

'I'll never do it. I'll never do it.' Giles mimicked an old man wringing his hands.

"Irvine told him . . . do as much as you can."

And they ran up the last flight of steps (avoiding a crouching circle of smokers sharing their last cigarette) and pausing at the top, polite at last, but only to each other, still laughing, they disappeared inside. I stood watching the glass doors slowly swinging. Sometimes I loathe this job. Whingeing punters. Wading through the opaque Crown Court bureaucracy with its silly targets and figures. Inane listing, truculent ushers, and lying police.

It's like going down a pit. All day in artificial lighting struggling to think of sensible questions, wrestling with legal argument, trying to dream up a speech. Listening to the moaning of a punter; avoiding his anxious relatives; dodging the criticism of a judge.

So why do it? And why, of all places, do it here?

Take a look at my card. Nicely set out in thick embossed lettering. 'Henry Wallace. Barrister-at-law', known as 'Harry' to his friends. One or two tried 'Wally'. But what sort of friends call you 'Wally'? I'll tell you. Friends who don't get a reply.

So 'Harry' Wallace a member of Whitebait Chambers – the only Chambers in Hull, or should I say Kingston Upon Hull? Because Hull is the name of a river. A muddy oily slick with the ramshackle city spreading out on either side of its slippery banks. But Kingston doesn't suit. Not the land of a million council houses and one ridiculous fort. Not the permanent home to bomb-sites, gutted buildings, and litter driven by cold winds off the North Sea bowling past you as you hurry down the street. One miserable market and pasty faces queuing up outside the dole.

I'd wanted London. The Middle Temple or Lincoln's Inn. Ancient stone and wisteria. A little evening's croquet. Popping in and out of the Old Bailey, a flat in Chelsea, poncing up and down the Kings Road. But that's not as easy as it sounds. Too many barristers chasing too little work.

Look a little further down my card. In smaller type. 'Specialist in Crime'. There's a rich vein of crime in Northern England and I've traced the mother lode to Hull. This is where the work is – the drug-crazed, binge-drinking, sex-mad, inbred, punch-drunk lunatics. A cancer of the estates whatever the Government may say. Breeding with all the profligacy and taste that only a cultural desert can bring.

Ignore solicitors, forget Jackson, put aside the luck of the draw. Meet my friends the punters. The beginning of the food chain. The men who really bring me work. My clients. My business and my pleasure. Read the final line, the small print at the bottom.

It gives you my telephone number and tells you when to call.

Don't tell me crime doesn't pay — it pays very well for me.

Chapter 2

I saw her as soon as I got through the door.

God. She was nice. Not bad at all. Short blonde hair. Very short, cropped hair really; probably dyed. I prefer it that way. Long neck; nice head; slightly shifty eyes.

She was tilted back on a chair near the window – bag on her knee, file on the floor, slowly swinging a foot.

I circled round to get a better look.

Pushing my way through the crowd of people studying the Court Lists, looking for their solicitor, asking for their barrister, trying to control their children, wondering whether to plead guilty or not guilty, wondering whether just to call it a day and fight their way back outside.

But who was this woman? Never seen her face before, she didn't look like a punter; more the air of an official.

Maybe a solicitor. Or a solicitor's 'runner'. More likely a witness. An expert witness perhaps. But an expert in what?

I leant against a column and lit a cigarette.

Hidden by the crowd I studied her carefully, twenty yards away, from the side. Short straight nose. Slightly protuberant lips. A lovely, almost classical profile – with an arched and elegant neck. She held herself well. I watched her breathe, her heavy chest rising and falling within what I could now see was a smart but well-worn, and almost certainly cheap, suit. Shoes were expensive though. I watched the swinging foot. Black, very soft leather with high heels and a slight lattice on the top. Probably Italian. Probably size six.

I edged forward. Large hands. Who cares about that? So far as I could see – no ring. And yes, I could just make it out, a straight row of tiny black roots.

I walked behind her and could almost touch the nape of her neck. She was reading a solicitor's file – the ones in a brown manila folder. Having produced a pair of glasses from her bag she was squinting at the pages with those tiny thoughtful eyes. Probably a party in a civil case. She looked too refined to be submerged in anything criminal. My spirits rose. Maybe a divorce case. Maybe she's getting divorced. But then that meant almost certainly she was involved with somebody new. Somebody else. Hanging around with some rich boyfriend. Somebody who could afford expensive shoes. But then, why the cheap suit?

I started to mentally undress her. The shape of her breasts; the width of her thighs.

I felt a tugging at my sleeve. "Mr Wallace, Mr Wallace, you're wanted." A bossy female usher started to pull me away. "They've called your case on in court."

She caught the line of my eye.

"Come on. The judge is waiting on the bench." So I got changed and went in, but I might as well not have bothered. I hadn't seen the punter and didn't know what he'd done. Was he pleading guilty or not guilty? I hadn't the time to find out.

The clerk read out the indictment. A string of dwelling-house burglaries – and from somewhere behind me a faint voice answered 'guilty' to every count.

Judge Irvine was sitting.

"Ah, Mr Wallace. Do you want to adjourn for a probation report?"

Who knows? I didn't. I turned to look at the punter and he miserably shook his head. That was a quick conference.

"No thank you," I told His Honour, "he wants to be dealt with now."

So I sat back and half-listened to the prosecution opening the case and finally stood to mitigate – the usual platitudes – has pleaded guilty at the earliest opportunity, has co-operated with the police, demonstrated genuine remorse. Wife, girl-friend, whatever, standing by him. Children waiting patiently in the wings. Means to give up the drugs.

Was it true? Was any of it? Who knows? Who cares? The sentence already pencilled in, I hadn't time for any of this nonsense, my mind was wandering off elsewhere.

"Thank you Mr Wallace. As ever concise. Stand up . . ." he

told the punter, "Very serious offences – take him down. Five years."

And I was off again leaving a bewildered punter wondering who it was I'd been talking about. He could have done it better himself.

And she was still there. Still rhythmically swinging a foot, now blowing smoke through those rather elegant nostrils. An excellent sign. There's nothing more sexy than tobacco on a woman's hot breath.

I stood looking at her. Nonchalant, relaxed, indifferent to the crowd ebbing and flowing around her. Waiting for something. Waiting for somebody. Waiting for somebody else.

"Mr Wallace. Mr Wallace." Another usher pulling at my gown. "You're wanted in Court Number three."

I looked back over my shoulder. I had to get to know her. I had to get her name.

But of course there's always the odd little problem. I had been happily married to Laura for thirty years. And I was wanted, rather urgently, in court.

Chapter 3

I bounced back onto the concourse after another memorable performance and, still there! The foot still rhythmically swinging, still surrounded by the eddying mob of burglars and petty thieves, drug addicts, drug dealers, dirty old men, dirty young men, maniacs behind the wheels of cars – drunken driving, dangerous driving, causing death by dangerous driving, causing death by drunken driving – a hundred different ways to cause death. Cruelty to children, abuse of children, abandonment of children, neglect of your child, paedophiles and gropers, homosexuals in public, buggery and rape.

Still there! Still elegantly dangling her file.

The Social Security fiddlers, handlers and robbers, armed robbers, breaches of public order, violent disorder, riot and affray, the punching, kicking and glassing, grievous bodily harm and the rest. All seething around her. Tattoos, earrings, nose-rings, shaven heads, dyed and tufted heads, ringlets, dreadlocks, a million baseball caps. The punters. Who are these people? They've turned into another tribe.

And the children. Why bring kids to court? Little miniatures of themselves. The same haircuts, the same clothes, the same identical piercing – little diamante studs in their dirty little ears. Running about, knocking down ashtrays; dropping wrappers; spilling drink.

The cleaners earn their money in this place. At the end of the day when the great doors finally swing shut, they wend their way through crisp packets, sweet wrappers, fag ends, even polythene trays and plastic knives and forks. They dust and hoover, and wipe away hand marks on the wall.

Needles on the stairs, syringes in the lavatory. Always, invariably, blocked.

A funny farm without the fun, run by idiots according to idiot rules.

I must be an idiot to care.

A Palace of Lies where sometimes punters answer their bail and sometimes Group Four (Global Solutions as they now like to be called), get their prisoners to court on time (even sometimes the right prisoners) where the evidence is sometimes ready and occasionally – very occasionally – the Crown Prosecution Service makes sense.

What brought her to court? What role in this circus was she expecting to play?

She was, in fact, a Legal Executive for Carter Cramner & Co. Solicitors of Kingston Upon Hull.

In other words, a runner. Freddie Platten (Cranmer's office boy) pointed her out. "Over there. The blonde. Pushing forty." Not the description that would have fallen from my lips. For a minute I thought he was talking about somebody else.

"What's she like?" I asked casually. In fact I could see what she was like. What I really wanted to know was, is she married? Does she have a boyfriend? Is she spoken for? As they say these days, does she have a partner? Is she in a relationship? More importantly, is she attracted to thin, chain-smoking barristers? Pushing sixty as Freddy might say.

"Not bad," Freddy told me, "only started yesterday. Doesn't know much. A bit thick, but Mr Tomkinson likes her."

Mr Tomkinson, Solicitor of the Supreme Court of England and Wales, and Head of the Criminal Department at Cranmers. Freddy's immediate boss. In fact everybody's immediate boss. The man who hires and fires at Cranmers. The man who sends his criminal work to Chambers. The man who decides which particular favoured barrister of the moment will have his name printed on the front of a brief.

Famous for his sneering snide sense of humour and his fruitless pursuit of love. There are those who try to avoid him.

I try to avoid him myself. I find it a strain trying to laugh at his jokes. Freddy doesn't have the same problem. His job depends on it.

"You two should get on all right," Freddy continued, "just show her what to do."

"I will, Freddy, I will." I patted his curly head. "She'll be fine with me." And then I said it. I didn't mean to, but I did. "Don't you think she's rather nice?"

Whatever else Freddy might be, he's not dumb. He gave me a glance.

"Not bad, I suppose, not bad. Not bad if you like middle-aged women that is. If you don't mind them knocking on a bit so to speak."

Knocking on a bit? Knocking on a bit? Come on Freddy, my eldest daughter's nearly that. At my age, forty is beginning to sound young.

"Name's Pauline Dawson by the way. Mrs Pauline Dawson." And that radar set within his mind detected that somewhere, somehow Mr Tomkinson was looking for him, had noticed his absence; was wondering what was taking so long, and Freddy was away, running, so as to be by the great man's side, and ready to hang on his every word – ready to laugh at his jokes.

I pushed my way through the crowd and introduced myself.

"Henry Wallace." I held out my hand.

"I think I'm with you."

She looked up and smiled. White even teeth (as it turns out not entirely her own).

"So you're Mr Wally?" she enquired.

Let it pass. Just for today.

"Wallace." I shot her a winning smile.

I was going to be especially charming. Debonair. Amusing. Tall. Good looking. Young. I would be anything. Do anything. Go anywhere for this girl. Go to the end of the world.

"So now what?" She put her glasses back in her bag. "Where do we go?"

"Why don't we go to the cells?"

She stood up and smoothed her skirt. We were about the same size. Maybe she gave me an inch. She bent over and stubbed out her cigarette in an ashtray. Perfect. Thin and slightly muscular legs.

"So what's the routine?" She was smiling again. "Mr Tomkinson said I should follow you."

So she should and so she will.

"Well, there is a set procedure." I thought I would take my time. "Every morning the prison van rolls up and delivers the punters. They want the lavatory. Or they want a cigarette. They want to see their papers or their girlfriend or their mates. Above all they want to be free.

So we go down to the cells to have a conference. What we do is make them see sense."

"Mr Tomkinson said we take instructions."

"No we don't. We give instructions. I tell them what to do."

My mind went back to happier days when runners were invariably retired policemen. Hard as nails and heard it all before.

"Don't give me the one about your look-alike brother. Nor the one about going to the lavatory on the roof. Come on. Not the one about finding the door open and going in to see if everything's all right. Don't tell me you were holding the gun for a mate.

I know you're guilty. Mr Wallace here knows you're guilty. You know you're guilty. And that's what you're going to say." And away to the pub before twelve.

Where are they now?

No doubt tending their allotments by the railway line. Or living in a bungalow in the middle of nowhere in Spain. Grey hair, white shorts, brown legs and arguing with the wife. These days runners are mostly women. Daft do-gooders with a touching belief in their clients. Worried, concerned, and stupid. Every last bit of barmy instructions written down. Every last ridiculous story believed, pens poised, faces etched with real concern.

"I've got a girlfriend. She's standing by me."

"I've got a job. I could start tomorrow."

"I'm a student. I'm on a course."

"What drugs? It's a plant."

"I wasn't there. If I was there, I didn't do it. If I did do it, it was an accident. If it wasn't an accident it was self-defence."

Ever onwards. Eternal excuses. Every last word recorded by the runner. The detailed jottings of a tiny mind.

I looked for the hundredth time at Mrs Dawson. Her first

21

day with a clean notepad ready. She gave me a confident smile. So I signed us both through 'Security' and once inside the cell area entered our names on the Register of Official Visitors noticing (not for the first time) that Donald Duck had already paid a call.

"Right Mr er . . ." I shot a look at my brief, "Mr Turner. Mr Turner it is." I tried to ignore his love bites, "You were found with the stolen property in a black bin-liner two minutes after the burglary took place.

It was three in the morning and, apart from your goodself, the streets were deserted.

You dropped your gloves and tried to hide the bin-liner by throwing it over a garden wall, and the police, more observant than usual, unfortunately saw it all.

You ran away and put up a fight when caught.

You bit a police officer through his blue serge uniform and your teeth penetrated the skin of his arm.

When interviewed you exercised your right to silence and to each question – no doubt on the advice of your solicitor – said 'No Comment' every time.

So for God's sake, let's stop fucking around and plead guilty."

Mr Turner leant forward in his chair, looking to me for salvation.

What a waste of time, I've been here before. Too many times. And so turning to the more sympathetic cast of Mrs Dawson's eye began, "I swear on my bairn's life . . ."

I sensed rather than saw Mrs Dawson's pen rise. Apparently, the note-taking starts here. But best start as we intend to proceed.

"Don't bother with that," I told her. "We don't need a record of this."

"But Mr Tomkinson told me to," she persisted. "He said it's very important to take proper instructions. Write them down. Get everything down. It helps the barrister."

"Not me it doesn't."

Just relax. Relax and enjoy yourself. Watch the Master at work.

"So what's the story then? The one you wouldn't or couldn't tell the police," I continued. "The one when you were interviewed you hadn't yet made up. The one you and your cell mates think's so fucking good."

Nothing like boosting his confidence and making him feel at home.

"Well I was walking the dog," he started again. (What dog? A dog has never featured before).

"A bloke carrying a bin-liner came up to me. Unfortunately I can't describe him. I have never seen him before. He asked me to hold it for him so, naturally, I did. At that very moment the police appeared. They were everywhere. Understandably I panicked and stupidly ran away. They were violent towards me. I was only defending myself. It's police brutality. It's all a big mistake."

"Yes and you're making it. Any idea what happened to the mystery man who gave you the bin-liner? Did he say, perchance, why he was giving it to you? Why did you take it? What were you going to do with it? Does it often happen that perfect strangers come up to you in the middle of the night and give you the proceeds of a burglary? And what steps have you taken to trace this offender who has got you into so much trouble? Have you got your mates, at the local pub for example, to ask around as to who he might be? Did the police by any chance come across anybody's prints in the house or on the bin-liner? Apart from yours. What happened to the 'look-out'? Did he leave you and run?

And, come to that, what happened to the fucking dog?"

I got the distinct feeling that our Mrs Dawson was not going along with this. Did I detect a faint sigh? A worried frown? A nervous jiffle? Fortunately she couldn't write fast.

"Look, stop fucking about. You've got fifty previous convictions – most of them for burglary. You know the score. Put yourself on the jury. What would you think?"

The reality is in this busy world I haven't time to hold his hand. Come to that, nor the inclination, my eyes drawn to the offending marks on his neck.

"Just plead fucking guilty. I've got an urgent appointment at one."

"All right Mr Wallace. You've persuaded me, but what do you think I'll get?"

The perpetual question. There is some consistency in this world after all. This is all the punter wants or needs to know, and I am going to tell him.

"Looking at your record – four, four and a half. Any more we might appeal."

I sat back in my chair and waited.

The moment of truth. Would he go for it? A little bit of money for me. Or rather a lot. Mrs Dawson hadn't the slightest idea what was going on. She thought we were trying to do justice. I knew I was trying to make some money. If this case went off for trial, I may be too busy to do it and may never see it again. Better a modest fee in the hand, than a larger one in the bush.

"Try and keep it under five. I'm happy with that. Do your best for me Mr Wallace. Don't forget I've got a job waiting. My girlfriend's pregnant. She's standing by me. I've given up the drugs. I know you'll do your best."

I most certainly will. Trust me I'm a barrister. And in the fullness of time and with a fair wind and good fortune may it please God I will do the same for Mrs Dawson who, I saw, had crumpled up her piece of paper and thrown it on the floor.

Chapter 4

Laura and I had been together thirty years. Thirty years of total pleasure, twenty five of them married. She was a lovely girl. Black hair and green eyes. Wonderfully kind. The best mother in the world to five children and countless others of their friends – many of whom stayed for months (one girl four years) in a large Victorian house overlooking the park that had been our home since the day we married all those years ago. She had furnished it from salesrooms with heavy Edwardian furniture. Large tables and large chairs; some intricately carved and now grown valuable, others less so and accordingly worth much less. Many bits and pieces still worth nothing. Not to others, but everything to her. And the pictures. The walls covered in prints, in oils, in water-colours. Still lifes and the odd view of the Lincolnshire Wolds. One oil of Lake Tanganyika, as it then was, of a hollowed-out boat and its crew waiting motionless for dawn. Some by Laura herself. She denied her talent but she had it, or at least to my untrained eye she had. For me she could do anything.

She was a wonderful cook, natural and instinctive. Cuisine from around the world.

"Indian tonight? Chinese? A bit of both?"

And all of this twenty five years ago when foreign foods were just beginning to penetrate London and light years away from Hull.

Laura bought (and sometimes tried to grow) herbs. She invested in books. She was the proud possessor of a pestle and mortar, a mandolin, a tongue press, a bain-marie, a fish kettle and a hachinette. She would take on anything. Pork pies, chitterlings in white sauce, round Christmas puddings boiled between 2 large white basins held together with a knotted tea towel. Béarnaise, Béchamel, Hollandaise, fricassees of game, cassoulet, pastas, paella, purees, poppadums, and pies. She even had an ancient wooden butter churn – but never managed butter.

If only someone, somehow, somewhere, had discovered her. She could have been a T.V. chef. One with actual personality. She was quick and she was funny. A natural star forever languishing in our forgotten kitchen where cooking would start sometime around midday, and by 5 o'clock, after the first bottle of wine and twenty cigarettes or so later, would still be nowhere near completion and still hours to go before the final triumphant pissed-up presentation to a kitchen full of family, dogs, cats and friends.

Happy days. Gone forever.

I often came home late, but there were reasons. Laura always waited. Sitting in the same chair by the long kitchen table, the lights turned low. A bottle opened and a glass waiting. A cigarette in her lovely lips and the phone cocked under her chin.

I felt the usual surge of pleasure seeing her there. The reassurance of a base, the welcome of a friend. And we were off,

"You'll never guess what happened today." I couldn't wait to tell her.

Her slow deep voice in reply, "Fuck that. The bank's been on again. And no . . . . no we have not received £25 from the Community Chest. Where does all the fucking money go?"

I suppose scrutiny of the ashtrays, empty bottles, and scattered broken toys might have provided a clue. But this was the best home in the world and the best woman in the world. A home at which, in those days, I was still welcome. But I knew the bank was beginning to drive her mad. They had been on to her for months. Phone calls, letters, trips to see the manager. I couldn't understand why it was worth their while to chase her tiny overdrawn account with such pitiless determination when they had lost millions lending money in the city to their friends.

I suppose they had to get it back from somewhere. They were finding it hard to get it back from Laura though.

We discussed the position. Or at least started to. It's amazing how a few bottles of wine can improve the financial situation. Hours later we had it all wrapped up, and so with my arm draped over her shoulder we laughingly rolled off to bed, carefully stepping over the cat sleeping on the stair, to slide between the warm duvet for one last fag.

Chapter 5

"Let's go see the judge." The first day of a trial. What a good idea, everyone agrees. The Crown Prosecution Service (CPS for short) are in support, so is the defence, not forgetting the defendant, or defendants as the case may be, who are the most enthusiastic of them all.

"Let's go see the judge and see what he thinks about guilty pleas to a lesser offence and the sentence he has in mind." A splendid suggestion. We can acquaint the judge with any little difficulties in the case – such as the odd absent witness, tell him the views of the victim and the police, run a little of the defence case past him, and after a little negotiation and a bit of mutual give and take, agree what if anything the punter should plead guilty to, and what in that case his sentence will be.

There is one small snag, one fly in the ointment, one something or other in the woodpile, a trace of acid in the wine. The Court of Appeal, that exclusive club of eminent persons that meets in the Strand and lunches in Chancery Lane, has forbidden it. Over and over again.

Prosecution barristers should refuse to take part and if they are dragged into the Judges Chambers they must not forget to switch on their tape recorders, take a full note, disassociate themselves from any discussion about sentence and not forget to make a full report to the Crown Prosecution Service immediately they return to court. What a load of bollocks!

Negotiating behind the scenes (and out of the glare of the public eye) is carried out in courts all over the world every day of the year. In America it is called plea-bargaining. As I see it, this involves some sort of upfront, wheeler-dealer, knock-down, best offer, bargain basement, series of trade-offs between prosecution and defence.

Remember, no defendant has ever done all that the prosecution says he has done. No defendant has ever done nothing at all. Eventually he settles for a compromise. A lesser sentence for a lesser guilty plea. His offence is reduced to a more realistic level, his sentence diminished accordingly and the cost, trouble and endless messing about of a trial is avoided. And everybody goes home happy.

The prosecution wins something, and the punter starts his time. The lawyer is paid expeditiously, and the judge gets an early day.

So what's wrong with that?

According to the Court of Appeal, a defendant may be persuaded by the promise of a lenient sentence to plead guilty to something he hasn't done. What rubbish. Innocent punters don't ask to see the judge.

But it doesn't end there. In England, justice must be seen to be done. This means saying everything in open court where the public can hear what is going on.

Public. What public? Apart from the odd relative or family friend or occasional pensioner seeking shelter from the rain there is nobody in open court. And what if there is? It's got nothing to do with them. Why shouldn't a defendant know what his sentence will be if he accepts his guilt? Why should he plead guilty blind, be forced to roll a dice, to play some kind of game of chance when it is so much more civilised, dependable, safe even, to make a polite enquiry and know what his number will be. At this late stage only one thing obsesses the defendant's mind.

Is he going to jail? And, if so, for how long?

If our learned friends can go behind the scenes, meander into the Judges Chambers and ask – then all is well.

"I was thinking of Community Punishment, or whatever they call it now. Putting back a little something into society by doing unpaid work to compensate for what he has dishonestly taken out."

Thank you very much. A grateful punter puts his hand up. The prosecution have their success. Money is saved. Witnesses return home untroubled and everyone gets on with their lives. An unnecessary trial has been avoided.

"I was thinking of three years."

Excellent. He'll only serve half.

"I think 12 months should be about right."

Wonderful. Even better. Under eighteen months prisoners can serve a mere quarter. Think about it. Just a quarter. Twelve months means twelve weeks.

The difference in actual time served – on either side of the various cut-off points is huge.

Perhaps the public are not aware of this. Perhaps justice is not being seen to be done after all. In fact, the truth is, short-term prisoners can get out even sooner. Leave aside day release, weekends at home, lunch with Jeffrey Archer. These days (at the discretion of the prison authorities) they are sent home early wearing an electronic tag. All they have to do is be at home before a certain time and be sure to stay in bed. A sentence of eighteen months can mean in real English only about three to serve.

So what is this, 'Justice must be seen to be done'? When just sentences so obviously aren't.

How useful if all this can be sorted out before swearing-in a jury and starting a long boring trial. A trial in which, remember, there is always a chance, however small, that the punter may for some mad inexplicable reason be gloriously acquitted and end up doing no time at all.

But the Court of Appeal is adamant.

No plea bargaining here. No creeping round to see the judges behind the scenes. Everything must be done in open court. No private discussions and the candour that might bring.

"Let's go and see the judge."

Things are done differently in Hull. We are a small court. By and large we trust people. London seems a long way away. The Court of Appeal out of sight.

Our system, the Hull system that is, is that both prosecution and defence barristers approach the court clerk. They ask to see the judge. Everybody knows what that means. Invariably he agrees. A procession forms of court clerks, defence and prosecution counsel, and an amiable discussion is held in the Judges Chambers which invariably results in the defendant in the Dock accepting some, albeit limited, guilt and everybody having an early day.

Our little procession duly forms up and marches away towards the Judges Chambers. Mrs Dawson bringing up the rear. No one has told her that these inner circle meetings are for the privileged few. She thinks – wrongly – as a legal executive representing the interests of the defendant on behalf of Cranmer Carter & Co. that somehow or other she is entitled to participate in matters affecting the future of her client. She is gloriously disabused.

"What do you think you're doing," the clerk demands, "where do you think you're going?"

"I thought I had to come. I thought he was my client."

Why did I not bother to tell her? I assumed she knew. Assumed she knew all about what we had been doing for years and she had been doing for days.

"I am afraid this is a matter that concerns only judge and counsel." He dismissively waves her away as we stroll on to enter the long corridor that runs behind, and interconnects, all five courts in Hull. It leads to the ushers' room, the clerks' offices and the jury rooms. It also leads to the Judge.

Judge Irvine welcomes us into his Chambers. It has been furnished to his taste. Mostly with books. They line the walls, block the window sills, and are stacked in tottering piles on the floor. Novels, books on history, sport, gardening and sex. In the corner the flickering screen of his old computer displays four hands of bridge. As usual he is sitting behind his cluttered desk doing The Times crossword. His breakfast tray lies discarded beside him betraying signs of sausage, bacon and eggs. He seems to have eaten the fat.

Once a county cricketer of some repute, and a matinee idol of Sloane Square, his famous chiselled features have slid away like wax down a candle. The blond curly hair long gone, beads of perspiration have broken out on his huge forehead as he struggles to catch his breath and adjust his expanding bottom to the Lord Chancellor's Department standard issue chair.

Those fingers, once famous for spin, now hold a permanent cigar. He has stopped smoking sixty cigarettes a day and now feels much better for thirty cigars. He can even taste his food. Judging from the tray there has been a lot of it to taste.

"Morning boys. What can I do for you?" He is as genial and engaging as ever.

"Henry. Don't tell me we're going to have a trial." We all laugh. Not much chance of that.

I make my pitch.

"It's the usual load of rubbish. Fight in the street at night. Young blokes. All in drink. Nobody too badly hurt. The usual sophisticated Hull criminal."

"What started it?" Judge Irvine enquires.

Who knows? Who cares? A careless push in a crowded club, somebody or other ordering a drink out of turn, somebody accidentally knocking over somebody's glass. Somebody looking too closely at somebody else. The other one catching his eye.

"What's your problem?" The inevitable question.

And the other eloquently responding, "No. You're the one with the problem." And neither, and here is the rub, having the courage – because it takes courage – to back down. And the inevitable clumsy punch or head-butt, and one or other, possibly both, going down – perhaps one of them catching their stupid head on the corner of a table, or a kerb.

"Any kicking?" asks the judge.

Kicking is bad news. It usually means jail. Kicking a man when he is down is dangerous. Particularly to his face, when his head is dangling helplessly in the gutter. Stamping is even worse. Deliberately stamping on an unconscious man's head when he can neither move nor defend himself causes brain damage. It can cause death. I am going to have to be careful.

"There is some evidence of kicking," I begin.

"Some witnesses describe the odd flying boot. But it is not easy to tell who they are describing as the owner of the boot. Descriptions vary. Everybody is drunk. A crowd has gathered round and there may be others involved. The prosecution cannot really say – so as to be sure."

I look towards Browne-Smythe, a member of my Chambers who holds the prosecution brief. He doesn't want a trial either. He has a big case coming up tomorrow which he is anxious to reach. The last thing he wants is to be stuck in our case for the next week being paid next to nothing by the C.P.S.

So it's time to do his bit. Gently nudge the rolling snowball down the hill.

"At this stage, judge . . ." he begins (and this is code for we shall be saying something different if this has to go to trial) "at this stage we are content to say there may have been some kicking but cannot with absolute certainty say that the defendant was entirely responsible. Certainly Wallace is right, there may well have been others involved. Yes. There may well have been others. At this stage that is."

My God; I pause for thought. Have you seen the photographs of his face?

"Yes," I pitch in. "At this stage the Crown is content with a plea on the basis of a little head-butting, punching, and strangling." We all laugh.

"However," I add with nice timing, "the victim seems to have made a full recovery. The odd little scar. Walking much better now. Recognises his common-law wife."

"Well," says Judge Irvine, reaching for a shortbread biscuit, "let's have a look. What's your man's record like?"

And here is the cruncher. My little ace in the hole.

"Nothing for violence. Never been involved in any violence before in his life." In this town, at his age, something of a minor miracle.

Bit of burglary, bit of handling, lots of motor cars. But, and yes, this is going to swing it, "Nothing for violence. Nothing for violence at all."

Judge Irvine smiles through the crumbs.

"No need to keep the prison van waiting boys. A little Community Service and Probation should do the trick."

And so it should. So it should. It is one thing for young men to attack and commit violence against old people (like my goodself) or women or, even worse, children, but for young men to fight each other, however violently, is something else altogether. Essentially it is a group activity entered into by consenting adults. Special stadiums should be erected for it. Areas could be set aside for binge drinking with walkways designed to enable each side to stare at the other. They could warm up on suspended dummies and kick blocks of concrete on the floor.

I daresay you could sell tickets to a grateful public anxious to watch these heroes trying to kill each other. On special occasions weapons could be issued. Perhaps wild animals could be involved. Marks given for content and style. My mind begins to wander.

Right now, the defendant has got what we lawyers call his 'indication'. He will be told by me what to do, and we will not be having a trial. We will certainly not be having a trial. The old age pensioner in the gallery can go home.

"Thank you judge. We're grateful. Have a very nice day."

We reform our little procession and march back into court where Mrs Dawson is impatiently waiting.

"All is well," I tell her, "point me at the punter." And when the three of us are gathered together at the back of the dock, I break the welcome news.

"Hands up to a little actual bodily harm and you won't be going away."

"What do you mean?" enquires Mrs Dawson. All this is a mystery to her. Sadly absent from Cranmer's training manual which she has so carefully absorbed.

"What I mean," I tell her majestically, "is our friend here, by my skilful intervention, and a little help from the judge, will now plead guilty, we will not be having a trial, and he will NOT, repeat NOT, be going to jail as he so richly deserves."

"But he's done nothing wrong," she persists.

Oh dear. She must have been whiling away the time reading his ridiculous proof. His account of the events of that evening. Worse. She must have believed it. Perhaps that's what the manual says.

We don't need any of this. I smile and squeeze her arm.

"Trust me." I say. And she does. And by God she will. And by God she should.

We have achieved another 'result'. We have brought home

the bacon. Another trial has been avoided, another happy punter, and another early day. And another space in jail for somebody else.

What a pity Mrs Dawson couldn't join us in our short stroll down the corridors of power – but she was not to be left out for long. Quick and clever she soon picked up the ropes. She never, unlike me perhaps, saw punters as a commodity to be processed with minimum fuss and maximum return. She always saw the human form beneath. Not that this stopped her giving strong advice, her notebook laid aside for ever, she would pitch in and give it to them straight between the eyes. For their own good; for the greater good; for our good. In the pursuit of Justice. In the cause of an early lunch.

And as we went from case to case together I began to sit back and let her take over for a bit, and then I would pick up the ball and run with it for a while and pass it back to her and she would put it in the back of the net. We became a team. We worked together wonderfully well and we had lots and lots of lunches, and in our wake, left lots of grateful punters far behind.

She was good company, a great partner, but no more. I couldn't take it any further. There was no way in. We exchanged confidences, we laughed, but I couldn't somehow engage her emotions. I couldn't get her to drop her guard, couldn't turn friendship into affection, couldn't even hope for the faint stirring of desire; some faint shadow of my own.

She simply loved her job. And of course I got to know about her family, the ages of her children, her ambitions for them, the little tales they used to tell.

What about Barry? Her husband Barry. "How's Barry getting along?" I used to ask. "Likes his new car does he? Thinking of putting up some shelves in the kitchen? Got round yet to cutting the grass?" Casual questions blandly asked. Too casual. She sensed my interest in her response. "Oh, Barry's fine. Let's not talk about Barry. You were on about him yesterday, and yes he does like his car, that's why he bought it; and yes he is still thinking about the kitchen shelves, been thinking about them for years and no, he never cuts the grass." What did I expect to hear? "Barry's wonderful. I love him dearly. What's all this about cars, shelves and grass? The perfect husband, I tremble at his touch."

What did I want to hear? "I hate the selfish bastard and I cannot bear his rough embrace."

What I in fact heard was her gentle fending off of my persistent questions and her easy glide into talking of something else. I learnt nothing. I knew nothing because she would tell me nothing, either way. I grew to assume that Barry was simply, if it is ever that simple, some normal husband at home.

Chapter 6

I didn't realise it was him when I saw him. How could I? He was nothing like the man she had described. Nothing like the product of my imagination. Nothing like the man you might expect.

I was hanging around in the central gardens at lunchtime opposite the offices of Cranmer Carter & Co. hoping to bump into Pauline when she left for lunch.

"Oh Pauline. What a surprise. Fancy meeting you here." You know. The usual thing.

I could remember the days when this area was a busy commercial dock. And then a less busy commercial dock. And then a derelict commercial dock. How had this arisen in a city facing Europe? God knows. At any rate they filled it in and planted trees and shrubs. Typists lolled on the grass eating their sandwiches and opening cans of coke. Solitary men sat on benches round the side watching them. Perhaps I was one of those men.

Anyway my attention quickly wandered to a big man in overalls standing on the grass. What did he want? He seemed strangely out of place. For nothing better to do I studied him. Huge shoulders and shaven head. The obligatory earring. Sleeves rolled up. Yes, the usual tattoos. What did he want standing by himself occasionally staring up at the buildings and offices that overlooked the park? He looked at his watch; shook his head and looked around. Nothing unobtrusive about him. He stared directly at the typists and they nudged each other and giggled back. I watched him take a sachet of Samson tobacco from his pocket and start to roll his own. Samson. It's everywhere in Hull. Not however sold in this country. Only available abroad. Not that I could talk. I smoke smuggled goods myself. When I can get them that is. Why should I pay all that tax to the Government? I looked around. To pay for projects like this.

And then I saw Pauline. Half running out of the big sliding door that fronts the offices of Cranmers. She saw me and immediately shook her head. Why? It didn't take long to find out.

She strode across the grass and tapped the big man on his shoulder and quickly moved back as he tried to exchange a kiss. I could see his frown. He pointed at his watch and was rewarded with a shrug. He looked around him pointing at the various buildings. A jobbing builder coming to price a job? A mechanic dropping off her car? Oh no. She told me later over a drink. This was the husband back home. The one I had asked so much about.

"He wanted to know where I worked," she told me, "wanted to know why I always made so much of myself in the morning. Why I always wore my best suit."

"Seems a nice chap."

She looked at me scathingly. "You had to find out didn't you? You had to bloody know."

"Just happened to be passing," I lied. "Fancy bumping into him. Anyway, what did he think of it. What did he say?"

I had seen her pointing up at Cranmers, that huge building looming over the park. Brand new; of a Georgian aspect. Rows of white framed windows rising into the sky.

"I showed him my office," she said proudly, "pointed out my secretary next door. He couldn't believe it. Couldn't get it into his head. Any minute I thought a partner might come out. Christ what would I have done then? Introduced him as my plumber no doubt. Anyway I let him know which floors the kitchens and dining room are on and told him about the gym. Not too pleased about that. I forgot I had promised to join the one on the docks. Not any more sweetheart. I've bought all the gear. Mr Tomkinson offered to show me around. Said we can exercise together."

Oh yes. I can see it now. Pauline bursting out of her Lycra. Tomkinson bursting out of his shorts.

I'd seen her start arguing with Barry, watched him getting angry and caught the odd word of what was obviously a quarrel.

"Perhaps he doesn't like the idea of you mucking about in the gym?"

"As you might imagine."

"Perhaps a little cautious about too much over-exposure."

She raised an eyebrow.

"Perhaps a little overawed by the place?"

"Well, he'll have to put up with it. He likes the money and I like the job."

I let it pass. Good news and bad news then. Obviously irritated with Barry. Not much affection there. A little widening of the horizons that might lead to a little parting of the ways? I wasn't so happy about Tomkinson though. Didn't like the idea of them sweating and straining together. Bumping into each other as they left their respective showers. Wet, clean, and slightly out of breath.

"Stop for another?" I asked her. "One more before you go?" But she was up already. Always in a rush. I leant over to kiss her but, like Barry before me, was just a little too late.

"Sorry. Got to dash."

"Got to get home to get dinner ready?"

"No, I've got an appointment at the gym."

Chapter 7

Giles Baring has called a chambers meeting in The Grafton Manor Hotel. One of those large houses dotted around Hull formerly belonging to fishing vessel owners now given over to restaurants, conference facilities, exercise spas and the rest. Bedrooms have been built on the side. A swimming pool instead of a lawn.

Members of chambers filter in. The younger members wear jeans. Those in the middle (and making the money), sport check shirts, sweaters and slacks. Those over the top wear tweed. Giles favours a blazer. He thinks it covers up the fat. His large bushy eyebrows meeting in the middle. Somehow he manages to leave isolated bits of bristle on his chin.

He parks himself at the head of a long table that has been arranged with agendas, pencils and notepads. There are coffee and juice facilities in the corner. Plates of biscuits are available. Sandwiches will appear at lunch.

Members are reassured of their own importance – and the hotel, or whatever it is, can justify its price.

"Item 1. Clerk's Remuneration." Giles begins. This is an almost permanent item. Now growing critical. In the old days when barristers were few and far between, each one chipped in 10% of his earnings to pay the clerk. In return the clerk 'clerked his men'. He fixed the lists of cases at court so that barristers could actually get to them; he negotiated fees; he bossed about the typists and junior clerks and generally ran the office. At lunchtimes he went drinking with solicitors in the hope of bringing back work. He was worth every penny.

As time went by chambers gradually grew larger from ten members to twenty to thirty. (In London to eighty and a hundred or more). 10% became a lot of money. The clerk became the biggest earner in chambers. Some clerks took home ridiculous amounts and lived accordingly. Cars, houses, holidays – Jackson was thinking of a yacht.

And chambers' other costs were growing. Rents racked ever higher, computers installed, more staff recruited. As members looked around to economise, clerks became the obvious choice.

Unfortunately most clerks had some form of contract. They resisted any reduction in their money and consequent decline from the style of life to which, over the years, they had become accustomed. They were better lawyers than their 'men'.

And of course no one wanted to be part of a failed minority voting for a clerk's wage reduction. Word would get back to Jackson and work would mysteriously dry up.

Everybody had to be for it – or no one, and getting everybody in chambers on board so far had been a bridge too far.

"We really can't let this go on," complained Giles. "Sooner or later Jackson has got to take a cut. Give us the figures Horace."

He calls on the man in the silver suit. Horace Pickles, elected treasurer at his own request.

"Not very good I'm afraid Giles. The usual story. Wages up. Rent up. Library up. And we need a new computer system to replace the one installed two years ago – predicted to be 'good for years' and now hopelessly out-of-date. Unless we reduce Jackson's percentage our chambers' contributions will have to go up. Dramatically. Last year we paid 20% of our gross earnings as each individual's contribution to meet the costs. This year it's 25%. Next year 30%. Who knows? It's either Jackson or us."

I look around. Not a difficult choice.

"But he's got a contract," chips in Browne-Smythe, prematurely balding with a round childish face. One of the sweater and slacks variety, but a good advocate. And he knows what to say to a judge.

"He will fight this to hell and back. He'll never surrender. Who knows, he might win. It'll cost the bloody earth."

Horace Pickles, as usual, disagrees. "It may cost us a bit in Year 1. Maybe Year 2. But look at the long term. Think of how much we'll save. Trust me, we'll be quids in."

And dear old Jackson no doubt quids out.

Actually I rather like Jackson. He has done well for me. To be totally honest, I am one of his best pals. Drinking together in our quest to find solicitors at lunch (he calls it 'looking for work') – we usually extend our search throughout the afternoon. Admittedly we don't seem to find any, but no one could fault us for trying. Younger solicitors seem to keep out of pubs these days. Some firms actually have rules against drinking in work time. We only seem to rub up against the older generation. Those who have retired or those who have graduated to "consultants" within their firm and do no work at all. We always seem to see the same people. Perhaps they are looking for us.

"What's in a percentage?" I ask.

"Does it matter how much he makes when last year we all made more?"

Perhaps I shouldn't have said that. Some might think I am the leak back to the office.

"We have got to grasp this nettle," says Giles, "and I should prefer we grasp it together."

McIntosh, another of Jackson's dwindling band of supporters, stays mute. It seems that our clerk is facing some modest diminution in his living standards. I unconsciously pat my wallet. This can only end in tears.

"I propose we reduce his percentage," Giles pauses, "as from next month." He clears his throat. "Uhm . . . Uhmm . . . to 5%. Do I have a seconder?" He looks across at Horace.

Our man in the silver suit responds on cue.

"In favour?" Giles looks round the table. A forest of hands.

Out of twenty members present and attending, all agree. There must have been some preceding discussion organised in rooms, or in our coffee lounge when McIntosh, Jackson and I were out 'looking for work'. This meeting is not the meeting. It has all been cut and dried before.

In the secure knowledge that our votes will not now cost us actual money, and as a vote of loyalty to the now impoverished Jackson, McIntosh and I raise our hands against.

"Carried" says Giles. He pours himself a glass of water. "Almost unanimously".

I know this is going to lead to trouble, but when I tell Jackson how I voted it hopefully won't lead to me.

"Item No. 2: Bar Mark." Giles presses on.

It is a sign of the times that as the Bar grows ever larger and more and more people of little or no talent (save to promote themselves) become members, the Bar's Trade Union (or Bar Council, as it likes to call itself), grows correspondingly bigger. It has expanded its offices in London. It has recruited new managers, 'consultants', new office staff. Appointed extra committees. Tripled its personnel.

All those people clocking in every day to manage our affairs. What can they do? Well here's a good idea. Let's get teams of Management Consultants, or Business and Financial Advisers, or whatever they want to call themselves to train chambers and their staff in good management techniques so that chambers might provide an even better service – yes an even better service – is it possible? – than they ever did before.

Chambers up and down England and Wales must submit to "efficiency auditing" at their own expense. Consultants arrive who check the filing of briefs, the contents of the library, the number of paperclips, the efficiency of the computer system, the method of 'returns' (whereby barristers already in court return their cases to other barristers in chambers), the work contracts made with staff, the clerk's contract, Bar Council Protocols, Health and Safety directives and what, if anything does our Mission Statement contain.

Our old friend Browne-Smythe is in charge of this hot potato. He outlines our "progress". Many chambers have already been blushingly awarded their 'Bar Marks'. Whitebait Chambers once more depressingly in the rear.

Browne-Smythe looks round the table. "Certain members have once again failed to fill in their forms." His ferret eyes seem fixed on our corner. "It is not that difficult," he piously complains.

"Every case now must carry its own form with a duplicate in the clerk's room and a triplicate in the filing room and a copy on the computer which sets out the progress of the case detailing, please, every item of work done and every contact made with instructing solicitors ensuring its progress and er . . . hopefully eventual success."

I fear I may be one of the miscreants. McIntosh the other.

Giles is feeling left out.

"We must get our Bar Mark," he interrupts, "without it we will not be eligible for legal aid."

Now this is a bit of a shock. Legal aid is our lifeblood. It is the way the great British tax-payer pays for his justice. It is the way we go home each month with money. For legal aid to be removed from either an inefficient or non-compliant chambers is a disaster. An absolute and total disaster. Without legal aid we are finished. Chambers bankrupt. The Bar on the dole.

As always, what started as a voluntary scheme for patting greasers on the head has become compulsory. What has become compulsory has now to be enforced. Penalties for failures to comply have become draconian. No legal aid. I can't believe it. We are looking at the wire.

Horace, our man in the silver suit, holds up his hand for permission to speak.

"I propose that if individual members of chambers fail to fill in their forms on time . . . properly, . . . or at all . . . then chambers hereby be granted the power to levy an appropriate and increasing fine."

Enough is enough.

It is time for me to go to the lavatory. I will not be coming back. I am going to 'look for work'.

Chapter 8

"Would you like to come for lunch?" I remember the first time I asked her.

Mrs Dawson looks up; pauses as if thinking, and agrees.

"Where are we going?"

I will take this girl absolutely bloody anywhere. Claridges, The Savoy Grill, Chez Nico, Ramsays, The Ivy, Wheelers, Chez Gerard, The Gay Hussar, The Pea Bung on Grimsby Market, Bob Carver's Fish and Chip Emporium, the local pie and mash.

We settle for Antonio's.

Antonio has set up his restaurant in the now defunct Fish Merchants Association Offices. Defunct because the fleet has nowhere to fish. It is a little chintzy. Scattered tables with a small vase of flowers and the odd candle in a silver holder. Discreet lighting. Cane chairs with cushions. A nice bar. He may or may not speak English, but he certainly knows how to charge.

I have read somewhere that partners to a business lunch sit facing each other. Conspirators to a romantic lunch sit at right angles. It doesn't take Sherlock Holmes to work out where I am going.

She puts on her glasses to read the menu. God, I love glasses. Her lips move as she reads the words.

"Prawns for a starter please and I think. . . ." long pause ". . . I think I'll have plaice for the main course."

This is getting serious.

"Antonio does do awfully big portions you know."

Anyway, all I want is a drink. Lots of drinks. I must loosen up. When I am with this woman I get serious. For some reason I feel my throat constrict. Normally voluble, I find it difficult to get words out. Naturally funny, I find my jokes fall flat. Even I can't laugh at them. She is driving me mad. She is wearing today another new suit, and yet another new pair of shoes. Where are they all coming from?

She does look good though. This is a girl who knows how to dress. Now about forty years old (or so Platten told me) and tending to wrinkle about the eyes, she is wearing – constrained by – imperceptibly moving beneath – a black sweater to her neck and a black suit which contains thin lawyers' stripes. Her shoes are high, her legs beyond belief.

I contemplate pressing against them but in spite of our partnership am too shy, or perhaps too fearful of offending her, or too frightened of rejection and of losing everything in a clumsy pass, so I lean back and light yet another cigarette.

"I really like working with you."

Did I actually say this? This weak, smarmy, coyly complimentary dross. Seeking to ingratiate at any price. What is happening to me?

She smiles, and I plough on.

"How are you liking the job?"

In what I later come to know as her blinding candour.

"I love it."

I'll bet you do. A life away from Barry and the children. A life in what passes for the commercial centre of Hull. A job with responsibility, working with nice (until you get to know them) people, the occasional lunch. Visits to the prison and the police station. Every day in court. Moving here, there and everywhere except (at this stage) to a judge's chambers. Nipping out in office hours to go shopping. Arriving home at night and taking calls on what has become her busy line. Turning her back on the kitchen. Hoovering a thing of the past. Moving slowly, inexorably away from Barry. Possibly, hopefully, in the general direction of me.

"Mr Tomkinson and I are having an affair," she says casually. "I thought you might like to know."

Chapter 9

I couldn't get over this Tomkinson business. There was I being nice – whilst he was being his usual clever self and exercising his giant fucking muscles alongside Pauline in the gym. I couldn't work it out. Nor did I get any help from Pauline. She is one of those people who, when asked a question they didn't want to answer, don't answer it. Not 'it's none of your business' or 'I never discuss my private affairs' or anything like that. When I say she didn't answer that is exactly what she did. Silence. Nothing. She simply carried on doing what she was doing as if she'd never heard.

It was exasperating not to be acknowledged, and annoying not to know.

She was not so reticent about Barry though. We were back in Antonio's when she dropped another bombshell.

The usual laconic beginning. "Oh by the way, Barry's gone."

I never know how to react to information delivered like this. I never will.

"Barry? Barry's gone? Barry's gone where?"

"Who knows? Who cares? I think I'll have the plaice."

Pauline was one of those people who, having ordered something they turn out to like, orders it over and over again.

"Plaice. You want plaice? You had plaice last time."

"So what? I like it. I'm not like you. I don't bugger about wandering all over the menu just to have something different and winding up with shit."

"Fine. Fine. Have the plaice. You were saying about Barry. I think you said he'd gone."

"Yeah. That's right. He's gone."

"Where?"

"Haven't we done this before? I thought I told you. I haven't the slightest idea."

"Why has he gone?"

"Because I told him to."

"Why? How? What's been going on?"

"God, you have to know every detail. I hope you've got plenty of time."

"When did he go?"

"Last night."

"Is he coming back?"

"No."

"Not ever?"

"Never."

"Jesus Christ." I reached for my glass of wine. It seemed to evaporate.

"You've been married fifteen years. It's a bit sudden isn't it?"

"Nothing's sudden. It just seems sudden because when it happens – it happens fast."

I poured another drink.

"So what happened. Fast or slow, what's been going on?"

She sighed and lit a cigarette. I can see her now. Leaning forward and rattling it off.

"He'd been drinking all afternoon. Supposed to be a committee meeting at that club of his."

"What club?"

"Does it matter? Oh anyway. The Harold Wilson Social Club – he's the chairman of social events. You ought to see them. Bouncing Brenda the lass from Barnsley. Streetfighters Incorporated. Hull's favourite group. Get the picture? Fun for all the family. Happy hour two till ten. Two burgers for the price of one – guaranteed made with meat. Extra chips before seven o'clock. Christ, the happy hours I've spent there."

A waiter interrupted her flow. "Would madam like her plaice with new potatoes, potatoes dauphinoise, mashed potatoes or chips?"

"As it comes. As I was saying," she ploughed on, "he'd been there all day. Carried on into the night. Obviously brooding about our state of play. You should have heard him when he came home."

"You never look at me. Won't talk to me. Never here when

48

I get home. Nothing on the table. When did we last have sex? You always turn your back. Sick of looking at your behind."

The man must be mad.

"Always turn away. Leave me looking at the wall. This is it. I've had enough. Let me remind you what it's like. It's time we watched our video. Something a little special. Remind us of old times."

"A video? A video? He wanted to watch a video? What sort of video?"

"What do you think? Use your bloody brains."

"A CCTV?"

"A CCTV? What are you talking about? A dirty fucking video. What else do blokes want to watch?"

"A dirty video. He wanted to watch a dirty video. What time was this?"

"What time? Does it fucking matter? I'd just got in. Nobody about. I thought he'd gone to bed. And then just as I was quietly rooting about in the fridge for something to eat, he staggers in through the door. I could see straight away the mood he was in. One look at his face. Knew we were in for trouble. Sure enough he wanted to get that fucking video out. Wanted to upset me. Wanted to make me ashamed."

"Ashamed? Why should you feel ashamed? I don't get it. Why should you feel ashamed?"

"Because I'm in it. That's the bloody point. Featuring me. Playful bloody Pauline with Barry in a walk-on role."

I couldn't get this through my head. I just couldn't understand. A mixture of interest and horror. I took another drink.

"But how? Why? Why are you in it?"

"Because I'm the fucking star. Because he's got a camera. Because he's a bloody pervert. Because he never let me alone. On and on. Day after day. You'd do it if you love me. Tony's missus does it for him. Just the two of us. Remind me what it's like. When we're old together we can always play it back. Over and over. He never let it drop. What would you fucking do? No don't tell me. I don't want to know. Anyway, in the end I agreed. Gave in. I suppose for peace. Don't look at me like that. What would you do with children and nowhere to bloody go? Anyway I did it. Got pissed on a bottle of wine."

"Did what?"

"Oh for Christ's sake. What do you think?"

"Not that. You didn't do that?"

"Fucking everything. In glorious technicolor. Barry was Cecil B. De Mille."

I didn't know what to say. My meal arrived but I couldn't eat it. I was amazed as Pauline tucked into her plaice.

"So Barry wanted you to watch it. Wanted you to remember what it's like."

"Oh yes. Very keen on a walk down memory lane our Barry. Went out to see where he kept it hidden in the shed whilst I locked the fucking door."

"You locked the door so he couldn't get in?"

"Yeah. You've got the idea. I knew he'd get angry. If anything it would make him bloody worse. You see it wasn't there. I knew where he kept it so I'd bloody had it away."

"Had it away? What have you done with it?"

"Put it on the back of the fire. I thought he'd be annoyed. Came back shouting down the path. Thought I'd better call the police. And, of course, as you so rightly observe, he couldn't get back in. Started kicking the door. Broke the fucking glass. Neighbours' lights going on all round the close. The kids were crying upstairs. I kept ringing the police. It's a good job they fucking know me. Anyway. Thank God they finally showed up. Turned into a bit of a fight. Only one winner though."

She smiled across the table, enjoying the moment.

"Only one winner. That's when it's three to one. Carted him off to the station. He was banging inside the van. Calling out to me. 'Don't let them take me away.' Well he can fuck off. Changed the locks this morning. Told the children. Made it clear. Told them their father won't be coming back."

"You told the children?"

"Yeah. And now I've told you." She was never one to waste food. "If you're not going to eat any of that you'd better give it to me."

Chapter 10

Pauline and I went to York. It wasn't much of a job. More of a day out really. Some punters or other had pleaded guilty to something or other on the day of their trial and, having adjourned for the Probation Service to produce the usual reports, we had now reached point of sentence and were simply following the judge who had no doubt given us his usual 'indication'.

Of course I had to go through the 'theatre', even though we already knew more or less what the sentence would be. I had to say something – we couldn't simply nod it through. I was going to mitigate, or pretend to mitigate, his sentence by the exercise of some platitude or other and after pretending to listen the judge was going to pass the sentence we had agreed in his chambers about four weeks before. Assuming I could concentrate that is.

I can't remember much about the case. I have some vague recollection of standing behind the square table in the well of Court No.1 and looking up at the beautiful fluted dome, and the judge coming through the tiny door at the back and popping up on the bench.

"Thank you Mr Wallace. Admirably concise", and then addressing the punters who never really believe they're not going to prison until they actually don't.

"Disgraceful behaviour. Street fighting at night. The public are heartily sick of it. They demand severe sentences, and I am going to oblige. Two years probation all round. Thank you. You may go."

And so did Pauline and I. I was with the reluctant object of my desire and jumping with excitement as we set out back together on the winding road to Hull.

At that time, before a by-pass intervened, the road twisted through Market Weighton, a town alternatively clogged to breaking point, or empty as a cemetery, depending upon whether it was a market day or not. That day was market day. It was also very hot, the sun beating down from a cloudless sky with barely a breath of wind. We had stopped in traffic. Conveniently outside a pub or maybe a hotel in the town centre. I can't remember which.

What I can remember is that soon we were both inside. Together. Sitting at a table getting drunk.

She told me Barry was being difficult. Her firm were handling the case. He had been excluded from the house, but she didn't want to live there anymore – she said she didn't feel safe – and had found a place to rent on the other side of town.

I can remember thinking at the time how unreasonably he was behaving. Why didn't he play the man? But then I had not experienced the bitterness of rejection. How resentment turns to hatred. How anything and everything becomes a weapon – even the children – to use to beat the other side.

He wanted the house (with mortgage), the furniture, the car (including hire purchase), his pension and everything else.

He wanted her jewellery such as it was, and for peace – anything for peace – she had gone round to the house one night, slipped the ring from her finger and pushed it through the door.

At this stage perhaps her eyes were fixed firmly on the future. She wanted rid of Barry at any price. And as fifteen years of marriage had not produced much in the way of material benefit, it was probably a small price to pay.

I can remember listening to all of this and drinking. I don't think I said very much. In fact, when Pauline was in full flow it was impossible to say anything at all. She hammered away at the detail, occasionally sipping her gin.

"Does he know about Tomkinson?" I thought I'd try again.

"What about Tomkinson? Not Tomkinson again. Listen." She leaned forward and looked me straight in the eye. "It was once. Only once. Months ago now. A watershed for me. A way of making things final. So there was no going back."

"But what happened?" I asked. There must be more.

I am interested. More than that. I am fascinated. More than that. I desperately need to know.

"So what happened?"

She sighed. Lit another cigarette. "I went to the firm's dance. Dolled up specially. He was there with his girlfriend. Told me I was reading too much into it. Told me not to be silly. Silly. I ask you." She rolled her eyes and shook her lovely head, "Left me on the dance floor, I had to pretend I hadn't noticed. Trying to dance with myself. Since then he's changed his mind. Never leaves me alone. In and out of my office, ringing me at home. Even been round to the house. Well it's over, and he's had it. In more senses than one. I told him to fuck off. He's had his chance and lost it. It's finished. And we're done."

And back to Barry. And the house. And the children, and the rest.

What did I feel? Outrage that a girl could be treated this way. Amazement that Tomkinson, that predatory lizard, could drop someone as precious as this. Walk away leaving her alone in the middle of a dance and then thinking he could oil his way back and make use of her again.

Admiration at her candour. Yes I was used. Yes I was dumped. But so what? I could not, still cannot, accept such stark rejection. Her honesty; her courage even, made me like her more.

And I felt relief. Did this present a window of opportunity? Was there a chance for me? My foot was already in the door, what might be achieved by a little steady application of the shoulder? Some persuasive salesmanship on the stoop?

I listened on, occasionally going to the bar for more drink. And through all my sympathy grew the hope that possibly, just possibly, there might be something in it for me.

I drove back to Hull drunk. Pauline lay back in the front seat, also the worse for wear. She seemed to be dozing but who knows?

Her skirt had slightly ridden up and her legs were apart. I was in a sexual lather. Suddenly without any warning I reached over and put my left hand on her knee.

She didn't move. No acknowledgement. Nothing. God knows what I thought I was doing. I held my hand there realising for the first time that she was wearing neither tights nor stockings. Her leg was smooth as silk, and slowly I inched upwards driving now in third gear and steering with one hand. This is not the way to drive on a motorway. Something seemed to pass very close. It might have been a lorry.

My hand now had a mind of its own. Infinitely slowly it eased itself upwards. As I've said, it had been a hot day. The inside of her thigh was slightly damp, as imperceptibly I approached the moist nylon of her knickers. Nothing could stop me now. Not a red light; not the police; not even a pile-up. I touched her for the first time and as she eased herself soundlessly upwards my fingers entered her and stayed. We drove on into Hull, neither of us saying a word. Whether passing motorists had any conception of what was happening I cannot say. I was totally absorbed in her and I could have driven one handed forever through Hull and into the sea.

"Drop me here." Pauline wriggled herself free and pulled down her skirt. As I pulled up she got out.

"Wait. Wait a minute." I shot round the front of the car regardless of the traffic.

"Can I see you? Can I see you tomorrow?" She paused to think.

"No. Sorry. I'm too busy." That was Friday out then.

"What about Monday? What are you doing Monday? Monday lunchtime. We could go to Humphrey's." (Yet another barrister who had left his wife and currently living alone).

She stopped again. She looked at me. I wonder now what sort of sight I must have been. Red-faced, desperate and drunk. There must have been pity in her somewhere.

"All right then. Monday it is."

She turned to go.

"But where? Where shall I meet you?"

I was panicking; desperate to know, but frightened of losing her by irritating her with detail. One more question and she might change her mind.

"Here. Pick me up here. One o'clock. Have a nice weekend." And she was gone round the corner with barely a wave, while I got back in the car and drove home elated. Cigarette smoke and perfume lingering in the car – her sexual smell still clinging to my fingers.

How did I get through that Friday and the long weekend? Strangely it was easy enough. I had fought and won a battle. I was a soldier leaning on his shield.

I was also hyperactive. I couldn't leave Laura alone. At first surprised, she quickly grew compliant. I must have made love to her more times that weekend than in the preceding six months. And I was kind, considerate and loving. I was all over her. Happy and excited, for once I felt alive.

Do not think that when one partner is having an affair he or she grows indifferent to the other. The opposite is true. Buoyed up by the excitement and pleasure of an affair the adulterer grows solicitous for the happiness of the partner he so treacherously betrays. An offering to assuage guilt? The pervading atmosphere of imminent sex? The world is warmer; colours brighter; every song is your song; the singer sings for you.

The weather remained hot and I pulled out the long table from the kitchen into the garden beneath the trees. We ate and drank outdoors, surrounded by our children and Laura's pets. Occasionally I would drag her upstairs.

Sunday evening found us once more in the garden. Laura at the head of the table. She was talking with a cigarette in one hand a glass in the other. I had not seen her so beautiful and happy for years. Some friends had dropped round (I cannot remember who), and, as ever, she was making them laugh.

Moths and flies circled round the lantern hung from the lower branch of a horse chestnut I had first grown at school. The dogs lounged under the table waiting for scraps, as the evening slowly wore on, I caught Laura's eye and she winked.

I rose slowly from the table and went inside. Our bedroom was cool and quiet. For a time I simply wanted to be alone. I could hear laughter wafting up from the garden to the window where I stood gazing into the park. I wanted to think. I wanted to think about Pauline.

Chapter 11

I had been impatiently hanging round chambers all morning unable to settle to work.

We occupy a beautiful, if rather tumble-down, old building set in a narrow cobbled street around the corner from the courts.

Passers-by can glimpse through the tiny window panes and see the stacks of briefs set out for that purpose. Unfortunately they can also see the staff in the typing pool doing their make-up and Doreen eating her crisps.

The entrance is impressive though. A huge black door with brass handles and brass knocker beneath a leaded fanlight with a wide brass letter box set into the wall.

There is more brass in the porch. The long plate inscribed 'Whitebait Chambers' that I watched our cleaner polish what seemed like months ago, with its list of members inscribed in order of seniority beneath.

I have been working my way upwards over the years, and now find myself three from the top. I always stop and look at it. Even after all this time it still gives me pleasure to study my name and check on those beneath.

Once inside, however, it is a different story. Humphrey, a middle-aged fool and friend of mine who fancies himself a thespian, volunteered himself years ago to undertake a complete refurbishment. It has been a disaster. In what dear Humphrey imagined to be a modern minimalist style he ripped out all the old panelling and architraves, and substituted beige wallpaper and stainless steel. He made a bonfire of the heavy old furniture and we now enjoy chipboard substitutes we screwed together ourselves. Upstairs in what Humphrey described as the amenity and recreation room he threw out all the old soft leather armchairs leaking stuffing – and replaced them with tubular chairs. The old card table went out the window. A pool table has been set up instead.

I ask you. A pool table. I wouldn't drink in a pub with a pool table, and now I am supposed to work and have conferences to the sound of balls clicking over my head.

Downstairs, near the clerk's room (the engine room according to Humphrey), is a row of pigeonholes, each one carrying a particular barrister's name. In effect, it is his post box waiting to receive letters, circulars, and most importantly, briefs. Every day or so (sometimes when desperate three or four times a day) each barrister will approach his pigeonhole with studied nonchalance to inspect his haul.

A passing spider seems to have weaved a cobweb over mine.

But no. An inter-chambers circular has arrived. It is from our old friend Browne-Smythe.

"Certain members of chambers are still failing to fill in their forms," he began. "Might I remind members of chambers that failing to secure our Bar Mark will inevitably lead to the withdrawal of legal aid. Might I further remind chambers that at our last meeting it was agreed by those remaining that persistent failure to comply with chambers requirements in this regard will result in the immediate imposition of substantial and increasing fines at the discretion of head of chambers and the recently constituted Fines and Levies Committee."

M. Browne-Smythe, Secretary FLC.

I wonder. Who might he be referring to? But frankly I couldn't care less. Today is the big day. Normally fastidious, today I am impeccable. Hair washed, nails cut and cleaned, lightly perfumed, a hint of egoiste. The groom preparing for his bride.

Actually marriage tends to put a little constraint on all of this. It doesn't do to leave home looking extra specially manicured and fragrant. Suspicions can so easily be aroused. Neither will it do to have suddenly invested in a whole range of new boxer shorts in some optimistic attempt to look like the models who feature on underwear boxes in all the shops. Deceit requires care. If your wife, for example, suddenly buys a new range of unusual lingerie, remember – it is not for you.

Nevertheless. Even constrained by caution I had still managed to turn out well, with shiny shoes and waistcoat, I headed for my car and within minutes was approaching the fateful corner where, only days before, we had arranged to meet.

But there was nobody there. Well not nobody, but certainly nobody resembling Pauline. I went round the one-way system, my heart in my mouth. This always takes time. Red lights, reversing lorries, the usual thing. What if Pauline turns up and I'm not there? She can't be as keen as me. Any excuse and she's off. "I got there. Waited for you. No sign. I can't hang around on a corner forever. Try again next year."

I nearly took out a pensioner buggering about on a crossing – you know the sort of thing, fluttering and dithering at the kerbside they suddenly dash across, and as you go to drive behind them they immediately double back. I was getting desperate. I went through a red light and round the block again. Still no sign. Where the fuck was she? If she wasn't coming why didn't she ring? Have I got the right bloody corner? I stopped on double yellow lines and Pauline serenely stepped out of a doorway.

"I was just about to go."

Always a chain-smoker I seem to have lit two cigarettes at once. And Pauline looks wonderful. More than wonderful. Ethereal. Untouchable. Magnificent. Wearing a yellow dress (she can't have been to court) and yet another new pair of shoes.

"Where are we going?"

I have not made reservations at a restaurant or planned a stroll in the park.

"To Humphrey's. I have to see you. I hope that's all right?"

She said nothing. Neither deigning to consent nor refusing to submit. As I was to learn, Pauline acquiesced to what she regarded as inevitable. Sex for her was a relief rather than a pleasure.

And now I can't find bloody Humphrey's. Having left his wife in spectacular circumstances he has now rented what he thought was a sophisticated bachelor flat on the waterfront – a place which I now find to be inaccessible by road.

I take the first left at the roundabout and end up in a

cul-de-sac. I can see Humphrey's block from here, the sun glinting on its windows. There appears to be a stretch of water between us.

I take the second left and then the third left. I had all morning out of court doing nothing. Why didn't I make a trial run? Why didn't I have the sense to check that I knew the road? Lunch or dinner or whatever it is will be over soon and Pauline will want to be off. Why didn't I just find out the bloody way?

But I am not myself. I cannot think, I cannot reason. I want to get inside and slowly achingly remove her dress. In my mind's eye, I see her playfully kicking off her shoes.

I try the final exit and magically, once over a bridge, we are there.

Where did I put the key? Standing outside the flat I rummage through my pockets. People are looking at us. Pauline calmly lights a cigarette and leans against a wall. Where did I put the fucking key? Is it in chambers? Is it in the car? Did Humphrey ever give it to me with, as I remember, the admonition not to make too much bloody noise.

It turns up in my waistcoat pocket. How did it get there? I pull it out on its string, and a condom flutters to the floor. Jesus Christ, how did that happen? I quickly cover it with my foot and stooping down to retrieve it I bang my head against the wall.

I get the impression Pauline is growing restless.

For God's sake, open the door. Get the fucking door open. I quickly shove the key into the lock but it will not turn. Maybe I put it in upside down. Unfortunately it will not come out. I am losing my air of calm sophistication. Falling backwards as it suddenly pops out, Pauline says, "You told me his flat was first floor with a balcony overlooking the dock. That's number six. Why are you trying to get into number four?"

I don't know really. There is no answer to this. Through the leaded window of the door I see the occupant of number four coming down the hallway, curious to see who is trying to enter his flat.

Pauline takes the key from my hand. She studies it. She bounces it in her palm, and then, as if decided unlocks number six and in an instant we are inside.

I follow her upstairs watching her lovely bottom slowly undulate beneath the shiny fabric of her dress. And suddenly, amazingly really, we are there. Together and alone.

Can words do justice to an act of love?

Yes. I did take off her dress. And yes. She did kick off her shoes. We lay together on Humphrey's bed.

I kissed her lips . . . I ran my fingers through her hair.

I kissed her neck as she slowly arched her head backwards into the pillow . . .

What is this thing that makes the world go round? A mixture of passion and tenderness reduced to a stain on the sheets?

We lay together afterwards but not bound together – really we weren't even close – touching yet oddly apart. I lit her a cigarette and, propping myself up on one elbow, placed it into her mouth.

"Pauline . . ." I began, but she was ahead of me.

"No. Don't even think about it."

"But Pauline . . ." I persisted.

She shook her head and rolled over leaving me to study her back. Suntanned but without the white strap marks that I have always found so sexy. Why do people assume they're not? So topless then. I don't like that either. Gawping bloody strangers on the beach. Just so she can gaze in her bathroom mirror and see no marks. I leant further over and kissed her shoulder.

"Don't do that. Not now . . ." She turned round and smiled, "O.K. I'll say it once. Yeah. If you must know. I'd say it was all right."

So this is love then. Perhaps I'm too sentimental and sentiment, apparently, doesn't guarantee success.

Time to act relaxed and confident. I smiled down on her upturned face. "I thought it was better than that."

The sad thing was we were both right.

Chapter 12

I didn't get back to chambers until gone three in the afternoon. Pauline slightly later to her office in the sky.

Jackson was waiting for me. Apparently I wasn't the only one to receive a circular. He had already been drinking and was in a mood.

"What do you think this is going to cost me?" he demanded, waving a letter from Giles.

I took it from his hand.

"In view of prevailing economic conditions it has been decided that, in a spirit of co-operation, you will be required to make a salary sacrifice of 5% of clerking fees."

Salary sacrifice, eh? Nice. Only 5%. Does this mean a reduction of 5% or to 5%. I think we know what it means. Jackson seems to have got the message anyway.

He glares around what is a strangely empty chambers. Our fearless advocates seem to have gone to ground, the pool table peacefully silent. The office staff, with heads down, are beavering away, crisps and make-up missing.

Jackson moved towards the door. "Come on. We're going looking for work."

Sitting opposite him in the pub I realised how old he had become. Thinning hair brushed straight back from his blotched red face. Hands trembling slightly as he put down another pint.

"I started this outfit."

True. Forty years ago. A young man with a moustache and thick black hair clerking two 'men' in Whitebait Lane. Photographs all over chambers traced his slow decline. With every man who was made a judge he had travelled down to London for the swearing in, and had posed later shoulder to shoulder with his robed protege in his full-bottomed wig, Jackson wearing his morning suit, the two of them together for the last time.

By strength of personality and mental agility he had controlled chambers for years. "This is not your brief sir," he used to say, removing a brief from some barrister who, because his name was on the front, had foolishly assumed it was his. "This is a chambers' brief sir. You may not be able to get to it."

But he had been good to me, and I suppose I owed him one. More than one.

"Do you realise how much this will cost me? How much you will cost me. Do you realise how much? Have you added it up?"

I am not in the mood for arithmetic. I want to think about Pauline. To slowly drift through an action replay of our time together. To wonder where we go from here. Perhaps I wasn't concentrating.

"Fucking millions. Fucking millions. Thank you very much."

Now I see the wisdom of voting against a motion already passed. I have officially registered my disagreement with a decision already taken; and have achieved both the moral high ground and the financial rewards. I have also ingratiated myself with my clerk.

"Not all of us agreed with this John. You know there were some of us against."

"Some of you! Some of you! Only some of you!"

"How many?" he cried. And more ominously, "Who?"

"Well, we needn't go into that." What was the point? He already knew, or sensed, that chambers were overwhelmingly against him. His pals had one by one left to become judges, retired, or simply dropped down dead, and me, McIntosh, and possibly Humphrey were all he'd got left. He knew who we were and didn't need to ask.

The rest of chambers – particularly the younger bar – didn't like forking out 10% for the privilege of being bossed about by a clerk who, because of changing times, no longer had the responsibility of negotiating fees and fixing court lists. The art, the style, the skill had gone; a computer could do it and usually did.

But Jackson was one of the old school, and he was going to

protect his 10% as a matter of honour, of greed, of defiance, of pride in his job. An amalgamation of them all; he would not give way to changing times and the minimising of his role. There was no way he was planning to settle for less.

"They have got no fucking chance. Not a fucking light. You know what they can do with their salary sacrifice."

I had a fair idea. But I was not in the mood for all of this. The sight and smell of Pauline was still upon me and I wanted to sink in the memory of her soft body. I could see her leaning over me as I lay on Humphrey's bed and I could feel her warmth and tenderness, her frenzy and her heat. I could smell her lingering perfume and still feel the smoothness of her skin.

I dragged myself back to Jackson.

"Why don't you negotiate? Look, you've got twenty five men. You can see that 10% from each might be regarded in some quarters as . . . .uhm as a little . . . uhm high. You can still make two hundred and fifty grand a year."

But he was not interested in what he was making. Only in what he was losing. "Fucking millions," he began again, "fucking millions."

Actually I would give 'fucking millions' to be back with Pauline – but was not about to say so.

As Jackson used to tell me, "Sir, a clerk is closer to you than your wife. I am your wife. You tell me everything. This way I know where you are and I can cover. I can cover. Remember, I can give you cover."

And I am going to need plenty of cover. I have big plans for this relationship, and Jackson as he so rightly observes, will need to know where I am. But today he doesn't seem to be concentrating on my case either. We both have more important business of our own.

"I am going to fight these bastards all the way. Salary sacrifice! We'll see who'll be making the fucking sacrifice. And it won't be me."

I hope it won't be me either.

Keep your friends close. Your enemies closer. And fucking sleep with your clerk.

Apart from us the Stag at Bay is deserted. Tables and chairs askew from the lunchtime trade. Ashtrays still full. We are enjoying the slack period before the cleaners come round and the evening crush begins.

Just the two of us. Two old men. Sharing a drink but with diverging prospects ahead. We chart our course by different stars, our eyes on different shores.

Somewhere amongst all this dark oak panelling there is a whiff from Elizabethan days of plotting and betrayal. And Jackson is in the mood for plotting.

"I am going to ring the Barristers Clerks Association." Another dwindling group. "They will want to see my contract."

"John," I said gently, "do you actually have a contract?"

"Not in writing," he sat and thought, his glass halfway to his lips, and then triumphantly "but then neither do they!"

So this is all by word of mouth then. No agreement about holidays, severance, salary, fees, even percentages; nothing. Nothing at all. And certainly nothing in writing.

This is the splendid way my learned friends conduct their affairs. Whitebait Chambers at its brilliant best. Not a document in sight that anyone can refer to – but everyone will be able to remember details clearly. And the details will be different on each side.

I can see this will be a long drawn out fight. Some clerk in Leeds had recently been paid out £150,000 for relinquishing some percentage point or other. John will know about this I am sure.

"And I'll be ringing Charlie Denby in the morning. We'll fucking see." John rubs his hands, warming to the fight. "We'll fucking see what this lot are made of. As if I didn't know. I've been trying to sell these so-called lawyers, exaggerating their non-existent talents, lying up hill and down dale about their imaginary successes for fucking years. They won't be getting so much fucking work now! Bunch of greedy cunts. We'll see. Oh yes, we'll fucking see."

Indeed we shall. I am going to need John more than ever. I can see which side I might be on.

I can see the months slowly stretching ahead. Do the odd case. Take the odd conference in chambers. Occasionally travel to prison for an interview with some forlorn prisoner or other. I see myself in restaurants ordering lunch whilst Pauline lights another cigarette and playfully toys with an olive. I see us together at Humphrey's waterside flat. I will learn to get there in under half an hour; remember where I put the key; learn to recognise the number, nonchalantly open the door.

Happy days that will last forever – and all the time good old Jackson sitting in his clerk's room at chambers loyally giving me cover.

My mind seems to have wandered off again. "Are you fucking listening?" he demands, "what's the matter with you today? This is war. Total absolute fucking war. Me against them. That bunch of fucking wasters and striped-arsed dilettantes. Are you with me or against me? Make up your mind. Whose side are you on?"

I think my mind has been made up, and rising to order one last round and conjuring up all the sincerity I can muster I tell him.

"John. You know you can rely on me."

How many more people am I going to betray today?

Chapter 13

Laura hadn't been very well. She'd not been well for a long time. In fact, she'd never been well at all. She'd never enjoyed the health you feel when you wake up in the morning wanting to punch the air. There was always something niggling away in the background – a migraine; a temperature; a constant dull ache in her neck. When we married twenty five years ago she was in her prime – startlingly beautiful with her straight jet black hair, green eyes, olive skin – even then when she was at her peak and slimmed down to eight stone two pounds – the perfect weight for the wedding – even then there was always something pulling her back and dragging her down.

She put up with cystitis which had her running to the lavatory twenty times a day to pass burning urine often tinged with blood. Her doctor had blamed me – forgetting we'd already been together seven years. He'd blamed me again for nephritis, the chronic inflammation of her kidneys which flared up from time to time, causing stabbing pain in her back.

And the children had been difficult. Both in conception and in birth. Each one, all five of them, delivered by Caesarean Section (a difficult procedure then) which had left Laura exhausted and ill, and each child with a perfectly rounded head.

And as the years wore on she developed spondylosis of the neck – a degenerative condition of the spine where the cartilage slowly wears away, and bone begins to rub against bone – grating when she turned her neck.

She became allergic, little by little, to mussels, to shellfish generally, to anything with nuts. She became terrified of insect bites which made her flesh rise in huge weals that hardened into irritating lumps that itched and wept for days.

Wasps were her particular fear and September was a dangerous month. I remember her sitting in a tent in France, her face a huge balloon, looking out through slitted eyes at more insects circling round the storm lamp hanging from the roof, a roll of newspaper in her hand.

I don't know why she lost her balance. No one could find an explanation for that. It just came over her. One day after visiting a friend she fell over in the street. Over nothing. A perfectly smooth pavement and Laura lying in the road, her ankle broken, unable to move, waiting for a passer-by.

She began to lose her grip and would sometimes drop her glass onto the stone floor of our kitchen, or find it difficult to use her fork, or lose control of her perpetual cigarette and scramble for it frantically down her blouse.

Her feet would swell, her knees would ache, and her head would flash with migraine. And never – never would she complain. These troubles – these embarrassments – became the background noise in her life.

She ignored, laughed at even, her doctor's advice to cut down on cigarettes which she enjoyed and couldn't do without.

"It's not the number that they kill," she would say, pointing her finger at him, "who cares how many thousands die? It's how old they are when they do!" And taking another glass of wine would press her argument home.

"Tell me then. Tell me how old they are, because if they're all dying at thirty then I suppose I'd better stop. But if . . . and this is the point . . . they're all dying at ninety five you better start yourself!

How old is the average age of death? Bugger how many. Do you get it? Do you understand? What are the figures? How old are they when they die? That's what I want to know."

But he had no answer to this. No one did. And Laura would triumphantly punch the air and wink at me and pour the doctor a glass of wine and light another cigarette.

I never thought it was the cigarettes that made her low and it certainly wasn't the wine. Perhaps it was worry. Worry over the children. Worry over all her bloody pets that were always getting ill or run over, or breaking out of the garden or wandering off and getting lost. Or perhaps it was the bank. Yes the bank. Endless worry over the bank. The bank that was driving her mad.

Laura had a little business. As a young girl she had run a couple of children's nurseries, or pre-school playgroups as they were called then. She'd been an overwhelming success because of her gifts with children and no doubt her attraction to the fathers who queued up patiently each morning to hand them over at 9 o'clock.

For some reason she had been loathe to close them down or let them go. But without Laura, now retired and caring for her own family, it wasn't quite the same and the overdraft rose and fell but never disappeared, and lately, according to the bank, a disconcerting trend had arisen. A slow but sure straight line diving ever deeper into the red.

The bank wrote letters. At the customer's expense. Something like £25 each to tell her that she needed a business loan, or a debt consolidation or another chat with her 'financial manager' – a youth about twenty five years old who had never run a business in his life.

They charged you for keeping your money; for transferring your money; for lending you money; for telling you how much money they had lent. They wanted to provide insurance. They proffered financial advice. They whispered at pensions. They were never off the phone, and with everything came a charge that bore down upon both Laura and her little business. I rang the manager once and offered to see him. Anything so that they would leave her alone.

"I don't come in Saturdays. I think more of my family."

I wish he'd thought more about mine.

This constant pestering was driving Laura out of her mind. She didn't like debt – wanted to be 'straight' as she put it. So why didn't I just pay them off? Why didn't I just bail her out? Because Laura wouldn't let me. It upset her more than the bank. It was her business and she wanted to run it. A vestige of independence perhaps? It was her debt and she would pay it. To her, it was as simple as that.

She was also having trouble with her teeth. Those beautiful

teeth that stand out so clearly on our wedding photographs. Laura looking straight into the camera smiling in that refined way. Laura turning to me and laughing. Those beautiful strong teeth. Why had they become looser and longer and occasionally so mobile she could move them with her tongue? Perhaps after the ordeals of childbirth her body was winding down and her sinews, along with her strength, beginning to unravel. Not that she ever gave in. As I've said, she never complained. But the household chores in such a big house were becoming difficult. Hoovering wore her out. She could no longer stand at the ironing board so I took over, amateurishly doing my best.

Eventually we got a cleaner called Val, a happy-go-lucky woman turning to fat. She was fine at first but rapidly became another 'Laura friend', and the pair of them would sit together all morning at the kitchen table drinking, smoking and laughing, and making even more of a mess. I used to complain, "I have to clean up after the cleaner. What's the point of that?"

But the point was it made Laura happy. What else mattered? She couldn't care less about the house being clean.

I just wanted her to feel well again. Not 100% fighting fit. I knew that was impossible. But just a little better. A little less stooped. I wanted to see some of the worry etched in her face fade away. I was anxious for her – probably more anxious than she was for herself.

I bought her a new bed. I invested in several changes of mattress. Anything to help her get a good night's sleep instead of the fitful tossing and turning and half-sleep half-waking that had to pass for rest.

I bought her a reclining chair that adjusted to any position in which she could relax in the bay window of our bedroom and sit and watch her garden and the park below.

Nothing seemed to help. The worry was getting her down. She was always worrying; always had something on her mind.

Was she worrying over me? No. I doubt it. Had she noticed my new-found smartness, the odd time I returned home late. No. I don't think so. It was the bank, the children, her aches and pains, those demanding bloody pets.

Not me. Never. She would have said. Or was she too smart to comment? Too proud to interfere? Or did it suit her? In some unfathomable way, was it what she wanted? A passing distraction that somehow fell in with her plans.

No. Never. I convinced myself. She would have told me. I was being stupid. How could it possibly be me?

Chapter 14

Pauline looked wonderful sitting behind me in court. Efficient, attentive, chaste. It was the contrast between that businesslike, untouchable, aloofness and the wanton moments of madness that added to her attraction and made me want her more.

I couldn't get enough of her. We visited Humphrey's more often than Humphrey – who always politely absented himself without complaint. I thought about it. I hadn't seen him around for days.

Meanwhile our lunchtime encounters had expanded to include lunch. We started earlier. Finished even later. Pauline would bring baguettes, cheese, tomatoes, strawberries and cream. I would bring wine and cigarettes. Occasionally oysters. It became a sort of indoor picnic. Lying on the bed, intermittently eating, raising the occasional glass, the radio tuned to music in the kitchen drowning out our laughter, a background to our love.

I never heard the two men come into the room. Not until the smaller one started shouting that is.

"What's going on here then? What's going on in here?"

A silly question really.

"Who are you?" I gasped. Words do not always come easily.

"Who am I? Who am I? I own this place," said the smaller vociferous one, "and this is the new tenant." He pointed to his larger gawping companion.

"But this flat belongs to Mr Humphrey."

"Humphrey! Humphrey!" my words seemed to set him off again, "wait till I find that bastard. He owes me six months rent."

Wait till I find that bastard too, I thought.

"But surely he is the tenant here. He's lived here for some time."

"Tenant! Tenant!" He had a curious manner of repeating

everything. "He's not the tenant. Left four weeks ago. This gentleman's the tenant. He's going to live here now."

"Delighted to meet you." I held out my hand, confidence returning. "Happy to be your guest."

"Guest! Guest! You're not a guest. You're a fucking trespasser. And who's that tart you've got in bed?"

Hardly a way to refer to the beautiful Pauline. Who had hidden under the duvet. I could feel her getting restless. An indignant stirring by my side.

"Tell them to fuck off," she hissed.

Easier said than done.

"Er . . . I thought we had his permission to use this place for lunch?"

"Lunch? Lunch? You call this lunch? You're supposed to eat it not roll in it. Look what you've done to the bed!"

"Look. Let's be reasonable. An understandable mistake. You wait outside while we get dressed. It won't take a minute; we'll soon be on our way."

But they didn't want to go, didn't want to leave us. They moved in closer, the big one fingered a pillow.

"Now, come on. Just you give us a chance to get our clothes on . . ." I was getting nervous. I knew what they wanted to do.

"Not so fast," said the little ferret, "don't I know you? What's your name? And who's that?" He pointed to the twitching mound that was Pauline and leant across to touch. I had to do something. I wasn't sure exactly what. And then it came to me. A flash of inspiration.

"Johnson. Clarence Johnson. Barrister. My name's Johnson. Contact Whitebait Chambers. Ask to speak to my clerk."

"Ah. Whitebait Chambers. Whitebait Chambers again, is it? No need to tell me the number. Clarence Johnson eh? I think I'll give them a call."

Why did I say that? I must be mad. I don't want this lunatic ringing chambers. Not now while he's got me like this. And what would Jackson say? The man who was giving me cover. Not somebody called Clarence fucking Johnson. Never heard of him. I could hear it now, 'sorry sir' and put down the phone.

Or would he cotton on? Twig it was me? "Are you referring to Judge Johnson? Mr Justice Johnson? My Lord Justice Johnson by any chance?"

Get us out of this mess.

Pauline was getting impatient. I sensed her gritting her teeth. I could feel her nails on my stomach. On another occasion pleasant enough.

"Johnson? Johnson you say your name is?" He produced his mobile phone. "Clarence Johnson eh? I think I'll give them a call."

Pauline had heard enough. Her head broke the surface. "Out! Get out! You pair of tossers. Coming in without knocking. You must have known we were here. Fuck off. Outside the pair of you."

"But this is my flat. This is . . ."

"And you're fucking welcome to it." She was incandescent. "Get your fucking self outside. And you . . ." she turned her attention to the new tenant, "going to live here are you? Going to pay him rent? Well good luck to you. There's only one ring on the cooker and the lavatory's fucking blocked. Oh and the shower's not working. Neither is the fridge. This place is a fucking tip." It didn't seem to bother her why. "So get out the pair of you. That's right. And close that fucking door."

Pauline turned to me with contempt. I daresay some women would find this funny. The sort of sophisticated woman who couldn't care less. One who might get out of bed to advise them to go. Treat them to a quick flash and wave a cheery goodbye.

"That fucking Humphrey. Your pal Humphrey. Why didn't he tell you? Why didn't he tell you he'd gone? When I think . . ."

She jumped out of bed. A glimpse of white bottom and she was dressed.

I couldn't find my glasses. Couldn't see my socks.

"For Christ's sake, hurry up. You're not going to a fucking wedding. Don't bother with the tie."

And thus it was in this way, walking barefoot and carrying

my shoes, shirt, waistcoat and jacket and blinking into the sunlight, I left Humphrey's forever. Banished from the Garden of Eden by the angry landlord and his tenant balefully staring at our backs.

But Pauline wasn't finished. Once outside she started at me again.

"Clarence Johnson. My name's Clarence fucking Johnson. Brilliant. Ask to speak to my clerk. Where do you think that would have got us? You stupid fucking fool."

No. We won't be having a good laugh about this in the future. A hearty chuckle together over a drink after work.

I didn't know it, but a new chapter had begun, tainted, I fear, in Pauline's mind by what had gone before. She never seemed the same again. Her confidence in me had evaporated; never to return.

Looking back, I could see that from this point on she had taken charge and that I had been permanently demoted to the ranks. No longer worthy of the authority of office; Pauline superseded my command and I was happy, relieved really, to let her make the decisions and arrangements which ordered our affair.

As for Humphrey, our erstwhile benefactor, that stupid, middle-aged, quasi–eccentric, amateur thespian, sunglasses wielding, trendy, parsimonious, cunt. That absolute cunt. He thought it was funny.

And, before I finally fathomed Pauline's reaction, so did I.

Chapter 15

Richard Grantham had an engaging smile, considering he had so little to smile about. Twenty five years old and sixty previous convictions. A record of which he was unjustifiably proud.

Starting at twelve years old with being carried in other people's vehicles taken by drivers slightly older than himself. Graduating to taking other people's vehicles and driving them himself. Driving whilst disqualified. Dangerous driving whilst disqualified, being pursued by the police at night. Going through red lights, round roundabouts the wrong way, exceeding the speed limit two and threefold causing, as they say, on-coming vehicles to brake and swerve and ultimately mount the pavement to avoid a head-on crash.

Assorted shop thefts. Then a little commercial burglary – returning to the same shops at night and, after putting concrete through their plate glass windows, running in and rifling the till.

Now – combining both his driving skills and interest in shops, a little ram-raiding. Also at night. This time putting another person's vehicle through another person's shop window and Grantham and his friends filling bin-liners with anything available – in full view of the video camera that, at this stage, they lacked the sophistication to destroy.

And the sentences escalating accordingly. Initially in the Youth Courts and placed under supervision, ordered to Attendance Centres, put on probation, required to complete Community Service Orders (serving in an Oxfam shop) and finally sent to a Young Offenders Institution for a short stretch inside.

And running in tandem with his sentences came his addiction to drugs. A little solvent sniffing at first. The occasional tin of furniture polish perhaps. Then a few pills – Diazepam, Tiazepam, the odd Amphetamine Sulphate, moving on to a little recreational Ecstasy at £10 a pop.

Smoking cannabis with his friends. Smoking heroin through a straw with his friends. Injecting heroin into his arm alone. The occasional rock of crack. And then of course it was the heroin that drove him. Burglaries of sheds at night taking garden tools to sell and, moving up a rung from sheds, to burglaries of garages taking power tools to sell, and graduating from garages to burglaries of houses taking videos, music centres, CDs, jewellery, anything to sell. Anything to pay for heroin.

Daytime dwelling-house burglaries with the husband at work and the wife at the shops. Smashing in through the kitchen window leaving glass all over the floor and ransacking his way from room to room – a trail of open drawers and filthy footprints tracing his route upstairs to look for rings and bracelets in the bedside cabinet and money in the bottom drawer.

Night-time burglaries with the occupants round the corner in the pub coming home to find their back door open to the weather, a trail of destruction and anything valuable (or indeed simply sentimental), gone. Everything gone.

Night-time burglaries of dwelling-houses in the small hours with the owners fast asleep in bed disturbed by a creaking on the stair and a ghostly shadow in their room.

Prison sentences duly followed. For longer and longer periods. The public must be protected, and of course (until he was released) they were. And whilst inside, and heroin still available, he mixed with others of his kind. Talked of girls at home allegedly "standing by him", and crime and more crime, and how crime can be made to pay, and how one day with just a little effort and a little luck he'll make the big time, do a serious job, get set up for life, and break his addiction to drugs.

Which of course he never would. Released from prison and back home with his family, comprising a girlfriend (also an addict) and two children (possibly his), a knock would come upon the door. An offer of a little heroin. A free sample, a little starter pack, impossible to resist, they always seek you out.

And within days he would be off again, running a daily £80 habit and paying for it the only way he could – breaking into other people's houses and ruining other people's lives.

So Richard Grantham smiled at me and Pauline as we walked into his cell. He seemed genuinely pleased to see me. Perhaps he was. He'd known me so long he confused me for a friend.

And again he'd committed the usual litany of night-time burglaries – only this time a novel addition. Escape. Grantham had been arrested from an upstairs room at a supervised residence for old people where (the prosecution would say) vulnerable people had been targeted and which he would say was an accident of chance. Whilst at the police station he was ill. Shivering, shaking, incoherent. Possibly withdrawing from heroin, probably trying it on. He had been taken to hospital, admitted, and placed in a single room, a policeman on guard at the door whiling away the time chatting and laughing with the nurse.

Grantham, left to his own devices inside, soon 'recovered'. Wearing a white coat left conveniently in a cupboard, he had softly opened a window and hair-raisingly climbed seven storeys down the hospital's face to the car park far below. Easier breaking out than in.

Still wearing his white coat he had strolled off round the corner and disappeared, only to be re-arrested three days later jacking-up on heroin with his girlfriend back at home.

"What will I get for this?" he wanted to know.

Always tell them more than you think they're going to get. This way they might be grateful for the sentence they were going to get anyway.

"Three for the burglaries and one consecutive for escape. A bit of unexpired licence. Say, four and a half." The dreaded long term sentence. He's going to be pleased when my brilliance reduces this to three.

However, in the meantime he was not so pleased with the forecast. "Christ. It's only burglaries. It's not rape, I'm not a paedophile, no one got hurt."

Several points arise out of this. It is true there is no sex. But to claim no one got hurt is not quite right. People who have their homes defiled by strangers are hurt. They feel personally violated. It disturbs the sense of security they had hitherto felt in their home. They become nervous. They can't settle. Their sleep is disrupted. They fret about the court case, about insurance, about the damage and the loss. About the little sentimental things that can never be replaced. Make no mistake, Mr Grantham, people are hurt. Burglary is an offence against the person. Don't let us forget that.

"Christ, I'm not a fucking armed robber."

We're on safer ground here. Nothing can compare to a person who points a sawn-off shotgun at a woman's face. Who carries tape to tie their victims up.

Although often idolised by fools in prison, and idealised by those who should know better, they are not glamorous gangsters or Hollywood look-alikes, who for their own maverick reasons, deprived upbringing, or sense of fun and adventure, take on society as rogues with a heart of gold. One of the lads. One of the gang. The goodfellas.

They are hard, calculating, cruel and greedy. They can watch a woman wet herself and cry. Hold a gun to another man's head. Cause serious mental damage. Serious physical injury. The lowest of the low.

"No Mr Grantham. We have not sunk that far."

Not yet.

It is not the effect of heroin that turns addicts into criminals. The effect is to render the user comatose in much the same way as cannabis does It makes him happy, sleepy and content. No, it is not the effect. It is the need to pay ridiculous prices to buy the effect. £10 deals, £20 deals. Three, four and five times a day. In the end, just to stay normal. Just to get by.

And the only way to feed a £40 or £50 or £80 daily habit is to turn to crime. To burgle, rob, and steal. To deal a bit yourself. Anything to raise the money to pay the price, any price, to satisfy a hunger that must be fed.

But it would be so easy to reduce the price to almost nothing. After all, poppies and cocoa plants don't cost much. Peasants grow them all over the world. Heroin is cheaper than sugar. The price of production is minimal, and, when refined, the costs of transport equally small. But by the time the prohibited substance has passed down the chain from grower to wholesaler and been divided and sub-divided, and cut a million times, and been foiled, or packaged in a Rizla or a freezer bag, and pushed out on the streets to the likes of Richard Grantham, the price has doubled, re-doubled, quadrupled and doubled again and comes out at £10 or £20 a deal and the farmer far away can eat his bowl of rice.

Pauline has used the time to pass Richard Grantham a letter from his wife and, nervously picking at his blackened fingernails, his chair drawn up tight under the metal table, he sits reading the large capital letters that she uses to convey her love.

What a wasted life. Locked up in his cell twenty-three hours a day with a rotating crew of strangers, whilst his children grow up on their estate without a father, and his lovely wife, in the grip of her addiction and at the beck and call of every dealer on the block, resumes her shoplifting and begins to think of going on the game.

It would be so ridiculously easy to stop all this. Simply lift the prohibition. De-criminalise drugs. Legalise the lot. Collapse the price. No more dirty needles, gang wars, or drug-related crime.

But the farce goes on. Addicts are jailed. Small time suppliers who supply to feed their own addiction are rounded up from the streets and jailed. Only to be replaced in the morning by others waiting in the wings, impatient to step in their shoes.

Both Pauline and Richard Grantham are looking at me. It seems I might have paused.

"No, Mr Grantham, you are only a poor bloody addict driven to fund his addiction and when normal, if ever that time comes, you will feel sorry for your victims and know that not only have you destroyed your own life, you have tried to destroy theirs."

I can see this is not going down too well. With either of my audience. Better lighten up.

"Don't worry Mr G. I'll keep it low. Have no fear. Trust in me."

No judge will hear me – not ever – complaining that our Mr Grantham is a victim, not only of his own weakness but of a system that is so deep-rooted and self-righteous that it is incapable of accepting the fact that for a moment it might – just possibly might – have got it wrong.

I look across at Pauline making a discreet 'wind-it-up' sign with her hand and watch her eyes roll as I get set to start again.

"Thank you Mr Wallace," she interrupts, "very informative I must say. I'm sure Mr Grantham is much reassured. Anything below four will do us fine." And turning to the hapless Grantham whilst pushing back her chair, "I'll be in touch with your wife. Tell her to try and keep out of trouble and come and see you when she can. I've got to dash now. And don't worry, you know Mr Wallace, he sometimes gets carried away. Everything will turn out fine."

Once outside she is not quite so pleasant. "What gets into you? You sit there day-dreaming and come out with a load of bollocks when you eventually wake up. Barmy." She shakes her head, and walks off down the road to where I'd managed to park my car about a couple of miles away.

I try to catch her up.

"But Pauline my love. I really must protest. Don't you see, if all drugs were legal, crime would fall by half." I clutch desperately at her retreating shoulder.

"Oh yes? Just remember this," she turns to tell me, "if that great day ever comes, so will your pay – and you'll be looking for another job. Your days of lecturing poor sods like Grantham will be over. You might have to try working for a change."

I nearly said it but I didn't. And you Pauline my love would still be stuck with Barry hoovering up his fucking mess.

It's amazing really how drugs can benefit us all.

Chapter 16

Laura didn't seem to be getting any better. She was now suffering from indigestion which always struck at night, causing her to sit upright in bed and rub her stomach to soothe the pain. We tried calcium carbonate pills of one brand or other and they worked at first. A couple of these and she was fine, and we would light up again and lie chatting for hours.

I told her, naturally, about Jackson and what had become a long drawn out fight to the finish between chambers in one corner and Jackson in the other with one or two members standing in the wings occasionally offering encouragement to one side or the other and pretending to be on both.

She was firmly on Jackson's side.

"What does it matter what he's making so long as everybody else is making theirs? They're a bunch of mean bastards in your chambers."

Probably in every chambers. But they're not my responsibility. I didn't ask them to buy executive style look-alike houses on new developments on the fashionable side of Hull. Fashionable side of Hull? Something of an oxymoron perhaps.

Nor did I advise on the purchase of all those BMWs and Mercedes currently occupying chambers' car park alongside town and country 4 x 4 offroaders that took up too much bloody space.

Nor had I counselled their marriages to chambers' wives – that godforsaken bunch of fat and grasping women that turned up at Law Society dinners and dances wearing expensive gowns and diamonds that might be real. I hadn't taken out subscriptions to health clubs, invested in personalised number plates or bought timeshares in Tenerife. I wasn't saving up to buy some naff villa on a golf course in the Algarve.

I wasn't paying school bills or buying golf clubs or going business class to Dubai. Nothing to do with me.

I was wasting my money on other things. Booking hotel rooms by the hour, and smoking and drinking to excess.

Giles had consulted chambers' solicitors in Hull. God knows what we occasionally charged them, but they certainly knew how to charge us. They told us we had a good case.

Jackson had consulted solicitors acting for the Barristers Clerks Association. A firm in London. They told him he had a good case.

The stage seemed to be set for everyone to make a lot of money. Except for us and Jackson that is.

I told Laura that Jackson had shown me a letter he had received.

"Your claim to what has become an unreasonable, preposterous, percentage payment on gross chambers' income is no longer sustainable or justifiable. Might we remind you that you have no written contract. It is an implied term of your oral agreement with chambers that your remittance be reviewed on an annual basis. This has now been done. We strongly advise you that chambers' offer to remunerate you at a gross rate of 4% (I thought it was 5% but battle lines seem to have hardened) is a generous one that remains provisional upon your prompt acceptance within a period not exceeding ten days."

Well things are progressing in the usual matey way. Nothing like getting solicitors involved to improve the atmosphere.

Laura thinks John should tell them to fuck off. He already has done. His solicitors have written back.

"Our client has a long-standing agreement with chambers, which incidentally he co-founded with two others over forty years ago, that his commission shall be calculated at a rate of not less than 10% of gross chambers' income excluding travel disbursements and to include N.I.C. payments and private health insurances for himself and his family to be paid by your goodselves, such agreement and binding contract having been negotiated many years ago when chambers was first created for and on behalf of parties who may no longer be members but whose liability remains on-going and transferable by reason of your membership of a body corporate."

Well you get what you pay for in London. How will our little firm of local solicitors respond to this? Robustly I imagine. Years of correspondence lies ahead. They could spin this out forever, until on the day of trial standing at the door of the court a compromise is cobbled together – and we agree what we should have agreed to years before. What would have been so easy with a little good sense and a touch of goodwill, and which any sane person would have known was inevitable, and could have been done with a shake of the hand and a spirit of, if not friendship, at least of mutual respect – and which might have been achieved if solicitors had not been involved, and inflammatory correspondence despatched and stances struck and enormous costs ran up.

But Laura is wincing again, and rubbing her stomach is not helping. She will have to go to the doctors and get it sorted out. As ever, she is reluctant to go. It is her nature not to bother people with what she regards as trivia.

"They are busy enough without having to see me at every touch and turn. Last time the waiting-room was crowded. Absolutely crowded. I was there ages. Probably came home with something worse."

"Come on Laura. Get it sorted out. It won't take a minute. It's not going to hurt."

God I love her so much. I lay my hand against her warm bottom when she turns on her side for relief. "Promise me you'll get an appointment," I urge her. "Come on Laura, get it sorted out."

But she has fallen silent. Lying beside her I know she is thinking. I feel her gentle breathing and I can almost hear her mind going round turning over the consequences of an appointment of which she is instinctively afraid.

Chapter 17

Pauline was now organising things, having promoted herself to being the one in charge of our affair. Ever the girl for a bargain – she has rang around town on the firm's phone and found a cheap hotel reasonably convenient to court. She has even inspected the room.

"£25 all in. It's called 'Pat's Place'. Round the corner from the Chinese. Stay as long as you like – but no breakfast. Cash of course."

I am not interested in breakfast, but I am more than interested in Pauline. I am beginning to lose my head. I arrive home later and later – occasionally dishevelled. Does her perfume linger? I don't know. I no longer have time for the precautionary post-coital shower spinning out, as I do (and often against her wishes), our short times together.

I would see her every day. Every minute of every day if I could get away with it. I think of her constantly. She floats before me businesslike with glasses and suit; I see her running between shops trying on shoes and pointing her ankle at the floor mirror; sitting in the pub behind a double gin and tonic; ordering lunch with that firmness and decisiveness that are her trademarks; abandoned in bed at Pat's. She is everywhere. She is everything. And as my obsession grows I sense her slowly pulling apart. As I wade ever deeper into the lake her blonde head is bobbing away towards the opposite shore.

Barry is being difficult. Naturally argumentative, he is intent on causing trouble – apparently obsessed with money. "I've given him the fucking lot already," Pauline complains, "what more does he want? Jesus Christ, he never leaves me alone. Telephone calls at home at all hours night and day, notes through the children, urgent messages at work. He's going fucking barmy. You tell me – whatever did I see in him? Whatever did I see in a cunt like that?"

Apparently there are credit card debts. Small matters of

clothes bills. Overdue council tax. Persistent mortgage arrears. He hasn't taken well to rejection – in spite of his having found another girl. Perhaps he had her all along. A small dumpy pleasant girl who apparently sides with – probably encourages – his ever more unreasonable demands.

I am lying in bed at Pat's listening to Pauline complain. I seem to be spending a lot of time in bed these days. Pauline is sitting up. Stabbing the air with her cigarette.

"For some reason . . . for some fucking reason he's contacted the Child Support Agency."

I study her naked back. Examine the moles. Run a finger down her spine in the faint hope of inspiring an encore. "Why would he do that?" I venture.

"Why would he do that? How should I fucking know? Money. Always money. He's always after fucking money. Because for the moment, just for the moment, my youngest are with him."

I have never considered Pauline's financial status before. I had always assumed that she was reasonably well off. Married for years and both working. Nice house in Beverley. Caravan holidays once a year. Occasionally off to Spain. Nothing special. Nothing extravagant.

"We never got out much," she used to say.

It sounded like they never got out at all.

"The Child Support Agency?" I enquire. "Is this the same firm that has brought us lunatic financial demands from absent partners? Letters that make no sense, 'professional assessments' that cause bankruptcy and suicide. Is this the outfit with which Barry has now so brilliantly involved us?"

Pauline is contemptuous. Livid. "They keep writing to me. They want to know everything. I ring them back but the person I am dealing with is out, or ill, or at a meeting, or 'on a course'. So I talk to somebody else. I explain everything again, and two days later I get another letter asking the same things that I have spent hours on the phone already explaining. So I ring back again. And now the last person I talked to is out or at lunch or ill or on holiday. So I talk to somebody else. I go all through the same fucking things again. And today.

Today. I get another fucking letter asking me to tell them all over again what I have spent days, fucking days, already setting out before. They are fucking barmy. They are driving me insane. All because of that fucking stupid Barry."

I have a brainwave. "Maybe Barry has not disclosed his real earnings. What about his overtime? What about the cars he fixes over the weekends for cash? What about the part-time butchering he does at his pal's shop when his pal is away?"

Pauline bites her lip. She is thinking. It may not be in everyone's interest to go down this road. I wonder, not for the first time, what Barry has got on her. What has she been up to herself?

"No. I don't think so. No." She makes up her mind, "No forget it. I'll just fucking kill myself like all the rest."

It never occurs to me to offer to help. Why not? I am not a mean man. Probably the opposite. I squander money. Generous to a fault. Always the first to buy a round and always tip the barmaid. Always picking up the tab for lunch. Laura and the children can have anything. The children's friends constantly in residence with us can have anything. I have never bothered about money. And for some reason the more I earn the more the overdraft grows.

So why did I never think to offer help? More ominously why did Pauline never ask?

After years of Barry, freedom must have tasted sweet. Another relationship underpinned by debt and gratitude made her shy away.

Or perhaps it was pride. She needed to stand on her own feet. Needed to know she could do it. Provide for her children and herself and be dependant on nobody. Despite Barry trying to drag her down with the dead malicious weight of his envy. She could do it. She could and would provide. And anyway, the last thing she needed was to get too involved with an ageing barrister with a wife. Her eyes were already over the horizon scouting for better things.

"I've got to go." I reached vainly for her retreating back. Watched her dress and disappear through the door with a wave. I listened to her feet clattering down the stairs and heard her footfall in the street below. Running, always running. Really a movement between walking and running. But lithe and quick and confident. And so within seconds I heard her reach the corner and her steps fade away towards the station, and I lay back and thought of her and Laura, but for some reason, I cannot say why – to my eternal shame I cannot say why – it never occurred to me to help.

Chapter 18

A huge brief had arrived in chambers. Boxes and boxes of lever arch files stacked in the corner of Jackson's office. He pointed at it with obvious satisfaction.

"Out of town, sir. St. Albans, sir. Your name on it, sir. Spoke to the solicitors yesterday. Good for ten weeks."

He made it sound as if he had obtained it for me personally. Perhaps he had. Yet another dividend springing from my judicious vote at chambers' meeting?

I told Pauline over lunch. "Could be away for three months," I mentioned casually.

"Enjoy yourself, dear." She was studying her nails.

Laura took it differently. She didn't want me to go. She couldn't see the point. "You've got lots of work in Hull," she complained. "I won't see you for weeks."

Well, actually, I hadn't got lots of work in Hull. I may have pretended I had. I may have told Laura I had. In reality my policy of 'looking for work' definitely wasn't working. However hard I tried.

Young solicitors wanted young barristers and old solicitors had retired and couldn't care less.

"Jackson thinks I should go," I said, playing my trump card. "He thinks it will do me good. Raise my profile. Bring me better work."

Laura thought about this. She never took Jackson lightly. "We don't need the money. I need you here with me."

I knew she had been to the doctor. I had forgotten to ask her how she had got on. "What did he say?" I rushed in. "How are you?"

She looked at me slowly. This was the first thing I should have asked. She made no comment. "Everything's fine. Don't worry. Just indigestion."

Oh well, I thought, that's all right then, and I got back to talking about myself and the fraud brief and the huge amount of money it was bound to generate. And inevitably I began to plan how to spend it. Spend it, of course, before I was anywhere near getting the cheque.

This is perhaps why the overdraft kept rolling up. I spent money when I got a brief. I spent the money all over again when I did the trial. And then gloriously I spent it all over again when I finally got paid.

Laura was looking tired. She didn't want a drink, she wanted to go to bed and lie down leaving me alone in the kitchen for almost the first time in our happy married life. But I couldn't settle. Soon I had joined her and was pestering her with the new brief and rattling on about my plans to stay in St. Albans. As ever, she showed interest and was kind.

I told Pauline again the following lunchtime. Perhaps she had misheard the day before. She was sitting opposite me staring over her empty plate at my full one. I had never known anyone eat so fast. She could swallow sausages whole. Sideways.

And I was never really hungry. I was full of nicotine and lager. I wasn't here for the food – I was here to see Pauline and nail her down for another visit to Pat's – interrupting regretfully yet insistently what was becoming her rapidly expanding social schedule and the ever-increasing demands upon her time.

She had made friends with the typists at Cranmer, Carter & Co. and with female runners at other firms, but her current favourite was Doreen, our very own telephonist. Another lonely heart. What had started as occasional drinks after work (each one buying their own) had slowly escalated into the occasional night out sharing a quiet meal together, to doing the local round of pubs and finally ending up in a club.

What could I do? I was powerless. I was at home in the bosom of my family whilst Pauline and her mate, in my mind's eye at least, were scouring the city looking for men.

"What will you do while I'm away?" I asked. (I had decided to go the previous night.)

"Away where?" she asked, "what are you talking about?"

". . . . St. Albans. I am going . . . . to . . . ." I spelled it out slowly, "St. Albans . . . for . . . three . . . . months."

She reached across towards my plate and took a sausage. "I can't bear to waste food," she remarked.

And so I left Hull for the great fraud trial. Laura in pain, and Pauline indifferent.

So what was this fraud all about? Even at the end when the jury retired to consider their verdicts, I still didn't understand it. Not fully, not so that my final speech made any sense. But then my final speeches have very little to do with the evidence. I never want to be fettered by the facts.

The defendant Jasbir Singh, otherwise known as Jas, a large, amiable, highly intelligent and non-religious twenty-five year old Sikh explained it to me. As much as I needed to know.

He was a broker working from Birmingham. Definitely not something in the city. He dealt in cars, or more accurately arranged deals in cars. Usually to car hire firms. Usually one firm. So the scam went something like this. A car hire firm was set up in London in the business of hiring out cars, vans and even lorries to the public from premises in the East End on the Roman Road.

Through Jas, the car hire firm got its cars from large main dealers who supplied brand new Fords, BMWs, Mercedes and even Bentleys "for that luxury feeling of real class", as the hire firm said in its blurb.

Jas was in charge of the contracts. Let us say 10 BMWs at a price of £35,000 each. A finance company to lend the money, repayable monthly over two years at so much a month. Everybody was happy. The main dealer was happy having sold 10 BMWs. The salesman at the dealer's was happy having made his commission. The finance company was happy to provide the loan and collect both commission and interest. The hire company was happy with the terms negotiated by Jas. Jas was even happier with his commissions which he apparently took from the dealer AND the finance company AND the hire firm as well. So where did it all go wrong?

Well actually the hirer wasn't really going to pay the

monthly instalments for the BMWs. Not ever. In effect it had free use of 10 BMWs for however many months it took the finance company or the dealer, or assorted strong men to get them back.

In the meantime the public had been paying cheap – call them 'competitive' – prices and the money had been pouring in. And Jas had not been idle either. He had been on the telephone to another dealer (preferably in Cornwall), fixing up another deal for another 10 BMWs to come rolling down the Roman Road to replace those that had been – from God knows where and in God knows what condition – repossessed at last.

Occasionally the car hire company changed names. Sometimes it moved to new premises. And always everything seemed in order because their books (the healthy profit and loss accounts and balance sheets prepared by a friendly accountant) showed a company with a record of successful and honest trading going back for years.

Meanwhile in St. Albans four men stood in the dock charged with conspiracy to defraud. Three menials from the hire company and Jas. As usual, the men at the top were absent. Absent without leave. No doubt enjoying the money (that had also gone absent) in warmer and friendlier climes.

I rang Pauline every day but was having difficulties getting through. As our hours overlapped she was always at court when I rang the office, and when I finally got through to her children in the evening at home she had 'just gone out'.

Laura was always there. She had been prescribed Gaviscon and was feeling much better. She told me not to worry, and so I tended to concentrate on reaching Pauline just to make sure she was all right. On the odd times I did get through she always seemed to be in a rush.

"We're run off our feet up here," she explained, "never known it so busy. A very important client. Got to go. Goodbye."

And so with a mounting sense of foreboding I let it go at that, and tried to read the mounting piles of papers and to do the best I could, in the circumstances, for Jas.

The trial was not going particularly well. Police experts had been belatedly going through his computer. More car hire company accounts had turned up. Not for this year, or last year or the year before that. Strangely and inexplicably they were for the future – two and three years literally down the road.

I needed to 'take instructions', as we lawyers say. I needed to know how it could be that Jas was so prescient. How he was able to tell that in three years time the hire company was still doing so well? How could he predict that once again it had changed its name to something similar, nearly the same, but not quite, and had once again moved on to a new address in the East End. An address that was not even on the market. And how was it possible to know that in three years time it would have made precisely £739,217.27 profit and, for example, had spent £832.60 on its post?

Jas laughed when asked for his explanation. "Perhaps our accountant can see into the future or he does them whole-sale," he suggested. "Gives a discount for bulk orders – saves going back every year."

The jury are not going to like this. Nor is his bewildered father who every day sits turbaned at the back of the court trying to follow the trial and meticulously taking notes.

Still. We must soldier on. So long as the defendant says, "I didn't do it", "Not Guilty", "I did nothing wrong", we must continue to defend, putting forward, in the best light possible, his defence. Whatever that is. Jas hadn't made up his mind.

The other defendants have a much better run. They are saying they simply worked in the office, or cleaned or delivered cars. How would they know whether or not the firm was keeping up with its payments? How did they know what the bogus accountants had said? Turning a blind eye, of course, to the hundreds of cars snatched back from under their noses, and never wondering why the firm was continually changing its name and address.

Others higher up the tree were in charge. Others like Jas. Our man who arranged the contracts and worked for commission and cash. Not me they said – but – it could be him. It could be Jas. And thus all three co-defendants were either directly or indirectly pointing the finger at their erstwhile friend Jas. What is known in legal circles as a 'cut throat' defence. And I had a fair idea of whose throat was likely to be cut, producing the dread result most feared by trial lawyers:

Defendant A – Not Guilty
Defendant B – Not Guilty
Defendant C – Not Guilty

Jasbir Singh – Guilty. Guilty of every single count!
The only one convicted out of four!

It would be difficult dressing that one up as a victory if I ever got home.

And as the trial wore on the evidence piled up. It takes a certain sort of barrister to prosecute fraud. One who, for example, understands accounts. One who is prepared to pore over figures for hours on end and sit up half the night getting their papers in order. One who does not necessarily sparkle in court.

Grovehill was such a one. Approaching sixty; thin beneath his shiny suit, bald beneath his wig, meticulous and humourless; overlooked for promotion; no doubt ignored at home. Sparkling was not a word which sprang to mind.

For me, the pleasure in convicting the guilty is not so great as that in acquitting the innocent, and doesn't get close to the pleasure in acquitting the guilty.

Grovehill didn't see it that way. It was his public duty to make sure that guilty men didn't slip through the net. He had devoted his life to it. He wasn't about to start doing anyone any favours now. On the other hand, his slow pedestrian style certainly bored the jury and (more importantly) irritated the judge.

I kept trying to make sense out of Jas's instructions. Why, when dealers raised obvious questions about the payment history and general viability of the firm, had Jas assured each and every one of them in that affable way of his that yes, there may have been some company with a dodgy reputation operating somewhere in the East End but no, it certainly wasn't this one when he most certainly knew that it was?

Why had he started negotiations for say 10 BMWs from the opposite end of the country when he knew – had arranged even – delivery of an identical 10 BMWs the day before?

How many BMWs does this firm need?

"Not too many at a time," he laughed, "just a constant supply."

I wondered, not for the first time, how this equated with innocence, and how he would eventually perform in front of the jury if I were ever driven to call him and put him in the witness box, so that he could give some evidence himself.

The prosecution team grew slowly more confident. They accepted that the menials might go free, and that the top men were probably enjoying the money in Tenerife, but it would be nice to get Jas – and send him away for a little while too. And so we became the main target, not only for our co-defendants but for everybody else, and by the time (it seemed like years) Grovehill closed the case for the prosecution our position had become so hopeless that there was nothing for it but to put up the main man himself.

And I have to say he was brilliant.

"Tell me this Mr Singh," said the relentless Grovehill, "Why it is . . . . why it is . . . . we find you saying this hire firm is sound, yes sound . . . . sound and profitable remember in a letter, let me see, yes a letter dated 27th October 2000 and signed by you – it is your signature I presume?"

And Jas was off the hook. Never ask two questions at once.

"Might I see it please," asked the genial Mr Singh holding it up to the light and pretending to inspect it while thoughtfully rubbing his chin. "Well, it looks like my signature, well a bit like it anyway, but then of course in a busy office one falls into the habit – I know we shouldn't – of signing for each other. I suppose it could have been signed by anybody."

"But surely you would remember the letter?" Grovehill was losing track of his original question. "Well I'm not too sure it is my letter. I write hundreds of letters. We all do. Often for each other."

"Well assuming it to be your letter," persists Grovehill.

The judge had heard enough. He had drawn the short straw in being given this case in the first place. No early days. No list of guilty pleas. No sentences to impose, or is it inflict, for at least twelve weeks.

Just days and days listening to Grovehill, and long nights of trying to make some sense of it, and hours of work lined up in preparing for his summing up which for all the notice the jury were going to take of it he might have polished off in five minutes.

"We cannot just assume things Mr Grovehill," he cautioned. "Either you prove it or he admits it."

Jas wasn't about to admit to anything.

The judge leant forward, "Is it your letter or isn't it?"

"Possibly," said the ever helpful Mr Singh, "let me think."

He held it up to the light again, squinting at the squiggle at the bottom and scratching his head, the jury watching his every move. "Yes," he finally announced. "Yes. That's right. Certainly it's possible, of that I am absolutely sure."

He managed to muddy the waters with unsurpassed success. He was courteous to the Crown. He never asked questions back and never sounded 'clever'. Always smiling at the jury. Attentive when the judge took over the cross-examination and in spite of considerable pressure still respectful and polite.

And, of course, an answer for everything. So gnomic and obscure that nobody could make head nor tail of it. But the thing was, and here is the art of it, he made everything, including the preposterous, sound absolutely believable. Not only believable but true.

How could anyone possibly believe he had done anything wrong? Trying his hardest, occasionally taking orders, trying to make the best out of the odd bad job, humanly falling into error, trying not to let the firm down, the customers down, his own little broken business down, dragging home a menial salary to provide for his family, but for God's sake, doing his best to keep going. Like all of us. Like you, members of the jury. Just trying to do his best. Trying his best to get by.

And you could see them think, "Well, I don't really understand all of it but I can see how difficult it can be and it does sometimes sound convincing. And he is a very nice chap."

And I daresay they were having difficulty in deciding who the real losers in all of this were.

So was I. I tried to work it out.

Not the great British public. They had enjoyed the use of cheap cars in the Roman Road for years. Certainly not the salesmen as they had already trousered their commission. Certainly not Jas who had charged commission both ends and sideways and whose bank accounts had never been traced. Not even the main dealers as they made their profit when they sold their cars to the finance companies.

So it must have been the finance companies then who were the losers when they bought and hired out a brand new car and recovered several months later a car with 10,000 miles on the clock and not an instalment paid.

But no, not them either because they were insured for loss.

So, I suppose, if I have got this right, it must have been the insurance companies who lost; but they in turn had re-insured with other insurance companies, who had re-insured with each other, and who had re-insured with syndicates at Lloyds who in turn re-insured with corporations in New York and so on in ever widening circles and when these tiny waves eventually broke on the edge of a vast and distant shore, their effect was imperceptible, and nobody really had lost anything at all.

The jury disagreed. They found all four guilty. The jury out for twenty-five minutes following a summing-up of two days, speeches for four days and a trial lasting twelve weeks. What miserable self-righteous bastards they must have been. They obviously wanted to be off in a hurry.

But it was 'not so fast' for the defendants. The judge spelt it out.

"It is essential the public have faith in, and can put their trust in, our financial institutions. That as a great commercial nation we maintain the highest standards of probity. That the lifeblood of the city is not polluted by foul corruption."

I seem to remember directors of public companies receiving

huge salaries, share options, fat pensions, 'success' incentives when their companies went bust leaving their shareholders with nothing. No matter. They were lucky. They were higher up the tree.

"You are a menace to society," the judge continued, "you have refused to plead guilty and maintained your ridiculous defence to the end and in the face of overwhelming evidence. You have, typically, tried to brazen things out. You have failed. Three years, each of you. Take them down."

I tried to ring Pauline to tell her the result but somehow couldn't get through.

Laura was sympathetic. "Bad luck. After all the effort you put in. You must be very disappointed."

I can live with the disappointment when I get the cheque.

"When are you coming home?" she asked. I have returned home the occasional weekend, but it has been a long time. I love her and I have missed her, and I want to see her. To be with her. I want to see how she looks and feels. I want to see if she is any better. I want to sit at our kitchen table and open a bottle of wine. I want to be at home.

Jas's father had been hovering in the background while I made my calls. Eventually he came up to me and with great dignity shook my hand and thanked me for trying so hard. Apparently he enjoyed my speech. He couldn't understand why the jury did not believe his son.

"He is a good son," he said. "He has always worked hard at his office. Always on the phone. He has always been very clever with figures. And do you know, he has always been able to do his own accounts – I wonder why that never came out? He always did his own accounts."

"I want you to go downstairs to the cells," he continued. "Please go and see him. Tell him not to worry. Tell him everything is going to be all right. He will be out soon. I shall do his sentence myself."

So I trudged down to the cells and gave Jas the good news. In the background I could hear him, as usual, talking and laughing. He was unabashed. He smiled when I told him that his father would do his time.

"Oh he means it you know." He grinned at a passing female prison officer. "Did it for me before. When we lived abroad."

"Well thanks for everything Mr Wallace." He put his arm round my shoulders. "Don't worry. I've got plans. Look after yourself, take good care Henry old pal . . ." I wasn't sure I liked the sound of this. "Just you take it steady – until we meet again." I liked the sound of that even less.

Something made me think I'd not seen the last of him. I was more than a little wary. What did he mean? Did he think I would be joining him in prison? Had he been talking to his father? Did he think a barrister who loses did some of his time?

Chapter 19

I am, once again, back in the Stag at Bay staring at the doleful face of Giles and putting away the odd pint of lager. He is drinking Chardonnay. He nurses his glass for comfort and never puts it down.

"Who would have thought it?" he moans. "Who would bloody Adam and Eve it? Who could possibly have known Jackson could be so difficult?"

I'm surprised he's surprised.

"The man's impervious to reason," he drones on. "He's up in arms. Won't talk to me. All he says is 'my solicitors will be writing to you' and closes his bloody door. I have to ring him up to try and make contact, and when I do finally get through to the bastard, all he does is give me his solicitor's number and hang up."

"And . . . And . . ." Giles continues, "I haven't seen a bloody brief for weeks."

Now there's a surprise. And here's one more. My pigeon-hole has been overflowing. So much so that Jackson has commandeered another one for me, ostentatiously glued my name on its polished wooden surface — and filled that up too.

"You seem to be busy." Giles eyes me narrowly. "Work coming in all right for you?"

"Not bad," I shrug. "Not bad."

How can I say this? Four pigeonholes kept so engorged that members of chambers have to walk round briefs that have spilled out onto floor.

"I've been getting a lot from Tomkinson lately."

"Tomkinson you say. Tomkinson." Giles eyebrows move up and down and then stay up. "You must have been laughing at his jokes. Can't understand it, always found him a stupid snide bastard myself. Anyway." Giles returns to his theme, forgetting for a moment the great dam that Jackson has erected in chambers that sends the crashing tide of briefs flowing my way.

"Anyway. What are we going to do about this bloody case that Jackson seems so intent on fighting? Our solicitors' charges are enormous. Now, contrary to expectations, we are going to have to put contributions up." With all these surprises I need another drink.

"Really. I thought the idea of all of this . . . . your idea," I stress genially, "was that it would bring our contributions down."

Giles sighs. "It was Horace's idea. The man in the fucking silver suit. He insisted on it. Jackson won't talk to him either."

Another empty pigeonhole then.

It's going to be easy to tell in chambers who are Jackson's friends.

"Well, I've been away," I stress. "Nothing to do with me. Wish I could help in some way." I am becoming the man in the white suit.

"I daresay it'll all blow over in a year or two," I encourage, "when Jackson settles for 20%."

But Giles is not amused.

"This could be the end of Whitebait Chambers as we know it. The end of an era." Giles always talks like he is addressing a jury.

"The end of one of the great institutions of the city of Kingston Upon Hull. One of the finest sets of chambers on the North Eastern Circuit. Possibly the finest set of chambers."

It must be something in the Chardonnay.

"And . . . And . . ." he concludes somehow pointing an accusing finger at me, "our downfall came about on my watch, when I was at the helm. During my . . . yes my . . . leadership of chambers." Leadership's putting it a bit high.

"Don't blame yourself dear chap," I say, putting my arm on his and knocking his Chardonnay over. "Let me have a word with Jackson. I'm sure it will all settle down."

Giles seems to cheer up. "Will you? Will you see what you can do. Try and get him to see reason. Sound him out. See if there's a chance to compromise."

And then as he lumbers to his feet and hoists up his striped trousers, he says emotionally, "I knew . . . I knew all along I could rely on you."

Now for the first time I really do find this surprising. So much for leadership. I watch him stagger away – no doubt to re-inspect his pigeonhole. And so with Giles' blessing I conduct my second audience of the day in the Stag at Bay. This time it is Jackson sitting before me. We are both drinking pints of lager, so I am going to have to be careful where I put my arms. I seem to have been in this place all day. Perhaps I have. Jackson is far more entertaining.

"I've got these bastards by the balls," he cries as a starter.

"This is going to cost them thousands, fucking thousands," he rubs his hands together and lights another cigarette, "and I haven't even fucking started yet."

It seems important to calm him down a bit. Let him see the pitfalls of litigation. Appraise him of the odds. After all he, the untutored clerk, is taking on an experienced team of highly qualified barristers used to giving the likes of Jackson a good stuffing, and then claiming their costs.

"What is all this costing you John?" I ask. "If you lose you face disaster."

Jackson knows his men better than I do. "Lose to that lot? That lot beat me? This is Whitebait Chambers you know," he laughs, "famous for snatching defeat from the jaws of victory and making ruin out of plenty. Anyway. I'm not paying. The Barristers' Clerks Association's shouldering the lot."

There is nothing worse than trying to persuade a confident litigant to settle when he has nothing to lose. Jackson's got a free run. He can go on forever. It's costing him nothing. And in the meantime until things are resolved he is still collecting his 10%.

I am loathe to jeopardise the happy flow of briefs that has recently been diverted in my direction, but a fresh thought comes to me. "What about the Bar Mark, John? What happens to our Bar Mark?"

He agrees. "Yes. More like fucking Black Mark. Bunch of barristers suing their clerk and. . ." he laughs triumphantly, "fucking losing again!"

"You tell Giles. It's going to cost him a fucking fortune. I hope he can find some work to pay for it."

And with that, he too joins the homeward throng pushing past the pub door in the rain-swept street and I am left alone at last to wonder why I can't seem to get hold of Pauline, and to worry about why Laura doesn't seem to be getting any better and is still holding her stomach in pain.

Forget chambers. Forget Pauline. I resolve to get Laura's little problem sorted out – it's gone on too long. What does it take to fix up an appointment to see a specialist, explain a few symptoms, submit to a few perfunctory tests and pick up a prescription on the way out? I am growing uneasy at her constant prevarication: more than that, I am getting suspicious. Why is she always so slow to make an appointment, and why isn't she wanting to see a consultant who, for a private patient, would find the time to fit her in tomorrow? If it were me, she would have done it already. Why is she taking so long to do it for herself? It's not as if she's busy. At home all day doing the odd spot of gardening and playing with her pets.

I have another drink and look around the empty bar. Drink-driving put paid to the after work trade. I can remember when this place used to be so full it was a job to get served, now even the barmaid has given up and gone upstairs.

What is Laura buggering about at? What is she frightened of? Why does she so persistently put off being told what I suspect she already knows and what I know, as I gaze across this empty room, is a truth too awful to accept.

I look at the usual charity collection boxes grouped competitively on the bar and, resisting the urge to make a contribution, set down my empty glass amongst them and make my way to the door. It's time I got home. It's more than time I took Laura in hand.

Next morning I stood at our kitchen window looking out into the garden. Not a large garden, just an ordinary biggish suburban garden, but running into the park as it did it seemed to go on forever, and beyond the hedge I could see distant trees swaying over the lake.

It was Laura's garden. She had planted everything and

knew the names of everything. Planted so tightly that you couldn't put a trowel in the soil to introduce another bulb or flower without digging up something else.

Heliobores and snowdrops in February, followed by thousands of daffodils in March and even more tulips in April. The air was heavy with lilac, jasmine and viburnum and throughout the summer roses and clematis hung from arches and trellises: even the trees that ran along the southern border were draped with honeysuckle and Russian vine.

Throughout June and July, Laura was tending and cutting back aquelegia, cranesbill geraniums, cornflowers, daisies and the collection of euphorbia that she had started about five years ago. She never planted in any particular order or worked to any particular design. Much of her garden was self-sown. Forget-me-nots were succeeded by foxgloves which gave way to towering hollyhocks in the Autumn, dwarfing the asters, wind anemones and phlox that grew beneath. She had made a pond for waterlillies and frogs and every available space had been so crammed with something or other that it was impossible to hang out the washing without knocking over a pot.

My role in this grand scheme had been limited years ago to cutting the shrinking circle of grass that was so overhung it was impossible to cut without cutting something else. I was now forbidden to weed unless strictly supervised. According to Laura, I couldn't tell a weed from a flower, and was prone to pull up something just planted or just 'coming through', and anyway I never knew where to put my feet.

I watched her back as she bent over the rockery. She was losing weight again. Not that there was anything particularly significant in this. Throughout our marriage her weight had constantly gone up and down. Our marriage photographs show a beautiful and wonderfully slim girl gazing adoringly into the eyes of a greasy-haired nerd-like creature who seems to have had too much to drink.

Several children later Laura's cheeks had plumped out and she was having trouble with her hips. The problem was she loved food so much. Eating out, eating in, the odd sandwich at two in the morning. For every pleasure there is an inevitable cost. As Laura used to say, "Little pickers make big knickers," and by the age of forty she had several collections in various sizes. We seemed to be on a down-slope now, and as I watched, she straightened her back, and putting a hand to her stomach gazed upwards at the sky.

I knew then that something was seriously wrong, and my tentative thoughts of the previous evening were suddenly confirmed. We have got to put this right. I walked towards her as she stood still deep in thought. "Laura. Come on. What is it?" I asked, "How do you feel. Tell me what's the matter."

And as ever she shrugged off trouble, "Nothing. Nothing at all. These wind anemones are taking over the garden."

"Why don't you see a specialist?" I pressed her. "It won't take long, and then we'll be able to put it right. We can't go on like this."

Laura was apprehensive. She had never liked going to the doctor. She had a theory that the body cured itself, and the medical profession claimed the credit. "It's nothing," she told me, "nothing that a spot of digging won't put right."

But I wouldn't let it go.

"Let me fix it up," I insisted. "Let me take you to the doctors now and get an appointment. We'll get the best man in the world."

Or the best man in this neck of the woods at least. But one never knows. One never can tell whether the expert you entrust actually knows what he's doing. The car goes into the garage to be followed by a phone call setting out its faults. How do you know these are real? Some mechanic or other purports to do the work and eventually you get and pay the bill. Did any of it really need doing? Was some, or any of it, done well or at all? Who can tell? Only other experts. When I see how solicitors aggravate cases by their aggressive correspondence and dilatory incompetence, and how barristers foul up a good case in court with their foolish questions and unnecessary antagonism of the judge, I wonder what other professions and practices are like.

The strange thing is that the clients are always grateful. The punter, after the case is unnecessarily lost, woefully sitting in his cell thanking his barrister for all he has done.

The civil claimant watching his easily winnable case crashing in ruins, and as he picks up the bill for the costs, gratefully shaking his solicitor's hand at the door.

The patient, perhaps, lying in his hospital bed thanking the surgeon for his kindness, even brilliance, grateful to be alive, blissfully ignorant of the remnants of his malignancy that have been left so carelessly behind.

But what can you do?

I am definitely going to get Laura to a specialist. I am sure, or fairly sure, there is nothing really wrong: no, I am not sure, not sure at all, but we need to be certain, and she needs some treatment that will not, of course never can, completely restore her health but at least give her some respite and relief from this constant nagging pain that is wearing her so low.

And it's not that difficult. Not difficult at all. One telephone call does it and a reply some minutes later confirming the date. I thought Laura might be furious and berate me for interfering but she is resigned and, laying aside her spade, accepts what, long postponed, has now become inevitable.

"Thank you," she says, "I know you've done it for the best."

And I finally managed to get through to Pauline. She was not particularly interested in the results of my trial, in Laura's illness, or if I was honest with myself, in me.

Barry was still playing up and Tomkinson was getting on her nerves, and – not to worry – she had to dash. Apparently some important client she had to see. In a last desperate throw, I managed to nail her down to an appointment at Pat's Place.

"All right. This Thursday," she conceded, "but I can't stay long."

Chapter 20

I received a telephone call from Jas in prison. These days punters have access to prison telephones. It sounds amazing I know, but good behaviour inside prison walls should be encouraged, and being allowed to call the outside world is one of the perks.

"Thank you again Mr Wallace for all you have done for me," he begins.

Where have I heard that before?

I wonder for a moment if Jas's case really was unwinnable. Did I really need to call that last lunatic witness from Leeds who said he could explain why Jas had ordered five Mercedes in the name of a customer long since dead, and how a dead customer could possibly make the monthly repayments for the next three years, but when cross-examined (by the judge of course) became so confused as to times, dates, names, and places, he couldn't tell the difference between five Mercedes and five bananas – nor the truth from his ridiculous lies.

And to be frank, was my speech really all that good? Jas's father said he liked it and I definitely liked it, but it hadn't cut much ice with the jury after all, and it did sound a bit glib, a little too smooth perhaps, a touch rehearsed and it had conspicuously tiptoed round the evidence. I suppose the tiptoeing had been inevitable, it was being conspicuous that had let me down.

Anyway, Jas is grateful, or says he is.

"I've been studying, Mr Wallace," he goes on, "looking up the law."

Oh please God, not this. I do not like the sound of this at all. This sounds like a prelude to yet another hopeless appeal – the punter basing his ideas on reading Archbold (the criminal practitioner's bible), copies of which circulate around prisons these days, and whose almost unreadable and certainly unfathomable contents seem to inspire the inmates with crazy theories, and over-optimistic prospects of success. I always tell them to throw it in the bin, or give it to another fantasist perhaps. I don't tell them how to deal drugs, download pornography, rob banks, lift weights in the gym. Don't tell me how to manipulate the law.

"I don't think our case is appealable," I say carefully. "I don't think the judge erred in his summing-up of what I understand to be the law. There was no material irregularity. The jury didn't seem to be confused — well not enough for our purposes perhaps. As to sentence . . ."

"No. Fuck all that. Not interested," Jas retorts. "I'm studying to become a lawyer. I want to be called to the Bar."

I can see it now. Sentence served; exams passed; oath sworn; convicted fraudster turned licensed fraudster. The good life beckoning beyond the prison walls.

But why not? He's done his time. He's paid his price to society.

He is clever, works hard, has never done anyone any serious harm. He is religious, a good family man and a pillar of his community. He certainly enjoyed his trial. I remember his gifts of advocacy that ran such rings round the prosecution that by rights, with a dafter jury, and a fairer judge, should have ensured a glorious victory — which I then could have claimed as my own.

But now, apparently, here he is in prison studying for the Bar. He wants to know whether or not he will be allowed to practice.

"Will they let me become a barrister Mr Wallace?" he asks. "Or will I have to change my name?"

I wonder if this call is being recorded. Technology can do anything these days. I am guarded in my response.

"I do not see that if a man has served his sentence, suffered his punishment, repaid his debt to society, he should not be allowed the free pursuit of wealth, health and happiness in the conduct of his chosen career," I slowly begin. Then I have a bright idea.

"I think it says something about this in the European Convention of Human Rights," I tell him.

"Really. Oh good," says Jas. "I'll look it up. As a matter of fact I happen to have the books right here. Human Rights eh?" Jas's mind is spinning. "I could be a test case. Imagine. Front page in the papers. Fraudster called to the Bar."

Hardly front page news.

"Not for the first time Jas," I say.

Pauline is also looking for justice.

No sooner has Jas put the telephone down than she is on the line. "What do you know about Human Rights?" she demands.

"What do you know about conjugal rights?" I ask.

"Listen," she tells me. "I've got a very important client. Doing serious time. This European thingummy. Doesn't it say something about a fair trial?"

Very likely. To tell the truth I haven't the slightest idea.

"Well . . ." once again I proceed with caution, "I daresay a careful examination of the Convention might lead to an appropriate conclusion regarding the requirements of fairness as they apply to criminal proceedings in a signatory country."

That should keep her quiet. But it doesn't.

"Listen. How can this be fair? He's an armed robber. Or supposed to be. Got twelve years."

"What's he armed with?"

"Sawn-off. Allegedly that is. Anyway, two girls pick him out on an identity parade. One says she's fairly sure it's him. The other says – no doubt after a bit of pushing by the police – she's only 99% certain. How can that be evidence? How can that be fair?"

"Only 99% eh? Seems fair enough to me."

"Listen – 99% is not 100% is it? If you're not 100%, you're not certain. If you're not certain, you're not sure. If you're not sure, how can a jury convict?"

God, I can do without this. "But you tell me there were two of them. The other is fairly sure. I suppose that's not 100% either. But take the two of them together. Bit of a coincidence if they've both got it wrong. Anyway, it's for the jury to decide. I daresay there was other evidence as well."

"Yeah. That's another thing. The fucking sawn-off. What

do you know about continuity? Isn't it supposed to be complete?"

"Well, it's like this. Say a policeman finds a shotgun. He hands it to another copper who takes it to the station and hands it over to the sergeant who books it in. A couple of weeks later the C.I.D. get a bright idea. What about finger-prints? So they get it tested by Scenes of Crime who manage to take some 'lifts' which in turn get transmitted to an expert who regrettably says that they and those of your client are a perfect match. You have to have statements from each one as they pass the gun between then. If there's a break in the chain then I daresay, if driven, the defence can argue that anything could have happened in the gap."

"Precisely. How did you know?"

"But Pauline, what's the point? If he's done it he should do the bloody time."

I wonder is there a moral problem in trying to overturn the proper verdict of a jury by trawling through the evidence of a trial trying to find a technical flaw. Pauline doesn't seem to think so.

"What's that got to do with it? Actually he's rather nice."

Rather nice. What's that got to do with anything? I don't suppose he looks so nice from the other end of a loaded shotgun. I don't suppose that Pauline is acquainted with the damage they can do. Not very nice at all. From short range in a rural post office they can blow your face away or cut you in half.

"Oh that's good," I tell her, "the Court of Appeal will be very impressed."

"More than you're impressing me I hope. Anyway I've got to dash."

"Will I be getting this case?" I slip in quickly, "it might merit a little more research."

"Not a prayer. Wants a London barrister. Somebody he can trust. Anyway, I'm seeing him later today, I'll let you know how it goes."

I can't understand why she's putting in the effort. The evidence sounds overwhelming to me. Dashing here, dashing there. Going to a top security prison, instructing barristers, press-ganging the European Convention of Human Rights. And what's this about being nice? I can see it now. A few jokes and a little laughter with some manipulative swine.

She rang me back the next day.

"All sorted. Going to London for another opinion. We had a long chat. I've decided to write to the local MPs, get some sort of campaign going. A gross miscarriage of justice. You know the sort of thing. Free the Humberside One."

I said nothing.

"Mr Tomkinson's not all that keen though. Wants to know if legal aid will pay. Came into my office when I got back. Sat on the edge of my desk shooting his fucking cuffs."

I can see it now. I know the way he performs. Time to jerk the reins. Let her know who's in charge. Time to gently pull those fine and invisible strings that their previous connection has, in his mind, put between them.

"Started asking about you. Wanted to know if we're still, as he puts it, 'hoteling it'. What's it got to do with him?"

Actually I would rather like to know myself.

"What did you tell him?" I asked her gently.

"Nothing. And then do you know what the cheeky bugger said? A reference to you no doubt. What's it like going out with an old man?"

What could I say? Am I an old man? I suppose I am to her.

"What did you tell him?" I asked again.

She laughed. I can see it now. The sweet but deadly smile. "Ask your girlfriend," she'd said.

Chapter 21

Pauline and I are back together again. In court that is.

Grantham is up for sentence. Having pleaded guilty to dwelling-house burglary, taking cars, and the Great Escape, he has been waiting for four weeks whilst the Probation Service writes a report before he can be sentenced.

I have read the report. It is not helpful. In happier days gone by the Probation Service would take a kindlier view. They would try to highlight the best in a person. Remorse; a firm and settled intention to break a heroin addiction; a willingness to attend an anger management course so that he would stop punching perfect strangers in the street every time he had a drink; an ambition to secure full employment and bring home real wages to his common-law wife and four children living in poverty on an estate. Anything really that might be seen as some possible sign of improvement, some prospect of a happy and productive life.

And in those distant days, prison was always the last resort, and they would try anything first. Probation (sometimes with a condition of treatment) or Community Service, or a deferral of sentence for six months to see if the punter could in the meantime keep out of trouble and maybe get a job. Even, as the last resort, actually impose a prison sentence – but suspended – the punter would only actually serve it if he committed another offence.

All were recommended. All were tried with varying degrees of success depending on the individual, his determination, the temptations that fell his way and the general rub of the green.

All this has changed. The Government has demanded a tougher approach. In response to public outrage at the rise in crime those few, those unhappy few, that band of outcasts who do get caught, in spite of efforts to the contrary by the police, and in spite of covert schemes for early release, are now to be made examples of.

The probation reports reflect this. Apparently Grantham, about whom so much good has been written in the past, has enjoyed a Jekyll and Hyde transformation. I read he is, " 'totally lacking' in remorse, 'has no conception of the trauma inflicted on his victims' and is 'irredeemably wedded to heroin and the life of crime'.

His home-life is a 'shambles'," the report remorselessly continues. "Albeit displaying some superficial loyalty to his common-law wife, he displays 'little or no parenting skills', and is 'feckless'. He has a capacity for 'self-deception'. He is 'showing violent tendencies'. He is a 'danger', and a 'menace to the public'. He must be locked up."

Well thank you for that. There's nothing like an optimistic report.

A visiting judge is presiding. A member of some Scottish religious sect, he has read the report and agrees with it. He calls it realistic. He welcomes what he thinks is its constructive approach.

Pauline is outraged.

"What's the point?" she demands, "what's the fucking point of waiting four weeks for some time-serving 'more than my job's worth' bastard to write a report like this?"

I am not too sure they do write reports. They all sound the same. Run off some computer or word processor with only the names changed to convict the guilty. "What a load of rubbish," she continues, "I hope you're going to straighten it out."

I stand to mitigate. But what can I say? He has pleaded guilty. He is getting older and hopefully his criminal tendencies are burning out. Notwithstanding anything in the report to the contrary, he is determined this time to break his addiction. He has 'seen the light', 'turned the corner', 'pulled up short', 'reached the crossroads'. Even 'been to the mountain top and looked over the other side'. He is now going to jail.

I concentrate on his unaided descent down the front of the hospital. I suggest he was driven to say a last goodbye to his family. A last ditch attempt to put his affairs in order, and to make some provision for his young children. It is hard to say this with a straight face. We all know he was looking for one last fix. I stress that the only danger was to himself. The public were not in jeopardy. The doctor's white coat was recovered and returned to him – his stethoscope intact.

He has plans for the future. Would avail himself of courses in prison. Would rejoin society with qualifications. All would be well. Just give him a chance. Let the sentence be not so long that the end is out of sight and all hope dashed.

I have said this in one form or another many times before. It is what I get paid for.

The judge has heard it many times before. In distant days when he too was a barrister he may have said much the same thing himself. But now his patience is running out.

"You have been given chance after chance," he begins. "You have taken none of them. The time has come for the public to be protected from you. For a long time. Mr Wallace tells me this monstrous flight down the front of the hospital did not jeopardise anyone's safety but your own. I disagree. You chose to descend above the public entrance. The danger of falling bodies raining onto the heads of people below cannot be underestimated. Had you lost your grip on that drainpipe and crashed to the ground who knows how many people you would have taken with you to the grave? A pensioner in a wheelchair, a crocodile of children, patients attending en bloc for their outpatients appointments, surgeons with the lives of others in their hands . . ."

I am hoping something is going to drop on this judge.

Pauline is tugging at my gown. "This is bollocks," she whispers, "can't you say anything?"

I think I have said enough.

"Five and a half years," says the judge triumphantly. "Take him down."

The evening paper is full of it. It reports my latest triumph as "WHITE COATED SPIDERMAN GETS FIVE YEARS." This is going to bring in lots of business.

I talk to his wife on the concourse outside the court. She has long black hair and large breasts. Not bad looking for a heroin addict. "Unfortunately he is a long-term prisoner," I tell her. "You won't be seeing him for some time." From the corner of my eye I see the curly head of Freddy Platten hovering nearby. What can he want with me?

Nothing apparently. He is here to watch the sentence. "Nice one Mr Wallace," he says, "couldn't have done it better myself."

He turns to the girl who has promised to 'stand by' the departed Grantham only a moment ago. Freddy has got to know the family during the course of the case.

"They won't let you see him," he tells her with easy familiarity, "they say they're too busy. Not allowing any domestics today." She seems to be taking it well. "Not to worry." She looks up brightly. "I'd like to thank you for all that you've done."

He puts his arm round her shoulder, "Can I offer you a lift home?" he enquires as he walks her to the door. "My car's waiting just round the corner." I watch them go down the stairs. He appears to whisper something in her ear and she throws back her head and laughs.

What do I care? I am off to Pat's Place to wait for Pauline. £25 for as long as you like. Pat must have missed the money.

I am in bed with the wine open when Pauline finally arrives. She is in a hurry. With barely a hello she starts to undress and in seconds has slid onto the bed. As always, I am left a little breathless by her approach.

Did she miss me? Is she acting like she has or is she just acting? It would be a stupid thing to ask. Unthinkable. What could she possibly say? I wouldn't lower myself to enquire.

"Have you missed me?"

"What?"

"Missed me. You know. While I was away."

"What?" She raised herself on one elbow. But what was she thinking? It was obvious. She was wondering whether she had.

"Of course I have. Dreadfully. I've been counting the days." She seemed to like this. "The hours, the minutes, the seconds . . ." Her mind drifted away.

"So how long was I gone?"

"Er . . . a fortnight? A month? Was it longer? It's amazing how time flies."

"Not for me it didn't. I was doing a trial remember. At night in a lonely hotel."

She said nothing.

"I kept ringing, trying to get in touch, to tell you how it was going." She was looking at the ceiling, somewhere over my head.

"I left messages everywhere. Why didn't you call me back?"

"I did call back."

"When?"

"Jesus Christ. You aren't the only one to be busy. I've got children. I'm rushed off my feet at work. Then there's fucking Barry . . ."

Why was I arguing? More importantly, why was I picking a quarrel when only I had something to lose.

She turned her back to me and began to study the wall.

"Do you love me or don't you?" I tried to put my hand on her shoulder but she shrugged and pulled herself away.

"Don't start that. What about poor bloody Grantham?" She turned to face me, "You told him three years. I hope you're going to appeal."

"Grantham. Grantham. I'm not here to discuss Grantham. I want to talk about us."

"All right. Of course I've bloody missed you."

"Do you love me?"

"Jesus Christ," she sighed again, "Yes of course I do." I went to embrace her. "No not now. It's the shopping, and the kids. The youngest one's on his own." And she rolled off the bed and scooped up her clothes from the floor, "Anyway, I'll see you tomorrow at our conference. A new punter. Coggins. Sex maniac." She paused, slit-eyed in my direction. "You two should get on fine."

"Do you love me?" I couldn't let it drop.

"Don't be silly. Of course I do." She was dressed now, a cigarette trailing from her mouth. "Why else would I bother to see you? Why else would I get you work?"

"Work. I don't give a fuck about work. Tell Tomkinson he knows what to do with it . . ." I began to get out of bed but she was too quick for me, and was out the door before I could stop her. I could hear her clattering down the stairs and the bang of Pat's front door. As ever flying feet along the pavement, if anything a little faster than usual, and round the corner and gone. I sank back on my pillow. Did she love me? I thought about it. 'Counting the seconds.' 'Of course I've bloody missed you.' Of course she had. How could I have doubted her? How could I? I must be going mad.

I decided to ring Laura and she picked the phone up at once. "How are you my love?" I asked her. I should have called her before. "How are you feeling today?"

"Fine. Fine. No problems. Where are you?"

"Just leaving chambers."

"When are you coming home?"

No point hanging around Pat's. £25 for nothing. She didn't even have to change the sheets.

"Not long. My conference finished early. As soon as I've . . . I'll be with you very soon."

She fell silent as if weighing up my words. "Let's have something special. I've already started the wine."

"Yeah. Great. I love you." I could sense her thinking again.

"You haven't forgotten my appointment with the specialist have you? It's this Friday remember . . ."

Well I have and I haven't. It's not exactly in the forefront of my mind but it's in there somewhere waiting to resurface when I give it half a chance.

"You are coming aren't you? You said you wouldn't let me go alone."

"Of course I will. You can rely on me."

"Yes." She paused again. What was she thinking about now?

I decided to cut it short. "Anyway I love you. Be with you very soon."

I thought of the specialist's appointment. Of course I was going with her. It's not a duty, it's a pleasure. She should have known I would go. Why did she have to ask? I wouldn't let her down.

Chapter 22

Paedophilia is rife in Hull. I don't know why. Perhaps it's rife everywhere. Even in Surrey.

There was a theory that it was something to do with the fishing fleet. In those days men were away for three weeks at a time trawling the icy waters of the Arctic Circle, and in desperate moments would relieve themselves with skate – a fish with sexual organs very similar to a woman's – colder of course, but otherwise indistinguishable in the twinkling world of the Northern Lights. When their feet touched dry land they were up for anything. That is, anything other than skate.

I had arranged a conference with Mr Coggins in chambers. An ex-fisherman, accused of sexually abusing his three step-daughters about twenty years ago.

Pauline had arranged to bring him over from Cranmer Carter & Co., and I was a little surprised when Freddy Platten turned up with an old white-haired man who walked with a stoop.

"Pauline couldn't come," he told me. "She has got some very important letters to write. This is Mr Coggins."

At least he knew his name, or was he making sure that I did?

The old man shuffled forward and offered me his hand. Limp but respectful. "Pleased to meet you, sir," he said.

Actually, I had read the papers. Frankly it was pretty standard stuff. When ashore, Coggins would sleep in the family home – a little terraced house off Hessle Road in the centre of the fishermen's quarter. He had taken up late with his wife who already had three young daughters. They had two sons together, who didn't really feature in the case. According to the statements of the three girls, Coggins had moved from one girl to another. As one girl approached puberty, he would take an interest in her younger sister and so on down the line. Genuine paedophilia then.

There is a difference in the obsession with children, and the sexual involvement with young women below the age of sixteen.

Children are undeveloped and innocent and the others are fully developed women not yet available by law.

According to the prosecution case, Coggins preferred them young. As young as five. In their little crowded house, in the early hours, and his wife fast asleep from drink, he would tiptoe across the landing to the girls' bedroom, and having gently pushed the door open would station himself beside their bed. Soundlessly he would pass his hands beneath the sheets to touch their flat chests and poke about between their legs.

If he chanced on one alone during the day, he would get her to hold his penis and, with his giant hand enveloping hers, get her to move it up and down.

They thought it was a game. "Our little game," he told them. "Tell no one. It's our secret." And to bind them to him and ensure their silence, he gave them money and told them they would have to go away and into care if anyone found out.

Not one girl knew he was doing it, or had done it, to the others. Only later in life, when they had daughters of their own and he had insisted on visiting, fearful lest he do the same to them, had the truth come out, and they had reluctantly informed the police.

"Why are they doing it to me?" he complained. "What have I done to them? I treat them like my own kids. No different. They want to get me sent away."

Their detailed statements are unremitting and explicit. As he groomed each one and persuaded them that what he was doing was normal, he was able to take things ever further to the point when in the kitchen perhaps, or in his car, or the garden shed, or on his allotment, he put his tongue inside their tiny bodies, and masturbated into their hair.

"These statements seem pretty similar," I said. "Do you think they might have got their heads together?"

"I don't know what's going on," he sighed. "We've been rowing about the house. Our house off Hessle Road. My boys still live there with me and my wife and I have decided to leave it to them. The girls don't like it. They think they should have a share."

A motive of sorts. It seemed pretty drastic to make up monstrous allegations like this for a fifth share in a fisherman's old house, but one never knows. Better than nothing anyway.

"They've been watching too much television," he told me. "It's on there all the time. You can get special channels late at night. Mrs Coggins won't look at it. She says its dirty, and, I have to say, she's right."

I had put in some time on these papers and knew that some of the allegations were time specific. For example, the younger one had claimed an incident on Christmas Eve 1982 and it might be possible to prove an alibi.

"That you were somewhere else," I explained. "Possibly away at sea. Do you still have your Fisherman's Books?" These record the comings and goings of fishing boats and their crew.

"You might have been at sea on that occasion. If we destroy one allegation it puts in doubt the rest. Starts to sow the seeds of doubt."

"Can you get your books Mr Coggins?" Freddy chipped in, "It might help Mr Wallace."

Coggins could certainly help. He said he'd kept them all. His record of a lifetime at sea. Excellent, we'll go through those carefully at another conference next time. "Bring the lot," I told him. "Put them in chronological order. We'll try and cover some dates."

He stood up, turning his cap in his hands, and made to shuffle off.

But I have one other item of homework for him. "Look up any photographs you might have of yourself with any of these girls," I instructed. "If they show one with her arms around you, laughing up at you, kissing you even, it might seem inconsistent with her allegations that you were a monster who abused her. Christmas cards and birthday cards couched in affectionate terms might also help. You know the sort of thing, 'To the Best Dad in the World' and lots of little crosses. Mrs

Coggins probably keeps them in the sideboard," I suggested. "Probably in a box."

Anyway it gave him something to do, but before he disappeared about his work I had one final question.

"Mrs Coggins. Is she with you or with them?"

The acid test. Somehow or other a woman always seems to know. Perhaps oblivious at the time, little things suddenly fall into place. That time I came into the bedroom when he was alone with little Susan. Why was he so red-faced? Did I really hear the zip on his trousers when I was coming up the stairs? Why was he always giving her treats? Why were the tops of her legs so sore? Why did she start to run wild? Why did her school reports suddenly go downhill? Why wouldn't she talk to me when I found her crying? Why didn't I take her to the doctors that time I found blood in her knickers when she was only five?

"Mr Coggins," I asked him again, "whose side is she on?"

"Mine," he cried defiantly, "never doubted me for a minute. She thinks the whole thing is disgusting. Says their husbands put them up to it. Says one's supporting the other. She can't believe what they're trying to do."

I shook his hand and thanked him for coming. This was going to be a tough case. Winnable – but loseable too. Hopeless cases are easy. One simply goes through the motions; no pressure – the outcome is inevitable. Other cases are either so trivial or so obviously deficient that the Crown Prosecution Service should never have brought them to court in the first place. It's the ones in the middle, the ones that could go either way, that cause the stress.

"A good case," I told Freddy when he'd gone, "but there is a lot of work to do. I want photographs of the house. Statements from relatives. Look up the neighbours twenty years ago. Take a statement from Mrs Coggins. Ask the Crown Prosecution Service, have any of these girls ever made similar complaints before? Do any witnesses have criminal records? Can we show dishonesty? Can we show connivance? Can we raise a doubt?"

Freddy was not very keen on all this work. I daresay he had his social life to consider.

"I'm a bit busy at the moment," he said, "snowed under really. But I'll do what I can."

I looked him in the eye. "Mrs Grantham get home all right the other day?" I enquired.

He laughed. "All right, I'll sort it. I'll get Pauline to help me when she's finished her correspondence. If she ever does."

Not a bad idea to get Pauline back on the team.

I was meeting her for lunch in the morning. A chance to bring her up to speed.

I wondered to myself whether or not Coggins was telling the truth. On the one hand there was a motive of sorts. On the other hand, if they really were all making this up together, why hadn't they gone the whole way? Simulated intercourse, actual intercourse, oral and anal sex. More importantly, why had they not supported each other? If they were inventing the story, why didn't they back each other up? One or other of them, peeping under the bedclothes, had seen him touching another? Why were they all so surprised all those years later when the revelations came tumbling out?

And what is Mrs Coggins like? Will she be the bright cheerful matter of fact no nonsense wife that is gold dust for the defence, or will I be meeting a dull, stupid, weak woman carrying faded bruises to her cheeks?

Freddy waved goodbye. "Oh by the way, Pauline sends a message. She might be a bit late tomorrow, says she can't stop long."

Chapter 23

Antonio's portions are only exceeded by his prices and Pauline has learned over the months to forego a starter whilst stoically sticking to plaice.

It is a little 'show-off' thing with me that I like the fish cooked on the bone and then fillet the flesh away at the table discarding head and bones etc. on a débris plate which is then removed by an attentive, and at Antonio's place, incredulous waiter.

"How would you like the plaice, sir?"

"Grilled on the bone with an extra plate at the table," I say. I am in a confident, nay imperious, mood.

"Oh no we don't," says Pauline. "I've had enough of this buggering about. Take the bones out in the kitchen." She doesn't say 'fillet'.

"Do it how you like."

I must say this is a little disappointing. I thought she enjoyed my mock sophisticated ways and I was careful, or so I thought, to deliver this little performance with the correct touch of understated self-irony. All apparently wasted.

"What do you think of the Coggins case?" I enquire pleasantly.

"Not had time to read it."

"Everything all right at the office?" I soldiered on.

"Busy. Very busy. Too busy. I shouldn't be here at all." Apparently not even for the benefit of a free lunch.

"And as for that fucking Tomkinson. Can't seem to get rid of him. Oily bastard. Always watching me, wanting to know what I'm doing. Worried in case we're not getting paid. Trying to be clever. Trying to be funny. I can't stand the twat."

She blows smoke into the air and knocks back her gin and tonic.

"Can I get you another one?"

"Not supposed to drink in work hours now," she says, and then defiantly, "Yeah, why not? Bollocks to them. Make it a double."

I manage to attract the attention of the waiter who, with all of two tables to attend to, has become simultaneously blind and deaf. I feel like another drink myself.

Pauline's plaice eventually arrives. As she has requested, it has been filleted in the kitchen and according to the waiter, 'pan fried' (what else would you fry it in?) to perfection. A 'garnish' of chopped iceberg lettuce and tomato clutters up the plate.

I reach across with my fork (as has become our practice) and try a little. It manages to taste both oily and dry. A good fish ruined.

"Not good my dear," I say, "too dry. And why fry it in olive oil? It obliterates, simply obliterates, the taste."

"For Christ's sake. It's all the same to me."

In retrospect, perhaps this was not the best time to introduce the topic of Pat's.

"How are we for next week? I can't wait to get you back to Pat's."

She sighs. She puts down her knife and fork. She pushes the plate away. "Look Henry. I'm not going to Pat's next week. In fact, I'm not going back to Pat's again at all."

"What's wrong with Pat's?" I ask, wondering why she's taken against Pat.

She looks straight at me. Those clear candid little brown eyes.

"There's nothing wrong with Pat's. It's you. Or actually it's us. It's us." A long pause. "And it's over."

Why had I not seen this coming? I feel sick. My stomach seems to twist. I feel an immediate pain at my heart. I cannot understand it. My mind is in overdrive but simply cannot connect to reality. I just cannot, absolutely cannot, get a grip.

"What have I done?" I am struggling to speak. This is pathetic. What am I saying?

"You have done nothing. It is not you. It is me. I don't love you anymore."

"But why? Why not? What has happened?" I feel absolutely stricken. Desolated. "Pauline, what is going on?"

I know this sounds pitiful but I was losing a wonderful girl and one, as I was realising through my shock, that I simply could not live without.

"Listen. We don't want a scene. I . . . don't . . . love . . . . you. Got it?" In an act of uncharacteristic kindness she reaches for my arm. "Put it another way. There's no spark any more."

"There is for me," I protest. Why can't I just take it? Lean back nonchalantly. Blow a smoke ring or two? Tell her I was beginning to feel the same and that our lovemaking was becoming repetitive, a touch too routine and that giving £25 to Pat was really becoming more than it was worth. Tell her I was tired of listening to her moaning about Barry and hearing the usual stories about Tomkinson and her efforts (if true) in trying to avoid him and the boring gossip about the dreary people with whom she worked. Why didn't I eat her bloody plaice or send it back or tell her to fuck off. But I love her. And this is being delivered remorselessly – hammered home looking straight into my eyes. I have never felt so ill.

"But don't you see. There isn't any spark for me. You don't do anything for me anymore. You haven't for some time."

I have to ask. I know I shouldn't – but I do. The weak words come spilling out. "Have you met somebody else?"

She sighs again. "Yes and no. I just cannot go on with you. You're a nice chap . . . ."

I cannot stand this. I may or may not be nice – whatever that is. I just don't want to be called nice. Not by Pauline. Jesus Christ, have I descended to nice?

". . . we can always be friends." Friends? Friends? Who wants to be friends? That tepid excuse for a relationship. Dry as dust. A consolation prize graciously handed down to soften the blow of goodbye.

She stands up to go. Hands straightening her skirt. Rubbing her cigarette into an ashtray.

"Don't go. Don't go." I have sunk so low, I am pleading with her. "Don't go. Not yet."

"I'm sorry. I've got to." She moves towards the door and

turns once before stepping into the street. "We'll still see each other in court."

I sit staring at my hands resting on the table amongst the unfinished meal. The drinks only barely touched, and now, the message delivered, hastily abandoned. I see Pauline's lipstick on the rim of the glass; her discarded knife and fork. The plaice, the rotten plaice, the fucking filleted plaice left uneaten on her plate.

I know. I know in my heart that my life will never ever cruise along in its former happy style, and that what is left will be blighted and infinitely sad.

Why do you always want the one you cannot have? Why pursue indifference? Why is the deepest love a love that's not returned?

I am old and getting older. I don't think I shall ever get her back.

I tell Giles later as we stand side by side at the bar of the Stag at Bay.

"She's left me. I don't know why. She told me it was over, and just walked out."

"Perhaps she's fed up with you," he suggests. "Don't forget, it's gone on a long time. She obviously wants a life of her own. Needs to move on as they say."

I just cannot accept what I know is an accurate description of our state of affairs.

"Giles," I say, clinging to his arm, "Giles I cannot lose her. I cannot bear to see her go. I tell you now Giles." I am well drunk. "I tell you now, I would rather die than lose her."

"Make up your mind," he tells me, "I'm not very busy next week. I could certainly use your returns."

This is not funny. I am caught in a tragedy, I do not use this word lightly, a tragedy, and Giles is dismissive of an event that he obviously regards as a run of the mill ending of an affair.

One can expect a little emotional pain, a little psychological stress perhaps, but I am in actual physical pain.

"Giles," I say, "Giles what can I do?"

He puts his kindly arm around my shoulders.

"Why don't you grow up and go home to your wife?"

Chapter 24

In the event Laura went to see the specialist on her own. I was in court that day. In fact, I was in court every day, burrowing through the work with which Jackson had overwhelmed me, and which I now used to try and blot out the constant appearance of Pauline in my mind as I struggled to accept the disaster of her matter of fact rejection of me, and the ending of our affair.

It is possible, just possible, that if I had never seen her again (say, for example she had immediately given up at Cranmer Carter & Co. and moved away) then over the months I could have gradually eased her out of my mind; and that perhaps, just perhaps, the pain would have gradually diminished to a dull and persistent ache and then just possibly, with luck, might have faded away (just for the odd day) and I would have had some respite (I cannot say pleasure) to help me forget my loss.

But she was everywhere. Popping up in court. In the street. Occasionally coming to chambers. I saw her in pubs and always she was polite; she smiled; she was friendly. Above all, she seemed happy. Always so happy. Why was she so bloody happy when I so obviously was not? I hope I had sufficient pride, or at the least sufficient self-restraint, to avoid lovelorn looks of reproach whenever we accidentally met, and that I carried a veneer of indifference that might have convinced her (had she been interested) that if I had cared once, it had soon evaporated and that even now I was weighing up the merits of rival candidates in her place. Frankly, she wouldn't have noticed either way, and even if she had, it wouldn't have made one iota of difference. She had made up her mind. Wallace was definitely a thing of the past. A relic on the beach, and she couldn't care less if another had stumbled upon it and was eagerly rubbing away the sand, or it had simply crumbled into dust. She had become completely indifferent, and any amount of play-acting on my part was performed before an audience that had already left.

She seemed to have put on weight. Not a lot, but enough to tighten the shorter skirts she now seemed to be wearing. And she had invested in clothes. Always wearing something different. Another new suit. And yes another, yet another, new pair of shoes.

She waved to me across the road.

"Everything all right?" she called.

Oh yes. Everything's bloody fantastic. Never felt better in years.

Laura had seen the specialist. He had given her what he called a full examination. They had had a long and leisurely chat.

"Mr Mitchell. A dour man. But a genuine man. Very decent. We had a good talk. He's happily married with two children. A house in the country, lovely wife."

Ah well. That's all right then. Another happy man.

"But did he say what was wrong with you? Did he get round to talking about you?"

I am part of chambers' private health insurance. For tax reasons it is a condition of membership. When you're paying privately I suppose consultants can afford to be generous with their time.

"What's the matter with your stomach?" I persisted. "Has he told you what's wrong?"

"Oh nothing very much," she said lightly. "Could be a sort of hernia or probably too much acid. Wants me to have a CAT Scan just to make sure."

"Sure of what? Acid's not going to show up on a CAT Scan."

"Don't worry, everything's fine," Laura reassured me. "A little blood pressure, a little overweight, kidneys not too good. The usual thing. Of course my health isn't great. But we've known that for a long time. Told me to cut down on the wine and to try and stop the cigarettes."

Easier said than done. Smoking and drinking are part of our lives. Initial teenage indulgencies became life-long pleasures became old-age dependency. Laura poured another glass of wine and lit the inevitable cigarette.

"I can see you intend to follow his instructions," I said.

She turned to me. Her large eyes seemed full of tears.

"What's the point, my love. What's the fucking point?"

Later that evening I was sat down in our kitchen thinking. Before me on the long table, still cluttered with the remnants of our dinner, was another bottle of wine. I could hear Laura coughing upstairs in our bedroom as she turned this way and that. I knew her pillow would be damp with sweat. I could see her in my mind's eye tossing and turning; trying to get comfortable, one hand rubbing her stomach, hoping to get to sleep.

I thought of the contrasts between them.

One warm and gentle, the other hard, nervous and irritable, always on the move. But they had things in common. They were both quick and funny. Reluctant proprietors of me.

Above all, they both had character. Strong, determined and tough. Ambitious for themselves and their families. Unremitting. Unforgiving? I wasn't so sure.

But women of high quality.

I had lost one. I was frightened of losing them both.

I sat there at the kitchen table into the small hours, moths circling and banging against the low lamp suspended from the ceiling. I occasionally scratched the head of my favourite cat.

I loved Laura dearly. Would never hurt her. I would do anything for her. Anything at all.

I opened another bottle of wine. Was it the second or third? I would die for her. She had never hurt another living thing. Not an ounce of malice. "Not a bad bone in her body" as my mother used to say. The love of my life. Loyal and true.

Loyal? Had she been loyal? I began to think about it and automatically poured another drink. Had she been loyal? How did I know? Loyal or very clever. And what did she know of me? My stupidities. Did she know, and had it suited her to ignore them? And why would it suit her to ignore them? Unless?

I pushed the cat away but it refused to go and persistently forced itself back.

How could I think of things like this? At a time like this. I thought of Pauline and felt the little kick of pain inside my chest. Welcome back old friend. Her matter of fact indifference. How much happier she seemed without me. A woman with a mission. She was never coming back.

I began to cry. I felt my shoulders shake and warm tears run down my face. It was pitiful I know.

I poured another drink.

I would never get her back. I had killed her with kindness. My absurd eccentricities had driven her away. She had found someone better, someone else.

I didn't hear Laura glide soundlessly through the door behind me. She must have woken up and wondered where I was.

I don't know how long she had stood there before she slowly moved forwards, and putting her arm around my shoulders, gently whispered, "Don't cry Henry. Come on. Don't cry. It's not that bad. You always think the worst. Whatever it is I'll beat it. Don't worry. I promise I'll get well."

Chapter 25

Coggins is fighting his cause. I had expected Pauline to be behind me but Freddy tells me she has had to go to some top security prison or other, and he is deputising for the day.

This is not a problem. He is bright and engaging and knows something about the case. Better than some gormless girl from the office who cannot take a note, talk to a witness, or follow the simplest instructions, and is forever disappearing, just when you might need her, to go to the lavatory to powder her nose.

Freddy knows what he is doing, and what he is doing at the moment is weighing up Coggins again. He is not impressed.

"Whingeing shifty little bastard. Going to be crap in the box." We shall see. At this stage the defence case is a long way off. "Why is it that paedophiles always look the same?" he persists. "Spot them a mile off. As soon as I saw him I knew he was guilty."

I have been searching everywhere for the barrister instructed by the Crown Prosecution Service – low paid lawyers who are living proof, if proof were needed, that you get what you pay for; hopelessly incompetent and collectively too stupid to recognise good advice. They like to dictate what happens in a case. It is supposed to be good for their morale. They do not welcome an independent opinion that does not accord with theirs, and so employ sycophants and place men. Usually from out of town.

I have a fair idea who it might be today and one look at the usher's list confirms it. Their usual choice for sex cases – an ingratiating middle-aged barrister, boring, long married, of limited ability and famous for doing what he's told. He is grateful for the work.

Many a trial is settled in the robing room. To be honest some are actually fought there. There is always some preliminary banter, some jockeying for position, before the trial actually starts, but this one has seen me coming and, having scooped up his papers, has disappeared into the CPS room out of sight. It has been impossible to prise him out.

We meet for the first time when he opens the case to the jury.

"Prolonged and systematic abuse of young defenceless girls too innocent to realise what he was doing was wrong, too trusting to complain, too immature to notice that he was doing the same thing to the others – as he was so persistently doing to them."

A fair enough summary I have to concede.

"Matters only came to light when they feared the defendant might turn his prurient attention to their own daughters and, confiding in each other, discovered to their horror that they had not been abused alone."

The jury are looking at the frail, pitiful Coggins with some distaste. Perfectly normal at this stage of the trial. It's how they are looking at him at the end that counts.

Our hero from Leeds in his fancy striped suit has made a good opening. He calls his first witness.

"Call Miss Susan Coggins!" She is a large red-faced woman in an expensive overcoat. She takes the oath in a clear confident voice and continues with her evidence in the same vein. She does not cry. She does not break down. She does not ask to give her evidence sitting down. She does not even break for a glass of water so that she might recover her wits. She is an impressive witness who has made a very good start.

I rise to cross-examine with some reluctance. One of the tricks of defence counsel in a trial is to memorise the initial statement the victim gave to the police (often many months earlier) and keeping it before him whilst the witness gives evidence, note down any discrepancies between what she said then and what she is saying now.

These inconsistencies are then put to the witness in an attempt to discredit her. I have some limited success.

"Do you remember giving your statement to the police approximately six months or so ago?" I begin mildly. "I suppose you were told to make sure everything you said was not only truthful but accurate?"

"What's the difference?" enquires Judge Irvine, breaking my flow. "Just trying to be helpful Mr Wallace. Don't want the jury confused do we?" He smiles benignly. "What's the difference?"

Not much. Obviously. If it's accurate it's probably true. If it's truthful it's likely to be accurate. But what if it's accidentally accurate when trying to lie? On the other hand a truthful witness can be wrong. I decide not to argue the toss.

"I don't think I need go into that." I can see who's going to be doing the prosecuting in this case.

"I wonder if I might get on? You signed your statement at the bottom. I assume you read it first?"

Miss Coggins nods. She is watching me carefully. She isn't looking at Coggins. Not at all.

"When you made that statement were you trying to tell the truth?"

"Of course. I always try and tell the truth," she adds, turning to the jury and the nodding smiling judge.

"Then why did you tell the police six months ago that he indecently touched you in the bedroom and this jury today . . ." I pause and point at the jury, ". . . this jury today that he touched you between your legs when you were downstairs in the kitchen and your mother was out?"

"Were you lying then or are you lying now?" She hasn't really got the point. Perhaps there isn't one; it's impression that counts and if the jury get the feeling that she has been telling two different stories they may reject her altogether.

"I wonder if this witness could see her police statement," Judge Irvine intervenes. "Have a good look at it," he advises her.

"Mr Wallace, I think is referring to page fourteen. Have you got it?"

"Yes."

"Well, read it to yourself."

Miss Coggins is no doubt grateful for the opportunity. She reads carefully and slowly with her finger on the page.

"Now," says the judge, "did you say that it had happened in the bedroom . . . . many many times? Is that the truth what you said then?"

"Yes it was," replies Miss Coggins, "over and over again. He was always doing it, he wouldn't let me alone. Some weeks nearly every night."

"Don't upset yourself," says the judge in his kindly fashion. "Let us now go to page twenty-three – about halfway down I think. Tell the jury what you said there."

Miss Coggins reads to the jury, "Although he was always at me in the bedroom it was a long time ago and occasionally it might have happened somewhere else in the house."

"Might that somewhere else have been in the kitchen?"

"Yes," she agrees.

"Might that have happened when your mother was out?"

"Yes."

"Well there you are Mr Wallace," he smiles genially. "I hope that's helped you clear it up."

"Thank you Your Honour. I am most obliged."

Thank you very much.

I start a different tack.

"Miss Coggins," I look at her severely, "you are familiar with the house off the Hessle Road where you then lived, and is in fact owned by your mother and stepfather? Yes?"

"And you are no doubt aware . . ." I continue, "that this valuable asset has been left in its entirety to your half-brothers? Yes? You agree? In other words Miss Coggins, you and your sisters have been cut out of the will. Cut off without a penny. Is this true?"

"Yes," she answers guardedly. She wonders where I am going.

"And that is why, out of spite and resentment, you are making these ridiculous allegations. It's all about money isn't it? Money that you thought was coming to you and your sisters, and now so obviously isn't. It's all about money isn't it? That's why you are telling these lies."

She pauses. She takes a deep breath. Her face is red with indignation.

"Do you think . . ." she begins, "do you think I would put myself through this? Go back to the terrible times all that long ago, upsetting myself and my family just to remember . . . just to remember how awful it was, all that . . . all that touching and creeping about and pain . . . yes pain . . ." She is becoming angry, "Just for a tiny share in a tiny house. Let me tell you, my husband earns good money – I earn good money. We don't need anybody else's. My half-brothers have got next to nothing, they still live in the house. It was my idea . . . my idea . . . . my mother should leave it to them. Call my mother to give evidence. Ask her. Ask her. She left it to them because that's what I asked her to do!"

The courtroom is completely silent. It can be a lonely place. Playing for time I turn round to Freddy who has dived for cover behind my back. "Can you think of anything else?" I ask him.

"Fucking hell," he replies, "this is going well. Why don't you ask her if she enjoyed it?"

I forbear from following his suggestion.

"Thank you Miss Coggins," I say. "You've been extremely helpful."

At the end of the day Freddy and I review progress in the Stag at Bay. I know he will report back to Tomkinson and I want to get him on my side.

"How do you think it is going?" I enquire, gently testing the water.

He splutters in his beer. He starts to choke. Eventually recovering his breath and fighting back the tears, he gives me his opinion.

"Terrible. Absolutely fucking terrible. The sisters were fantastic. You never laid a glove on them . . ."

I am not pleased to hear this. Freddy is too bright. He can recognise a disaster when he sees one.

I wish now I was in the company of one of those gormless girls. They can't tell a good question from a bad one. Answers pass over their heads.

Back in the office they report that Mr Wallace asked lots of questions. So that's very good then. The punter will be pleased. Never mind the quality, feel the width.

". . . and in those few, those rare moments when you got them on the ropes," Freddy continued still laughing, "old Judge Irvine, your supposed mate, stepped into the ring and bailed them out. We are fucking finished. Absolutely fucked."

"Thank you Freddy," I say, "so you don't think it's going too well then?"

"I think he's got two options," Freddy tells me confidentially. "He can either plead guilty in the morning and save something from the wreckage, or jump on the ferry and fuck off to France."

Next morning Pauline is back again. She seems tight-lipped. She must have been talking to Freddy. "Not too clever then?" she enquires. "I heard we're going down the tube."

Our own enquiries have led nowhere. His Fisherman's Books proved nothing. Well, nothing helpful to us. And there were no photographs. No affectionate Christmas or birthday cards. Enquiries revealed all the neighbours to have moved away or died years ago and the girls, none of them, have ever made similar complaints before.

Naturally, they have never been in trouble with the police, and are all ladies of good character, highly regarded by all who know them, pillars of their small but respectable communities; honest in every way.

And of course, I am going to have to call Coggins. He doesn't have to give evidence. He can stay in the dock. But the judge will tell the jury that they can hold this against him. One more grain of sand to put in a balance that is tilting dangerously away.

And of course he is as pathetic as Freddy predicted.

I lead him through the evidence. "Did you indecently assault Susan Coggins in the bedroom?"

"No."

"Did you indecently assault Susan Coggins in the kitchen?"
"No."

"Did you ever indecently assault Susan Coggins any-where?"

"No."

"Anywhere at all ever?"

"No."

"Did you indecently assault Tracey Coggins?"

"No."

"Did you ever, at any time, anywhere, ever indecently assault Mary Coggins?"

"No."

We don't want "No". We want shock and horror. We want "absolutely fucking no. Absolutely fucking not."

We want: "I loved those girls. I loved them as if they were my own. How could I possibly have done that without anyone knowing? There were three girls in one bedroom. They often had friends sleeping over. This is a small house. Two young boys running about. My wife in the bedroom next door. How could I possibly have gone creeping about in the night – nearly every night, year in year out and nobody, but nobody notice? It is absolutely bloody ridiculous. I have never been in trouble in my life. I don't know why they are doing it. It is a nightmare and it's driving me fucking mad."

We want him collapsing back into a chair and asking for a glass of water. We want the jury rising and filing out whilst he is given time to recover, and on their return crying out, "And anyway, when did I have the time? When am I supposed to have done this? I was either pissed or fishing or both."

We get instead a series of monotone "No's". No indignation. No protest. No challenge. No explanation. Nothing. He stands there, head hanging down looking at his feet. Avoiding everybody's eye. I have to let him go. As usual I am going to have to give the evidence in my speech.

To be fair, our pal from Leeds doesn't fare any better.

We go through the whole process again. Coggins is in reso-lute denial. A litany of "No's" without a word of explanation. There's no colour, no life, no passion. Whatever impression does he give?

"Is that another 'No' Mr Coggins?" the judge enquires, "you're saying 'No' to that again are you? Do you have much more of this?" he enquires of the prosecution, "I think the jury has got the point."

"One last question if I may," and turning to Coggins for the last time and by way of closing his cross-examination with a little speech rather than a question asks, "Why would they say it if it wasn't true Mr Coggins? Are you listening to me? Why would these three ladies make these dreadful accusations if they were not true?"

"No. . . ." and then, at last, the slightest reaction, "perhaps I wasn't as good a dad as I thought I was. I was always at sea. We only got two days on shore. About every three weeks. I didn't bring them very much home. Well, I didn't bring them anything home. I can't remember really. . . ."

At last. A glimmer of a reply. The prosecution attempts to shut him up by sitting down. "Thank you Mr Coggins, that will be all."

"Let him finish," I intervene.

". . . it was a long time ago." Coggins continues as if talking to himself. "I was more interested in getting drunk when I got home. Always kept a taxi waiting. And we were off around town. Sometimes we had to be carried back onboard just before the boat left to catch the tide . . . I don't know . . . perhaps I wasn't much of a father. We didn't have much money. Spent most of it on drink. I don't know. Perhaps I did favour my boys. Perhaps there were a few rows with the wife. Perhaps they did resent me. Perhaps they missed their own father. Perhaps they still blame me for taking his place. I don't know. Perhaps they didn't like me very much at all. Perhaps they've never liked me. I don't suppose I showed them very much love. But I'd never touch my kids. How could I? I was never there. I wish I'd been a better father to the girls . . . I don't know. It's too late now. I didn't know they hated me so much."

That final question. It's often the case. One question too many and the floodgates open. Has Coggins finally raised a doubt?

His wife is much the same. Only sixty-two but she looks much older. A frail, care-worn, washed-out woman in a head-scarf; she has to hold the edge of the witness box and lean forward to try and hear what is going on.

"He was hardly ever home. Always at sea and when he came back he was out. I never saw him sober in twenty years," she tells the court. "He wasn't like that when I met him. He was nice then. That's why I left my first husband for him. He was a nice young chap, but then they all turn out the same. My first husband was upset. He went away somewhere. I don't know where. We never saw him again. It's a long time ago. And no I don't remember our Susan suggesting we give the house to the boys. I think it was Mr Coggins put it in my mind."

The jury are going out in the morning, but there is no visit to the Stag at Bay for me tonight. Pauline says she has got to be off, and I walk back to chambers alone. There is a message from Laura waiting for me, so I go to my room to return her call.

"How are you my love? Has it been a long day?" she asks.

I start to explain about the trial but she stops me.

"Listen carefully to what I have to tell you," she continues, "and please – don't worry."

I know something is wrong, and I know what it is. I don't have to ask but I do.

"What is it? What has happened?"

"Well you know I had to see the specialist again today" she tells me, "to find out the results of my tests. Well, it's cancer, I've got cancer of the stomach. Don't worry. Everything's going to be all right."

I sit holding the receiver. I'm stunned by the dreadful news and the matter of fact way Laura is able to say it. The ground seems to move beneath my feet, the room sways and I want to be sick.

"What are we going to do?" I manage to ask her pathetic-ally. "Laura, my love, I am so sorry." I don't know what to say.

"What are we going to do?" I hear her voice rise emphatic-ally. "I'll tell you what we're going to do. We are going to fucking beat it. Just like I told you before. Piece of piss. Don't even think about it," she warns me, and in my mind's eye I can see her finger raised, "I will do what needs to be done. I've done all this sort of shit and I am not – absolutely fucking not – going to be beaten now. So don't you worry that's all. Don't you be going and doing something stupid. I promise you we are going to beat it. Just get a fucking grip. And Henry . . ." she adds and then a long pause, ". . .please come straight home tonight. No drinking. Promise me no drinking. No anything. Just come straight home now."

Laura and I sit together in the kitchen. We are seriously drinking. Laura is chain-smoking.

"It's a bit late to stop now," she says cheerfully. "Now is definitely not the time to stop. I might try when it's all over."

"Mr Mitchell wants to see you on Friday. Wants us to go together. He thought you might have come today, but it doesn't matter if you're busy, I can go on my own."

There is to be no more 'going on her own'. Laura has done enough of that.

"How bad is it?" I ask her gently. "Just tell me. What are we looking at? What are the odds?"

"Oh, it's not too bad. Not that bad. It could be worse. The scan shows a hard edge – nothing too diffuse. That's a good sign. It shows it hasn't broken out."

"So it's contained then, they can see can they, exactly where it is? They could tell, could they, if it had spread?"

"Oh yes." Laura is as confident as ever. Reassuring. "They can tell anything these days." She smiles at me. "Everything is under control."

How can she be like this? So calm. So brave. I would be going bloody mad. Feeling the pain in my stomach – that dreadful thing growing inside me – killing me from within. Tiny bits breaking off into my blood and being carried away to the brain. I can't bloody stand it. It is the most revolting, unnecessary, unfair, utterly cruel thing.

Laura just sits quietly thinking. Planning ahead.

"Don't tell the children. Any of them. I don't want them to know. There is no need for them to know. There is nothing they can do. I don't want them worrying. In fact, don't tell anybody."

I am trying to pull myself together and she puts her hand on mine. "Henry. It's going to be all right. Now come on . . ." and she repeats that phrase of hers, one that she has used for as long as I've known her. "Come on just get a fucking grip. Chin up and get a fucking grip."

So I try to get a grip. She is facing an ordeal so terrible it is beyond my imagination. She is going to need every last shred of strength to look after herself and she cannot continue to carry me as well.

"But Laura. Laura my love. What are they going to do? Will they operate or is it radiotherapy or chemotherapy, whatever they call it? What are the odds? When do they start?"

"It's easy. Mr Mitchell will tell you all about it when he sees you. Probably Friday. The plan is that next week I start chemotherapy. First of all they put in a Hickman line."

What is all this? What is a Hickman line? We are looking out over a new territory. A strange and foreign country, containing terrible things.

"Henry, just listen. It is nothing. A plastic tube straight into a vein in the neck. It allows them to put drugs directly into me. Saves lots of injections. But you must be careful with it. Don't be clumsy. Don't catch it or pull it. Be careful when you turn over in bed. You understand, don't you?"

It is slowly dawning on me just how difficult and dangerous this is.

"And Henry . . ." she continues, ". . . it has to be clean. It must be kept clean. The whole system of tubes and valves and all the rest of it must be cleaned out regularly, we don't want any infections. Do you understand? I can make an appointment with the McMillan nurse every two days. Alternatively you can do it for me." I have no idea what a McMillan nurse is but let it pass.

I look up into her large clear eyes. I'm not sure I can handle this. I don't know whether I've got the skill or the finesse or the sheer bloody guts or the persistency, the regularity, the reliability even to be there day after day ready when required, the patience, especially the patience, to make sure the job's done well.

"Do you want me to do it?" I ask her.

"You know I do."

"Then I will."

We sit together. We hold hands, and silently gaze out over the darkening garden where the last of the summer's hollyhocks bend gently against the evening sky.

"You knew this all along didn't you?" I ask her. "You knew from the start."

Smiling as if to herself she draws deeply on the remnants of her hundredth cigarette. "I had an idea, it was in the back of my mind. The truth is I didn't want to know, I just couldn't face any more trouble." She pauses. The bats are coming out and perhaps one of their number fluttering too close to the window has caught her eye. "I didn't want to open up another front until I was ready. Best to fight one thing at a time."

We look at each other. Now is not the time. There will never be a time. She squeezes my hand. "Don't worry. It's not your fault."

"But it is, I should have made you see the doctor earlier, insisted on it, I should have made you find the time . . . you see I knew as well."

We continue to sit together in silence, still holding hands and it is quite dark now and the silhouettes of the trees and flowers have all faded away, but our thoughts are tracing out another landscape where we are looking out over a precipice towards a long weary trail winding away into the distance. With no idea where it is going to end.

Chapter 26

"Do you swear to take this jury to a private and convenient place and suffer no one to speak to them, nor to speak to them yourselves, save to ask if they have come to a verdict upon which they are all agreed."

The clerk intones the time honoured oath given to ushers through the centuries.

"We do."

And the two black-robed ushers, having sworn their oath, conduct the jury through the side door of the court and away along the back corridor.

"I make the time 10.35," says Judge Irvine. "The defendant will be remanded in custody." He stands to leave the court.

"Court will rise," commands the clerk. So we all rise and bow, and counsel, solicitors, runners, CPS representatives and one solitary member of the public make their way to the door and, awaiting deferentially for each other to file through, hang around on the concourse for the eventual verdict which could take five minutes, five hours, or five days.

As Pauline is busy I am meeting Jackson for lunch. I am going to have to tell him about Laura, and have cleared it with her in advance. My clerk must know everything. I will not be working too much from now on. Anything I do will have to be tailored around Laura and I depend upon Jackson to arrange it, and I know that he will.

He takes the news badly.

He and Laura have always been close. Ever since that time when I first joined chambers and, looking for a family home, they went together to view a house (as it turned out, something of a mansion) near Beverley and she introduced him as her father.

Now he passes a liver-spotted hand across his brow – his blotched face a ghastly, sickly, yellow. He dabs his eyes with the handkerchief he has always worn at his breast pocket, and reaching out to embrace me we stand locked together, my damp cheek against his.

"Christ," he says, "I don't believe it. I don't believe it. How bad is it? Jesus Christ, what are her fucking chances now?"

The truth is, I won't know until Friday. That is if they tell me the truth. What are anyone's chances with stomach cancer? And what are you like if you survive? I have lost interest in Coggins. I just want the jury back so I can pack up my gear and go home.

"Bad luck you had to come in today," Jackson says. "Is anyone with her?" I hadn't really thought about it. "Just her cats and dogs."

We drink for a while in silence. I know what he is thinking. He is not a selfish man. "Christ," he says, "this could happen to any of us."

"How's the case going?" I ask him. "The unequal case of Jackson versus his barristers."

"Still paying me 10%," he smiles, "I can spin this out for ever."

But our hearts aren't really in it. What was interesting once is now unimportant, and what was fun then, now seems merely sad.

"Better get going," he says, finishing his drink – my introspective mood driving him away.

"I'd better get back to chambers. I have to ring Laura."

I carry on alone. I have a lot to think about. Poor Laura who has done nothing in her life to deserve this. What is going to happen? Will she survive? And – I have to confess – although this should have been the least of my worries, what am I going to do about money and the overdraft? If I'm not in court I earn nothing. We have been extravagant. I owe tax and probably VAT. I have fallen behind on my chambers contributions, and of course I owe Jackson his 10%.

I have another drink. How will this affect Pauline? I must tell her. And these are shameful thoughts; will it drive her back to me? Will the thought of possible future prospects make her reconsider and, after a respectable interval, ensure her eventual return. How important is a spark now? And was there anything I should have done to prevent this happening? Should I have pushed Laura more? Why didn't I drag her to a specialist sooner? Was my delay deliberate? Dare I think it – do I secretly want to be free?

I wander back to court. Pauline is waiting for me on the steps. "We had a verdict an hour ago," she screams, "where have you been?"

"You'd better apologise to the judge," she continues to hector me. "For God's sake try and walk straight and suck this fucking mint."

News of the verdict has spread and the court is now full. I notice the three Coggins sisters in the public gallery waiting with their partners and their friends. Mrs Coggins is there. She sits apart and alone.

The press are ready in the front row, and as I enter, they exchange glances. I see Coggins in the dock at the back with his head down; a prison officer stood on either side. The benches behind counsel have filled up and Pauline, who has been looking for me and lost her place, sits with the probation officers neutrally waiting at the side.

We all rise as Judge Irvine enters, and staying on my feet as the rest subside, I apologise (as I have many times before) for keeping the court waiting.

"Not at all. Not at all Mr Wallace. You haven't. I had an urgent case in between." What a star! What an absolute star! Has Jackson rang him? I wonder.

"Send for the jury please," he asks the clerk and the jury file in. They do not look at Mr Coggins. They seem surprised to see how much the crowd has grown.

"Will the foreman please stand?" says the clerk, and a thin intelligent looking middle-aged man in glasses rises to his feet. It is not difficult to spot who will be selected the foreman. It never is.

"Have you reached verdicts upon which you are all agreed?" asks the clerk.

"We have."

"Upon count one. Do you find the defendant Guilty or Not Guilty?"

144

A long pause. He clears his throat. "Not Guilty." There is an audible gasp – but we are still a long way from home. There are nine counts: three for each girl; and I have been around long enough to know that juries are capable of anything, and on long indictments often perversely save their guilty verdicts to the last.

Not on this occasion. As each count is read out the foreman, growing in confidence, his head up looking across the court, acquits Coggins of every charge.

There is a moment of silence whilst the message seeps in.

This has been an emotive inter-family struggle and battle lines have been irreversibly drawn. Partisans of either side often cheer or cry out in disgust. Occasionally fists are shaken and people rush for the doors. Not today. In dignified silence the divided Coggins family files away and I ask that Mr Coggins be discharged and released from the dock.

"Certainly Mr Wallace," says the judge and then looking carefully at me, ". . . and I'm very sorry."

There is a crush outside as the press gather for unguarded comments from either side. Pauline has disappeared. No doubt on the telephone to Tomkinson.

I shake Coggins' hand. He seems bewildered. His wife stands beside him and I kiss her cheek. I cannot leave them here unprotected in this crowd, and having taken them to a side room I listen to their stilted words of thanks. I want to be away but dare not leave them alone.

Suddenly Freddy Platten bursts in. He is oblivious to their presence.

"How the fucking hell did that happen?" he cries.

"How did you ever get that dirty bastard off?"

"Oh, hello Mr Coggins." He is unabashed. "And you Mrs Coggins," he says cheerfully. "Bloody amazing result."

Does he expect them to agree?

What does he expect them to say?

"Oh yes Freddy truly fucking amazing and old Coggins here been at it for years."

They stand bemused. Now grown into a quiet dignified couple. Freddy claps them on the shoulder. "Come on.

145

Cheer up. Off the lot," he laughs, "and I thought it was stitched on."

"I wonder Freddy," I begin, "if you would be so kind as to help Mr and Mrs Coggins find their way out. Try and keep them away from the rest of the family, and don't let them talk to the press."

"Oh I'll talk to the press," he says, "tell them I never doubted it for a moment. Ask them why do the police and CPS persist in bringing such bloody hopeless cases? Fucking hell," he shakes his head, "who would have believed it? Come on you two," he turns to his clients, "back to the Hessle Road."

Later when I am alone with Laura I tell her the events of the day. It is a distraction for her. "Did he do it?" she asks.

In truth I don't know. These allegations are easy to make and after twenty years difficult to disprove. The girls were magnificent witnesses. They were sure in their own minds that what they were saying was true. A witness who has convinced herself can be convincing. On the other hand, could one imagine all that illicit secret sex in that tiny overcrowded house and never a word of complaint? Put into the scales Coggins's last blinding defiant answer — it might just have tilted the balance his way.

I don't know. I will never know. It is not my job to know. It is not my job to care.

I tell Laura how I went to the window overlooking the main door to the court and saw Mr and Mrs Coggins going down the steps together (Freddy having immediately deserted them), and stand still on the pavement below. They had waited there for a minute or two and then, pulling themselves together, had slowly disappeared around the corner. No one had come up to them. No one to offer congratulations. Perhaps to suggest a celebratory drink. No one.

They had simply slowly walked away together — but alone.

"There are no winners in these things," Laura tells me, "everyone loses. The jury might have thought after twenty years 'who cares'. Is it really worth it?"

"Well is it . . ." she persists, "is it worth it? All that worry, tears and trouble. The family split in half. Washing your dirty linen in public and the papers full of it. Is it worth it?"

She pauses for breath, and looks down at her lap where one of her cats lies curled, now slightly stirring in its sleep at the intensity of her tirade. "Is it bloody worth it? What do you think? Is it bloody worth it? Don't you think that life's too short?"

Chapter 27

Laura was right about Mr Mitchell. He was dour. A man of few words, he seemed ill at ease. Standing before an illuminated screen holding up Laura's scans and tersely pointing out what they so gruesomely displayed.

"You see here?" He pointed out 'a hard edge'. "That is good. Very good. But what worries me is this bit. Do you see that? Where it's all fuzzy, I don't like that. That is an area of active growth." He pauses, scratching his chin. "No. I don't like that. Just there. Do you see it? It could be breaking out."

"Well Mr Mitchell," I interrupt the flow, "don't you think we should get started perhaps? I mean the sooner we stop it the better, don't you think? What, please can you tell us, is taking so long?"

It seems to me — it would to anyone — that now we know that 'heartburn' (apparently this was the G.P.'s diagnosis) has turned into oesophageal cancer, and is showing signs of 'breaking out' and spreading, we should be doing something to stop it. Now. Today.

There doesn't seem a lot of time to lose.

Dr Mitchell sighs. "I know how you feel. But this is a delicate, indeed a dangerous, procedure. We must do some tests. We must select the correct medication. We have to review progress as we go. I cannot just charge in. This is not a bullet wound."

Laura puts her hand on my arm. "Be patient," she says. "Mr Mitchell knows what he's doing."

But does he? I am going to find out.

"Look Mr Mitchell, please don't take this the wrong way. I do not mean to be offensive. But in my game I know certain solicitors tell punters, 'I am going to get you a barrister from Leeds' or indeed 'I am going to get you a barrister from London.' Now the truth is, the local Bar is as good as they are — but punters like to hear that their solicitor is bringing a big man from out of town. Usually they are no good at all. Else why would they travel so far? But a punter can't tell the difference. What I am asking you is, are you any good? Are you a bloody good local man as good, if not better than, anyone else. Or put it this way. Do we go to London? I'm sorry. It's best you tell us now."

He doesn't flinch. Doesn't react at all. Instead he pins a sheet of paper over the screen and draws a stomach and oesophagus rising from it. He etches a dark circle where they join. "That is the cancer," he says, "the size of a rather small orange. These are the blood vessels," he continues stabbing at the paper with his crayon, "they pass very close. I am going to resect this section of stomach after having cut and raised the ribs. All this will go." He slashes across the bottom of the ascending oesophagus and the top half of the stomach.

"I may dissect out the lymph glands. I may go further, and follow any extensions if I must. But the trick is, the difficulty is, I must – I absolutely must – keep these blood vessels intact. These feed what is left. Do you understand? These blood vessels allow the stomach to survive. I don't say grow. But to heal, to recover, to function. God willing, they will save your wife's life."

He threw the crayon on his desk. "Nobody, but nobody can do this better. I do not often say this. I usually don't have to. But I have the best record of anyone doing this operation in England. So tell me now before we go any further. What are you doing. Are you staying with me. And with my team," he adds, "or are you going shopping somewhere else?"

And I thought he was a man of few words.

"I am staying," Laura ignores me. Her deep voice never wavers. "So when do we start?"

"Monday. As an out-patient. The Hickman line goes in. We wait a day or two and check it, then probably Friday chemotherapy. That's when we start. Four courses. Each course lasts one week. Then a scan. By this time you will feel, frankly, terrible. Eventually the tumour will start to shrink. Hopefully it will become very small. After six weeks I operate and take out what's left."

I have to ask. I don't want to ask. I don't want to know. But I do want to know. We have to know. I have to know what the chances are. What are the chances if we do nothing? What are the chances if we stick with just chemotherapy? Or what are the chances if we forgo chemotherapy and go in and do the surgery now? What are the chances Laura will survive the operations? I don't want to know. Don't tell me. I can't bear it. I don't want to know.

"What are the chances?" asks Laura. "I think I should like to know."

Mr Mitchell is now talking to her. Back to his usual brusque style. "If we do nothing – six months. If we just take the chemotherapy – about twelve. The operation has a 10% mortality rate. That is, 10% of patients do not regain consciousness, and if they do they don't last long. If you survive the operation you have approximately two years. If you get past two years you may go on for a further five. If you get past that, and some do, you will have recovered and will live a normal or nearly normal life. Your chances of survival are about 20%. As I have said, if we do nothing, you will be dead very soon."

Laura smiles, "Not a lot of choice then. Starter, main and dessert. Book me down for the lot."

Mr Mitchell nods and turns to open the door. "Dr Hussein, have you got a minute?" he shouts through and immediately we are joined by a small doctor in a white coat with greying hair and, in contrast to his colleague, a voluble but kindly manner.

"Dr Hussein will explain the chemotherapy to you," says Mr Mitchell. "He is the expert in that."

It is quite simple really. They are introducing a chemical poison to the body that in theory, at least, poisons the cancer faster than it poisons the patient. It's a bit of a race. They give enough to kill the cancer, but not too much to kill you.

"It's a matter of balance. Of fine-tuning," the softly spoken Dr Hussein tells Laura. "We monitor as we go. But you will lose your hair. All your body hair will fall out. Eyebrows, everything. Even the hair in your nose. And you will feel ill.

Very ill. Constantly sick, cramps and vomiting. Your body will ache, even your eyes will ache. Your joints will swell. So will your feet. You will want to die."

Laura sits weighing all this up. She is motionless.

Eventually she looks up at the hovering doctors, takes a deep breath and smiles. "Listen boys," she says with her usual easy familiarity, "I know the odds. I've got the message. But this is a tough game. For all of us. I'm a private patient and we're all in this together, so you two remember this . . . No win . . . No fee!"

She shakes a finger and starts laughing. And we all start laughing.

And so laughing together we walk into the abyss.

Chapter 28

Giles has called another chambers' meeting and we are back in the Humberview Executive Suite of The Grafton Manor Hotel where the usual pencils, notebooks, water carafes and paraphernalia have been carefully laid out. Judging by the size of the agenda, it appears that Whitebait Chambers is deep in trouble again.

"Thank you all for coming," Giles begins, and nodding at me, "especially Henry."

I am only here at Laura's insistence. "Go to it," she said. "It'll get you away for a bit. When you come back you can tell me all about it. And don't forget. Do your best for John."

"Item One," begins Giles. "Report on negotiations with the clerk. Bring us up to speed Horace."

And still wearing his silver suit, the one that he doesn't seem to have changed since the last meeting, Horace Pickles reports, as we all expected, that negotiations have not been going well. Indeed, they have not been going at all.

"Contact, for the time being at least," he tells us, "seems to have broken down. I can't get inside his room and he won't pick up his internal phone. I have to call him from a public phone box in the street," he complains.

"Well we're suing him aren't we?" says Browne-Smythe picking at his balding head. "Perhaps that's why. Or is he suing us? No matter, I trust we're on the winning side?"

"Not entirely," says Horace. What does 'not entirely' mean? It has an ominous ring.

"Our solicitors seem to have fallen down a bit I am afraid. Been out-smarted by that London lot. Made some admissions that I . . . . certainly I . . . . did not authorise. Perhaps Giles can help here?"

"Nothing to do with me," says Giles folding his arms.

"Ah well," says Horace resignedly, "somebody according to our solicitors, somebody in these chambers; and I'm trying to find out who, told them to admit that each member has an individual, an individual, oral contract with Jackson, and that there is no such thing as a collective contract with him upon which we can either defend or sue, but that we are individually bound, or not bound as the case may be, by what we have individually agreed, expressly or inferentially, by our individual course of dealing with him over the years."

I wish I had stayed at home.

"I want you all to know that I have investigated these claims very carefully," says Horace. "Indeed I have researched the law, and I am happy to be able to tell you that by no means, not by any means, not by any means whatsoever, is everything lost. My recommendation, indeed my strong recommendation, after having considered this case from all possible aspects, is that we, without further ado, issue fresh proceedings. Yes . . ." he waves down a growing murmur from around the table, ". . . Yes fresh proceedings. For negligence. Yes, negligence no less. Against our own solicitors!" He ends triumphantly. "We sue our own solicitors for their stupid advice."

Oh, absolutely brilliant. We are now suing the solicitors who we have instructed to sue our clerk, who, needless to say, is in his turn, suing us.

"Oh dear," says Giles. He seems to be bursting out of his blazer, "I don't like the sound of this. Let's not be too hasty Horace. I suggest we proceed with caution. What do the rest of you think?"

True to form, Humphrey favours not paying the bill – but a consensus is growing; slowly forming in the nucleus of the giant mind that is Whitebait Chambers that after much careful consideration the best course yes, the best course – is to do nothing at all.

Probably what we should have done in the first place.

"Let me look into it," says Giles. "I'm sure something will emerge."

My guess is a huge bill will emerge – and chambers' contributions will be going up to meet it.

"Item number Two. Bar Mark. Now young Browne-

Smythe . . ." says Giles, ". . .I hope you've got some good news for us here."

"Sorry Giles," begins Browne-Smythe from his new position at the head of the table, "I've got a letter here from the Bar Council which seems to indicate that a preliminary study by their Management Consultants has disclosed certain hitherto unknown defects in our procedures. We don't seem to have held a fire drill lately."

In fact, chambers is so cold we don't seem to have had a fire recently.

Giles is nonplussed. "A fire drill lately," he repeats. "We've never had a fire drill at all. Why do we want a fire drill?"

Browne-Smythe is a patient man. "Perhaps in case we have a fire. But the real reason is to get our Bar Mark in order to get Legal Aid in order to get paid," he tells the meeting, "just something we have to do I'm afraid."

I've had enough of this. "Give me the forms," I tell him. "I'll just fill them in. Tell them we have one every year."

"Not good enough, I fear," says Browne-Smythe. He is becoming irritating. "It has to be observed by a qualified Executive Fire Officer I'm afraid. And on top of that we do not have smoke alarms, water sprinklers, or sufficient, indeed any, fire extinguishers, emergency lighting, nor self luminous exit signals nor an automatic unfolding chute from the second floor, nor a fire escape, indeed any fire escapes, from any of our rooms, common staircases, passageways or marked routes of egress.

On top of that, I'm afraid our entrance door opens inwards when it should open onto the street. Our furnishings unfortunately will also have to be replaced as they are not constructed from non-combustible materials and we will need to construct a special reinforced storeroom in which to enclose all inflammatory materials overnight.

The building will also have to be rewired as all main fuse boxes and ring mains are not protected by fire repellent materials and we shall require a special ramp into the car park to allow the safe exit in an emergency of all disabled members and visitors, including the CPS.

All windows of common rooms will require replacement as they are neither fire resistant nor shatterproof and special fire doors will have to be inserted at statutory intervals along the corridors. Oh and I forgot. The staircase. It's a hazard. Yes, I know. But a fire hazard as well. It'll need to be enclosed."

"Any legal aid that comes our way is going to be absorbed by re-building the whole fucking premises," I tell them. "Why don't we put up the insurance and simply burn it down?"

"Oh and there's something else I forgot," says Browne-Smythe shuffling his papers. "We need to appoint a Fire Marshall. Might I suggest Doreen? Of course she will need to go on a course to receive training. I'm afraid we will have to pay for that, plus travel and her overnight accommodation for one or two days. Oh, and the Bar Council recommend an appropriate increase in her salary to reflect her new qualification and status-upgrading."

Horace is getting impatient. It's a long time since he spoke. "You'll be glad to hear I've held preliminary discussions with Doreen and she is in broad agreement with our proposals. She would, however, like to select her uniform herself."

Giles passes a weary hand over his brow.

"Don't you go talking to her too much," he advises Horace. "We don't want another court case. And you Browne-Smythe, perhaps you could get the architects to come round and give the old place the once-over. Nothing too elaborate. Perhaps not the best materials. Certainly not in the clerk's room. Give us some idea about the cost." He waves away further discussion. "Then we can all look into it."

Young Browne-Smythe has more, much more, to discuss but Giles has heard enough bad news for one morning and, ignoring his upraised arm, presses on.

"Item Three. Correspondence from the Lord Chancellor. What's this all about Horace?"

"More bad news I'm afraid Giles. McIntosh, as chambers will remember, was put in charge of our Race Relations Equal Opportunities Submission. Another part of Bar Mark. I am afraid he has not done well. He disappoints in fact."

We all turn to stare at McIntosh, dressed as smartly and eccentrically as ever in shooting jacket and plus fours. I am rather taken by his cravat. He gazes indifferently out of the window and reaches for a small cigar.

"The Lord Chancellor writes that he is concerned that some chambers might, unknowingly, or unbeknownst to them as he puts it, have come to be 'institutionally racist'. It is important that chambers actively recruit at least 10% of their membership from ethnic minorities. Those with a different sexual orientation should not be overlooked. Your chambers' response to my little questionnaire designed to test racial attitudes is nothing short of disgraceful. Scandalous even. I am instituting an immediate enquiry. In the meantime, I strongly recommended that a member of your chambers describing himself as McIntosh N. be immediately suspended. A team of specialist investigators will be with you shortly."

"Doesn't sound too good," Humphrey agrees. "What exactly has McIntosh done?"

McIntosh looks around the table with an indolent, contemptuous gaze. "Bloody fools in London sent me some puerile forms to fill in. Something about testing our attitudes . . . Couldn't take it seriously, something about subconscious negative feedback. All bloody nonsense. Took me hours to fill it in. Hundreds and hundreds of stupid questions. Let me give you an example. Question 903 if I remember right, 'What are black men good at?' "

McIntosh raises one eyebrow awaiting an intelligent response.

Giles is looking at him aghast, "So what did you reply McIntosh? What did you put on the Lord Chancellor's form? What did you bloody say?"

"I seem to remember inserting", drawls McIntosh, "playing the bongos", he pauses for effect, "into the appropriate box."

Humphrey has pushed his designer sunglasses to the top of his head.

"Something else for you to look into Giles," he says laughing.

Giles has had enough. He is no longer to be trifled with, let alone laughed at – particularly by that designer clad, dilettante, smart-arsed Humphrey. His stained blazer hangs open and his purple face is bursting above his collar.

"And here's something else for you to look into Humphrey. Something that just might concern you.

Item Four. A letter to me personally. A Mr H Goldblatt, landlord of 6, Waterside Mews. You Humphrey apparently saw fit to give Whitebait Chambers as one of your references before moving into accommodation there. You apparently have failed to pay any rent. Mr Goldblatt is holding us responsible."

Somebody else suing us then.

"And there are damages," Giles continues ferociously. "I ask you. Damages! Soiled bed linen. A smashed wicker basket chair." (One of my more adventurous suggestions). "Cigarette burns on the bedside cabinet, irreparable stains to the edge of the kitchen table by what might be a dead oyster. Broken bottles in the sink."

Giles is staring across the table at Humphrey. Humphrey is staring back at me. I am staring at the door.

"Disgusting food debris under the bed, and to cap it all," continues Giles, "to cap it all . . . damaged shower equipment and a blocked toilet."

I hadn't realised I'd enjoyed myself so much.

"Mr Goldblatt has not finished yet," says Giles. "Oh no. By no means has he finished. Apparently when visiting his premises with a potential tenant one lunchtime he was confronted by the sight of a member of these chambers . . . Whitebait Chambers . . . cavorting on the bed with a blonde tart. According to Mr Goldblatt – some depraved sexual activity that seemed to involve rolling in food. He was subjected to a stream of obscenities by the female party and ordered to leave his own flat. He has lost a potential tenancy and claims damages for harassment and distress. And so yes Humphrey, certain matters do require looking into. And you can help us for a start."

Giles' eyes are popping from their sockets, great beetle

eyebrows rising in pursuit of his receding hairline, veins throbbing at his temples, he waves a fist at Humphrey seated across the table scattering his glasses, agenda, pencil and pad. He may have an erection but fortunately, so far, has remained sitting down.

"Why have you not paid your rent?" he demands. "Why have you left 6, Waterside Mews in such a disgusting condition? Why have you permitted the said premises to be used by a member of these chambers for lunchtime fornication? This man, this member of these chambers, when challenged by Mr Goldblatt, gave his name as Johnson. Who is this man? Name him immediately. He is looking at an enormous fucking bill."

Humphrey, thank God, has had time to recover his nerve. His sunglasses are back in place. He is in complete control. "It's bugger all to do with you Giles," he begins. "An entirely private matter. Give me that letter immediately. The landlord is a lying grasping bastard and there is nobody – certainly nobody in these chambers – with the initiative and balls to do anything more exciting in his lunch hour than to play darts. Give me that letter immediately, and you can all fuck off."

"Hear. Hear," I cry, "Well said, Humphrey. What's it got to do with us?" Perhaps I protest too much. "Whitebait Chambers has got enough on its plate already."

But Giles will have none of it. "Besmirching the name of these chambers! Leaving us open to yet another fucking claim. Bringing the good name of Whitebait Chambers into disrepute," he repeats.

Giles bangs the table with his fist. "Failure to honour your due debts! Counterfeiting a reference! The loss of a possible client."

Giles is back to the things he knows best. Naturally our man in the silver suit agrees with him.

"Write to Mr Goldblatt, Giles," Horace suggests. "We must have further and better particulars. We must trace this Johnson chap. He must be brought to book and made liable."

Humphrey is on his feet. "I warn you! I warn the lot of you! Stay out of this. This is a private matter. If you, if any of you, do anything to interfere I shall refer you . . ." he points round the table, "I shall refer you all, every bloody one of you, to the Disciplinary and Complaints Committee of the Bar Council. And I tell you now, I shall be looking for damages."

Looks like another court case then.

Hopefully, one in which the mysterious Mr Johnson will not intrude

Giles refuses to be intimidated. What is another court case more or less? Between friends, so to speak.

"You have forged a reference Humphrey. You have forged my signature when you knew, knew full well that I for one, knowing you as I do, would be wholly disinclined to vouch for you for anything. Apparently in this reference, you have so glibly and falsely composed, I am offering chambers as surety against rent and damages, and – get your pomaded head round this – we are not talking peanuts. This Goldblatt fellow is looking to us for £75,000 plus. So why don't you fucking look into it Humphrey, and sit your fancy arse down and write him a cheque?"

Humphrey is looking at me as I am now making for the door.

"Not leaving are we Henry?" he asks. "It's Laura," I tell them, "told her I wouldn't be long." I turn at the door. "Why don't we give Humphrey a chance to sort his own mess out?" I catch his eye. "With goodwill on all sides, I am sure this will be easily settled. Let Humphrey fix up a meeting with this Goldblatt chap. You won't need me to attend of course. Make him an offer Humphrey," I suggest, "perhaps a little contribution from this Johnson chap, whoever he is, might help. A token contribution that is . . . er . . . without any admission of liability that is . . . er . . ." I catch Humphrey's eye again, ". . . well perhaps something a little more than a token, but anyway fix up a meeting and give that ferrety little bastard (have I said too much?) some money. You can fucking sort it out."

"I think I should attend." Horace is also on his feet. "We most certainly don't want any legal problems to arise later. Browne-Smythe here can take down the minutes and report back to Giles. I shall of course immediately alert our solicitors." Giles groans, his head in his hands, ". . . I am required of course to put our mortgagors on notice." Horace presses on. "As you will all no doubt know, the terms of our mortgage require that they immediately be notified of any pending legal action affecting their security on these premises, and further, it is my considered opinion that the Bar Council be kept informed."

In those far away happier days I would have gone 'looking for work', but now I must get back to looking after Laura. This meeting could go on forever. I pick my way carefully down the stairs to the sound of distant shouting and totter out into the bright sunlight and wander away across the lawn. There should be enough material here to entertain Laura and maybe make her laugh. Without introducing the subject of Johnson that is.

Chapter 29

Laura is impatient to start her treatment. She broods upon the malignancy growing inside her and is terrified that while she waits, it is spreading its poisonous tentacles further into her stomach, along her oesophagus and into her neck, where she is continually and fretfully poking about for 'glands'.

She has been told, or heard about, metastases and worries about these tiny clusters of cells that break off at the edges and are swept away in the blood and lodged like tiny seeds in some far away capillary where they put down roots and grow another colony. She wants to get started. She is available any time. Every day that goes by is a day when this tumour might slip its leash.

Two days later the Hickman line is inserted. This small but delicate operation goes well and Laura returns home from hospital with her tubes inserted below her neck and taped to her chest. For a few hours she is happy. She senses things are moving on and her sense of urgency is shared by those who hold her fate in their rubber-gloved hands.

But of course there is always delay; a further four days of waiting to make sure the connection remains open and stays free of infection until at last the cancer nurse (the McMillan nurse), arrives with the equipment and after months of Laura putting off seeing her doctor, putting off ringing the consultant, waiting for an appointment with the consultant, arranging the tests, having the tests, waiting for the results of the tests, making another appointment to be told of the results, deciding what to do about the results; finally the treatment can start and Laura belatedly, physically weak, but strong in spirit, assumes the offensive and takes up arms as she sees it against the enemy within.

She is carrying her chemotherapy prescription in a pressurised plastic ampoule worn at her waist in a small velcroed bag which connects to the Hickman line by a series of tubes and valves. It is my job to clean this system every two days. The procedure has been carefully explained to me – demonstrated to me over and over again until I become relatively adept – by the small, bright businesslike nurse.

First of all I wash my hands in hot soap and water. Then I swab them with alcohol before sliding my fingers into talcum-lined thin plastic gloves. I set out my sterile tray: arranging the phials of saline and disinfectant; opening the needles; removing the syringes from their sterile packaging; preparing more alcohol swabs to rub the ends of the tubes; and (lining Laura up in the light of a large window overlooking her flowers outside) I cautiously begin my routine of sluicing out her tubes and valves one by one, always remembering – this is very important I am repeatedly told – to make sure there are no bubbles of air before infusion begins.

Between us we are getting along quite well. All right, there have been a few tense moments. Once I knocked over the whole tray from the top of the piano where we keep it out of the animals' reach. Sometimes I get taffled in the tubes. I remember dropping a syringe onto the carpet and, absent-mindedly, recovering it from under the table, carrying on with the injection regardless until Laura's cries of protest brought me to my senses, and discarding the syringe into the 'Sharps' box, I began the procedure again. Famously I tried the process with a cigarette between my teeth and saw a delicate plume of ash powder the valves as I checked whether they were open or closed. "Fucking marvellous," Laura interrupted. "Intravenous tobacco. You think of everything, a cigarette straight to the head."

We had been warned of the side effects, but nothing can prepare you for this. Her hair is coming out in handfuls. Every morning I discreetly collect it from her pillow; brush it from her cardigan; scoop it off the kitchen table. It is everywhere, and Laura impatiently waiting the arrival of her wig – she has defiantly chosen blonde curls – is now wearing a white sun hat or her mother's old head scarf to cover her embarrassing bald head. I had never realised it was so small. Every night as I watch her trying to sleep I keep tugging at her scarf to cover her naked scalp. And of course she is in pain – both from the cancer and the perpetual aching in her joints. She suffers wild temperature swings, and is forever in the bathroom, her contorted body writhing on the floor as she tries to vomit down the lavatory.

Periodically, the exhausted ampoule was changed for a full one until at last, another milestone, she was ready for the introduction of an even more powerful dose which unfortunately – because of the possible side effects – could only be given under the constant observation of the local hospital, and the immediate supervision of Dr Hussein.

It took some time to get her ready. I had to pack her suitcase while she watched me from the bed. The nightdress; the change of nightdress; the underwear and the change, or rather changes, of underwear; her dressing-gown and slippers; the toilet bag and the second toilet bag; the magazines and books; her outdoor clothing. Why?

"I'm not going into hospital wearing that. And I'm coming out in something different. And don't forget the wig."

And yes, the change of wig.

She wanted me to check her tubes. Clean the ends or something, or make sure the tape was holding fast, or really, in spite of the time it was taking, not to leave her alone.

I thought I might give them one more sluice. But for some reason I got halfway through and forgot the next step I was supposed to take.

"For Christ's sake, concentrate. What's the matter with you? Your memory's going to pot."

For some reason this stung me and we began arguing. Perhaps it was the pressure. The worry of what she was going through – of what was coming next. But I have always prided myself on my memory. All right I might be a little clumsy or lazy, or have the odd bad habit or two. But memory? I could remember everything. There was nothing I forgot.

"There's nothing wrong with my memory. It's bloody perfect. I remember everything. Everything . . ." I was moved to exaggeration. "Why, I even remember being inside my mother. There's not many people who can say that!"

Laura raised an eyebrow. "I wouldn't be so sure."

But I finally got her there and helped her through the swishing electronic entrance where we followed green arrows on the floor to the queue waiting at reception. One girl behind the counter was having difficulty with the forms. Laura leant her head patiently against my shoulder fiddling with her tubes and trying to get herself comfortable as we inched forward imperceptibly (rather like a check-in at a foreign airport) until eventually twenty minutes later we finally arrived at the front.

"I'm sorry, your bed is not quite ready. If you'd like to take a seat."

Laura was to stay a few nights on the cancer ward. Imaginatively called C1.

A nurse finally led us inside.

I looked round at the patients. They seemed to be half asleep, propped up against their metal frames; hands lifeless on the sheets, gazing at the flickering blue screen of the television parked at the end of the room. Their faces ghastly – a sort of washed-out grey, worn and miserable, old before their time. A solitary nurse was bent over an old lady doing something with a catheter, a patient who seemed already dead.

I could see the panic in Laura's eyes. "Don't leave me here. For Christ's sake, don't leave me here."

But there was nowhere else. The private hospital with its French cuisine, separate rooms and flowers, didn't have the equipment – the medical equipment that is – to monitor her 'cure'. There wasn't any choice.

"You'll be all right." I tried to be reassuring. "It's only a couple of nights." But the smell, the sweet indescribable smell of death was driving me away. I gently prised her fingers from my wrist.

Anyway, I had to meet Pauline for lunch.

She had taken to frequenting a new brasserie, the first brasserie to open in Hull. It didn't do much business. Apart from Pauline's that is. And those like her. Aspirants to something more, without quite knowing what.

She was wearing what I took to be a new suit. A business

suit in light grey with a white blouse. I avoided looking at her shoes.

"Where have you been? I've been waiting ages. Anyway, I've ordered. Put it on your tab."

I'd not seen her since the triumphant ending of Coggins' trial. Perhaps I'd expected some congratulation. At the very least some curiosity as to how it came about. But no, she pitched in as usual.

"What do you think happened at work today? And wait till I tell you about Barry. That idiot. What do you think he's fucking done now?"

But I cut her short. Obviously she'd not heard about Laura. It was about time she did.

"Jesus Christ – I'm sorry."

What did I expect her reaction to be? Shock? Indifference? Sorrow? Suppressed elation? Sympathy for Laura?

Perhaps some sympathy for me?

I didn't expect her to be moved.

"What are you going to do?"

What can I do? What is there to do? Never one to let a bandwagon pass me by, I found myself clinging to her hand.

"Look after her," I told her. "Make her comfortable. She'll be left with half a stomach. An invalid, if she's lucky to survive."

Pauline was upset. She was frightened of illness, but it was more than that. Perhaps she felt that she had injured Laura indirectly in her deception with me and that Laura, the wholly innocent party, had suffered enough, and that out of the three of us (four if you include Barry), Laura was the least deserving of this fate.

"You should be with her. Why aren't you with her?"

"I just thought . . ." a waiter was hovering with my plate, but Pauline waved him away, "I was wondering . . ."

"Forget it. You should be with her now."

When I got back to the hospital, and it didn't take me long, Laura was already changed into her nightdress and lying back in bed with a drip (soon to be a constant companion) trailing from her arm and up into the saline bottle mounted on a mobile metal stand. Its lights were flashing. The alarm was pinging away.

It wasn't the only one, so were several others up and down the ward.

"What does that mean?" I was glad of the diversion. "Is something going wrong?"

"God knows. I don't think so." She looked up and down the ward. "It's been doing it for ages. It's the noise that drives you mad."

"So where are the nurses? Where are they?" I was getting irritated. "I thought they were here to nurse."

I know it doesn't do to antagonise the staff. Not when they were looking after Laura. Or supposed to be. Take it easy, I told myself. Try and be polite. I walked back down the ward looking for the nurses' station and, pushing through the swing doors, found it at the top of another flight of stairs.

There were three or four nurses drinking cups of coffee, laughing and listening to the sister tell a joke.

"Excuse me . . ." I was placatory, "alarms are going off and lights are flashing." They looked up in surprise, biscuits in their mouths, "I'm surprised you can't hear the noise."

"Don't worry lovey," the sister stopped her flow, "be with you in a minute. Just as soon as we've finished here."

So these are our Angels of Mercy. Another date for lunch.

"But . . ." words weren't coming easily, "but . . . what about the patients? Some of them . . ." I thought of Laura newly arrived and doubly left alone, "are getting upset."

"They'll be all right. Can't you see we're having our break?"

She turned back to her companions, "As I was saying . . ."

"You must come. You must. This is a cancer ward. They shouldn't be alone."

"And they won't be." She didn't call me lovey. "Just as soon as we've finished our break – which will be in about . . ." she consulted the watch hanging from her lapel, ". . . ten minutes. So you go back to your wife and tell her we'll be with her very soon."

What could I do? I couldn't drag them, I couldn't force them. I couldn't stand there arguing the toss. But I did.

"Ten minutes! Ten minutes! God knows how long you've been here already." I thought of the patients lying helplessly in their beds. "Some of them are dying. For all you know, they may be dead."

But it was no use. I thought of the dusty ward with its grimy windows and dirty toilet, the oppressive smell of neglect. Where did all the money go? What happened to all the targets? The promises. The good intentions. Where did the money go?

"Didn't you hear me? Nothing to worry about. Nothing out the ordinary. Just go back and wait."

She dismissively tossed her ginger head. What more could I do? It wasn't my day for parting shots. I made my way back down the stairs looking for the doors to C1 – they all looked alike – and after one or two false tries, finally found Laura and told her I had seen the nurses and they were very busy, but not to worry, they would be with us very soon.

And eventually they were. They made an impression of being very energetic. Running from bed to bed, changing lines and bottles and making a great show of reassuring their patients, until one finally came to Laura – saving her for last.

That night I stayed by Laura's bedside holding her hand and occasionally whispering words of encouragement. I told her about the chambers' meeting. It made her laugh. I mentioned McIntosh and his glorious indifference to the Lord Chancellor's letter; and I told her about Giles and Horace and how not only were we suing John, but it was possible that we might be suing our own solicitor, and how Humphrey was suing us. And through the small hours I explained the glorious nonsense of Bar Mark and how chambers was going both mad and bankrupt in trying to meet it, and how Doreen was insisting not only on a uniform but actually picking it herself.

Laura cheered up, and when I finally left near midnight – I left her soundly asleep.

But I was back again next morning. And the morning after, and the morning after that.

No more cases or conferences or lunches. No sudden trips to Hull.

And I was still there when she was finally unhooked from her drip. I got her dressed and down in the lift to a taxi. I loaded up her luggage (somehow it seemed to have grown) and took her home to her bed.

And in this way, this small way, perhaps I was able to expiate some of the guilt I felt at my persistent treachery, which in its own way was coming to reflect the tenacity of her cancer and proving just as difficult to cure.

Chapter 30

I went to see Mrs Coggins in the little terrace house that had caused all the trouble. Or might have caused the trouble, it depends on whom you believe. She showed me into her living room and switched the television off. She didn't turn it down.

I suppose I had to go and see her. It seemed the least I could do. She brought in two cups of tea on a tray and a little plate of biscuits, and I asked her if I could smoke.

"Use his ashtray," she said, "a present from my eldest boy."

We sat there for a while in silence until I indicated the window. "Is that the one they put through?"

She nodded. "And a couple at the back."

I had read about it in the papers. "It must have been frightening." I was trying to comfort her. "I hope you told the police."

She said nothing; playing with her hands in her lap, her grey head staring at the carpet, her tea untouched.

"Do you see anything of the children?"

She shook her head. "Nothing. None of them. Not since the trial."

I was amazed. "What, none of them speak? None of them? Nobody said anything?"

"Oh yes. As we walked away they called me a bitch."

"But I thought your sons lived here. You all lived together. You must see something of them."

"They'd gone by the time we got home. Not even a note. He thought he saw our youngest in the street once, but couldn't be sure. His eyes were failing you see. Anyway, he tried to catch him up. Told me he shouted his name. Anyway, whoever it was simply walked faster. Disappeared into the crowd."

She had started talking now and once started couldn't stop. "We never went out much you know. Not after the verdict. Everyone knows us round here. I've lived here all of my life.

All my friends, my family, nearly everybody I know. Nobody would talk to us. Nobody would let us in. At first we used to go round to see them but nobody would come to the door. He would be banging on the knocker and I could hear them inside. Once I saw a boy peeping through the curtains. Another time somebody stopped the hoover, but nobody answered the door. We used to stand there knocking but nobody came, and eventually, we never said anything to each other, we used to walk away. Then he would go to the pub. Well he did at first. But he was never gone long. Not like he used to. Back in half an hour. Nobody would talk to him he said."

"I can't believe it. It doesn't make sense. What gets into people? He was acquitted."

"Was he?" She looked up but wouldn't meet my eye. "Was he? Not round here he wasn't. And nor was I. Being ignored by everyone. Just simply ignored. It's like being invisible. It's like you're not there. If they knew us they wouldn't serve us in shops. Not even the fish and chip shop round the corner. We've been going to it for years. He told me about it. Dinner-time Friday. It's always busy. You can wait for hours. Anyway he waited. He'd got nothing else to do. And when he got to the front they wouldn't take his order. They wouldn't serve him. Just ignored him. He just stood there while they carried on with the next ones behind him in the queue."

She began to cry, soundlessly, her shoulders shaking, twisting her handkerchief in her hands.

"But that wasn't the worst. It was bad enough, but we could cope with it, or we could have done for a while. It might have got better. People might have forgotten in time. No. That wasn't the worst of it. It was the shouting that was the worst. As soon as they saw him they would come over and stand in our way. Men. Young men. I'd never seen them before in my life. Didn't know who they were. But they knew us. Different people. Not always the same ones. Not always men either. You won't believe it, but women also shouted. Dreadful things. Terrible. Things I couldn't say."

What do you do? Is it best to bring it out? Get it off her

chest. Or would she be embarrassed. Ashamed? Sad to have let him down.

"Tell me," I leant forward and pressed her knee. "You can tell me anything. I've heard it thousands of times. Nothing offends. Nothing surprises. I've heard it all before."

She looked up and I could see the tears. Two tracks down the folds of her shrunken face. Now she looked me in the eye.

"Not to your face you haven't. Nobody said it to you. Fucking nonce. Fucking beast. You dirty fucking animal. And that bitch with you. What do you do to her? We'll burn your fucking house down and you inside it. We know where you live. One night we'll be round. We'll put your fucking windows in." She paused and waited, still twisting her hand-kerchief in her hands.

"And they did. That's what they did. Glass everywhere, and the curtains blowing outwards into the street. We used to call the police. What's the use? They never came round. Not when you wanted them that is. Used to turn up later. Next day. The day after. Next week. Took statements. Filed a report. What's the use of that? There was paint all over the door. There still is. Paint on the bricks. You must have seen it. I tried to scrub out the words."

She paused and noticed the tray. Her manners, her sense of what was proper shining through. "Drink your tea," she said. "It's getting cold. Help yourself to another biscuit?"

"How did you cope with it? What did you do?"

"We did our best. We stuck together. We saw more of each other in six months than we had in thirty years. He used to go to his allotment. He spent hours there. Made it nice. You should have seen his shed. Like another home. A little palace. Took some furniture from the boys' bedrooms. Well they didn't want it anymore. Even a little bed. Put down carpets, a couple of easy chairs. I used to go with him myself. I don't like being here on my own. We listened to the radio. He used to like shipping forecast on the BBC. Would join in with the names. We both did after a while. I suppose it was something to do. And you should have seen the vegetables. Never seen so many. Rows and rows of sprouts. He had carrots, potatoes, beans on canes, lettuces, the lot. Funny really, the only time we had all that food, there was no one left to eat it. Couldn't even give it away. Nobody would touch it. But it kept him busy. Gave him something to do. I used to like it there. Nobody around. Peaceful. Just the birds."

She fell silent, her shoulders hunched, her head shaking from side to side. I waited. To pass the time I played with a biscuit and lit another cigarette. I'd read about it in the papers. Not the trial. They'd been unlucky there. Front page night after night. A bad week for news. Nothing else to report. No, not that. The later report. Famous again, but only for a night.

"It was just another day. Nothing different. Every day was the same, but we used to get up later and later. There never seemed much to do. He went off to the allotment and I started tidying up. It took me longer than I expected. I can't remember much about it. I may have had a little doze on the settee or I might have had another go at the walls.

Anyway, when I finally got there and managed to open the door, he'd got a hook in the ceiling and his feet were brushing the floor. I could see what he'd done." She stopped and cried again. "Been dead hours. His face turned blue. For some reason he'd put his slippers on and tidied up his desk. I sat there with him for ages. He was never really still. Just slowly spinning around. I don't understand it, why he couldn't rest."

We sat there together. There seemed nothing left to say.

"Did he leave a note?" I asked as gently as I could.

"Oh yes. Two notes in fact. One to me. The Coroner read it out. He couldn't stand it anymore. Wanted me to have something of a life. He'd got it into his head, with him gone the children might come back to me. But I don't want them back. Not now. Not ever. What they did killed him and it might as well kill me. Anyway. You must have seen it in the papers. What he said about the offence . . ." She paused again and looked up to me for confirmation. "Yes," I said, "that's why I'm here."

"Well, as you know, he denied it. I never did it he said. I would never touch my kids and I would never touch anyone else's. I can't admit to what I haven't done. And I believed him. Always have. If it were true, he'd have said so. What's he got to lose when he's dead?"

"The other note?" I pressed her. "I don't remember reading about that."

"No it wasn't in the paper. Not a lot of point. I gave it to the police though. One of them laughed and gave it back. I've still got it. Anyway, it's for you."

She took a crushed piece of lined paper from the sleeve of her cardigan and carefully flattened out the creases before handing it across.

'To Mr Wallace, Pauline and Freddy,' I read. 'Thank you for all you've done. Herbert Coggins.'

What did we do I wonder. He'd be better off in jail.

Chapter 31

Laura was delighted. Absolutely elated. She had lost nearly two stone, her skin hung in dry folds at her neck, she was sick five and six times a day and she had lost every single hair on her body.

She cocked her tiny head beneath the auburn curls of one of her growing collection of wigs and laughed. "I've just had Mr Mitchell on the phone with the results of the final scan!" She gave me a thumbs up.

"There's nothing to see! Absolutely nothing. Well . . . nearly nothing." She hesitated. "Absolutely fucking clear. Well . . . nearly clear. Do you understand what this means?"

She looked up at me from the wicker basket chair where she was sitting in her garden, but didn't wait for an answer.

"I may not need that operation after all! Not my skin cutting, ribs breaking, half my stomach hoicked out." She could be very graphic when excited. "Buckets of blood and shit. Christ knows what. I may not need it. Paul, I have got this thing fucking sorted." And she punched the air in her characteristic way, her little fist waving at the sky.

"That fucking cancer's disappeared. Well . . . to all intents and purposes. Fucking gone. Mr Mitchell's delighted. Absolutely fucking delighted. He can't believe it. Never seen anything like it in his life. Just a tiny scar. That's all that's left, a tiny scar. Well . . . so far as he can see. Just a little scar and fucking nothing. Can you believe it? I told you I'd beat it and I fucking will!" and punching the air again, she fell back into her chair, exhausted. Her two sleeping dogs jumped up startled, the little terrier barking. "Shut up you silly buggers. Mother's getting better," she said.

Mr Mitchell had also put a tube down her throat and into her stomach. He wanted to see what was happening, what effect the cocktail of poisons was producing inside. I rang him back and spoke to him myself. I wouldn't have used the word delighted. More cautiously pleased. Perhaps satisfied is a better word.

"Laura is fantastic," he told me. "What spirit. She wants to carry on the chemotherapy into a fifth session. This just isn't possible. We have given her all we can. Most people don't go past three. Any more and we'll kill her. I've spoken to Dr Hussein. We just daren't do it. And Henry," he was on first name terms by now, "this is the moment of truth. It's shrunk to a little scar. That's all I can see. Of course, you understand, there may be more, but anyway not very much. Do we go in or don't we?"

How do I know? How does anyone know? What if we don't operate and it grows back? Where are we then? More chemotherapy? And Laura so ill, operating is no longer an option. And what if he does operate and she dies under the knife? Why didn't we leave it? Why did we take the risk? She was getting better anyway.

"What do you think?" I ask him. After all he is the doctor. The surgeon who has been here many times before. Knows the risks, can calculate the odds. It's all a gamble really. There are no certainties in this.

"We'll do whatever you think," I tell him. Only a few weeks have passed and already Laura and I have total faith. I remember how sceptical I was in the beginning. Now imperceptibly, day by day, I have been converted to total trust, more a blinding faith. Is it always like this? I wonder. Is everybody the same?

"We'll do anything you say. Whatever you think best." I sound penitent almost. "Tell us what to do."

He pauses. I can hear his children in the background shouting to each other – possibly quarrelling. In my mind's eye I see his young wife leaning against the front door of his large house dangling the car keys and asking him, mouthing to him actually, are you going to be long?

He clears his throat. Calls me Henry again. "I think we should operate. I want to operate. While she's still fit enough. I think we should do it as soon as possible. I think we should do it next week. Talk to Laura. Try and persuade her – she may not want to – but try and persuade her. Persuade her we do it next week."

And he is gone. Away with his young family for the weekend. And why not? Enjoy what moments you can. Nothing lasts forever.

I lean over Laura and kiss her full, soft lips. They feel flaky and dry and I see her teeth pushing through inside. They seem to have grown larger. In fact, her whole face has changed. Those beautiful plump cheeks have all but disappeared, and beneath the remnants the sides of her mouth have shrunk and fallen in. Her large luminous eyes, now looking up at me, have grown enormous.

"Have a rest." I kiss her neck. "Go to sleep for a while. We'll talk about it later."

And she sinks back further into her chair smiling silently to herself, her body poisoned and wrecked, but her mind fast and active and delighted – delighted that this tiny shell of a body that is all that is left to her is somehow, in spite of it all, on the edge of success. How she would have detested herself only one year ago. The lines, the wrinkles, the fallen hair.

For some reason I kiss her wig. I want to touch her. Squeeze her. Encourage her. But I am afraid of hurting her frail body with my clumsy and belated devotion. So I sit by her side perched on the end of a garden bench and watch as she dozes and her tiny chest, just a rib cage really, rises and falls with every breath – taken it seems at agonisingly longer intervals. Eventually she opens her eyes. I am still there. She smiles.

"So let's have a drink," she suggests, "let's celebrate!"

It will be better if I give her Mr Mitchell's news when we're drunk. I cannot face it sober. We lift our glasses and clink them together.

"Cheers me dear!" she cries. "Happy days!"

It is much later and the sun much lower over the trees in the park when I broach the subject I have circled so cautiously all afternoon.

"You know, it might be better to have the operation anyway. Just a thought really. You know. Like taking out

176

insurance. Can't be too careful. Better safe than sorry . . ." Empty words that trail away.

She looks at me. Those knowing eyes. Why am I so far behind the game?

"Of course I'm going to have the fucking operation. I was just pissing about this morning. Enjoying the moment. Pretending to myself. I've not come this bloody far to back out now! They can take the bloody lot out! Let's fucking rock and roll." And the fist waved challengingly at the sky again. Was it the drink talking? I don't think so. She had decided months ago. Prepared herself months ago. The veteran of five caesareans, chronic kidney disease, brittle bone syndrome, God knows what else, she'd been there before, seen it all before and she had the guts to do it all again.

And I'd been tentatively to-ing and fro-ing all afternoon waiting for the right moment; waiting to slip into our drowsy conversation, the possibility – just the possibility Laura my love – that we might just think of having the operation (made of course much easier by the cancer's virtual obliteration) just to be absolutely sure, 100% certain; so there were no doubts, no doubts at all, of eventual success. And I would have said 'We'. 'We' would be having the operation. Just to make it a collective enterprise between the two of us so that she would not feel totally alone. But she had travelled way before me, and she was totally alone, and knew she was alone, and was ready to be alone and take it on whatever it was and however much it hurt.

Within her broken body she had the spirit of a giant.

"I want it soon," she said. "Let's get it over with. Give Mr Mitchell a call. Tell him I'm ready now. Try and persuade him to do it next week."

177

Chapter 32

Anything for money. But we needed it.

Bills kept dropping through the letterbox as the overdraft went through the roof.

I left Laura and went over to Hull to 'crack' a trial. Another trial lawyer's term. When a case has passed the formalities of the Magistrates Court, and the directions hearing in the Crown Court (or what some fool has now christened a 'case management hearing' with a bigger, dafter form) it is listed for trial, and given a date to start.

At this stage it can collapse for any number of reasons.

Witnesses change their minds and sign retraction statements, or just simply disappear.

The Crown Prosecution Service, belatedly and under the pressure of a looming trial date might re-assess its evidence and realise what it should have realised weeks ago, back in the Magistrates Court – that the evidence was paper thin and the victim probably a liar, and the police not much better, and inevitably some Crown lawyer (as they like to call themselves) or other gets cold feet and pulls the plug, and a letter is written to the defence called (rather grandiosely) a Notice of Discontinuance and the case is quietly dropped.

More frequently it is our dear friends, the punters, who get cold feet. Bold and fearless whilst the trial is weeks away, as the appointed hour approaches their courage fails, and the inflated bladder of innocence springs a quiet leak. They realise with mounting apprehension that they might not be quite so 'not guilty' after all. Their solicitor (usually Cranmer Carter & Co.) writes that their client is having second thoughts.

"Does learned counsel consider that the Crown might be persuaded to take guilty pleas to a lesser offence?"

Does he? You bet your life he does! I have contacted the barrister for the prosecution. Our old friend Browne-Smythe, who seems to be doing more and more work for his pals in the C.P.S.

We have discussed the case. Looked at the pitfalls for either side. Decided what I can squeeze out of the punter, and what he can sell to the invariably gung-ho, unrealistic idiot of a Crown lawyer. The stage is set. This is not going to be a trial at all. The jury (unbeknown to themselves) are on a fool's errand condemned to sit around all morning in their waiting room, never told and never knowing that there will be no trial; that Browne-Smythe and I have settled it days ago; that effectively it has 'cracked'.

And by twelve o'clock, and after a little intervening trip through the corridors of power and a small stroll down memory lane with our old pal Judge Irvine – just to tie up any loose ends, and little local difficulties – not to mention the matter of sentence – we have 'pleaded the punter up', patted him on his head and seen him safely off to start his 'Community Service' so that now we are safely ensconced in a place more familiar to us than a court room, none other than the saloon bar of the old Stag at Bay.

Pauline was standing next to me, her elbows propped up on the low copper bar. She looked as smart as ever – white blouse, possibly silk, a dark grey herring-bone suit with matching shoes and bag. Am I becoming an expert on fashion?

I confess I had telephoned her earlier to let her know I was coming, and that drinks were available but no lunch (I won't try that again) at what used to be our usual hour.

It was funny, but since our relationship had ended, we seemed to be talking more and more. I never had any trouble getting through to her at work, and when I called her home she seemed to have stopped 'slipping out to the shops'.

"So it's this week then?" She looked at me over her glass. "Laura's operation. Why is she having it if the chemo's such a success?"

"God knows. She knows the bloody risks. Wants to be sure. So does the surgeon. They both do . . ."

"It's a 10% chance of death."

"Christ. Poor bastard." She took a thoughtful pull at her drink. "What has she done to deserve this?"

What has anyone done to deserve this? However mean and low. What could anyone do to deserve this?

The pain. The blood. The loss of dignity. Hopes raised and dashed. The bleak, desperate despair. The tests and more tests. Endless tests. I could see it stretching out for years.

"How's she feeling?" Pauline was studying my face.

"Oh, as fucking feisty as ever. Worrying about her children and the pets. Ordering me about. Telling me how to look after the house. Not too many fags and drink. She never thinks of herself. Or if she does, she doesn't show it. Wants to be out in a week."

We stood together at the bar in silence. Two old pals. Browne-Smythe had joined us for a quick one, but soon ran off to chambers to read his next great case.

"Anyway . . ." Pauline lightened up. "Here's some good news. I've bought myself a house. New development. Bloody good area. At least not bloody bad. Three bedrooms. Big enough for all of us. I signed for it today."

I wonder. Where is she getting the money from? She must have found the deposit from somewhere. And then there's the furniture, curtains, carpets. Setting up home from scratch can't be cheap. Where's the money coming from? I look at her. Beautifully turned out as ever. The suit is extremely expensive and, I have decided, the blouse is certainly silk. Shoes I may not have seen before. I am losing track of all this. Where is she getting the money from?

"Where are you getting the money from?" I asked. "Tomkinson doesn't pay you much."

Pauline is a very private person. More than private. Secretive. She ferrets away in the background plotting and scheming, seeing little opportunities here and there and pouncing in whenever the chance arises. I'd heard she was doing some part-time waitressing at weekends. Some fashionable place or other in Beverley. Probably working for cash. But even then, with the most liberal tipping scheme in history, where has she scraped up the deposit for a house?

"Never you mind," she tapped the side of her nose and winked. "Never you mind. There's ways and means. There's always ways and means."

How can this be good news? Obviously she has found a provider. Some bloody rich boyfriend or other. And what is she doing to get it? I don't want to think about it. I could see her when she was mine, thrashing about in bed at Pat's.

I don't want to think about it. I can't stop thinking about it. The pain is right back where it's always been and just as fucking sharp. But I am going to be casual. Nonchalant even. Brush it all aside.

"You've got a fucking boyfriend," I screamed. "You've not waited fucking long! I bet you've had the bastard all along. Who is it? I don't want to know. Who is it? Don't tell me, I don't want to know."

She must have known how I would react. She had experience of my nonchalance before.

"Steady tiger, calm down. What I do is my business. My business. Not yours. But . . . as you're my best friend, well . . ." she thought about it, ". . . one of my best friends, I think I can tell you this. I've borrowed a bit from my Dad and Mr Tomkinson has been very generous with the rest."

Mr Tomkinson? Mr Tomkinson eh?

I looked her straight in the eye but she blanked me.

"Don't be silly. When you get to know him he's really rather nice. But it's nothing like that, so don't you go thinking it is."

I continued to stare at her face. She seemed to be able to re-write history. What had happened to that twat Tomkinson who had previously let her down?

"Anyway . . ." she snapped her handbag shut, "he insisted I let him help me. What did you want me to do?"

God knows. It wasn't her style to turn down money. She couldn't afford the luxury of saying no.

But I had to get back to Laura. This had gone on long enough. There was Laura getting ready for her operation, and there was I in a pub, as usual, with Pauline, as usual, working myself up as usual about what she was up to, what she was doing, where she was going, was she still trailing around with that sex-mad bimbo Doreen? Had she got somebody else? Was she sleeping with somebody else? Was it fucking Tomkinson? Or was he just coughing up in the hope?

I didn't want to think about it. I wouldn't think about it. I could think of nothing else. Everything as usual. Just for a fucking change.

But this time I was going first.

She sensed me getting ready to leave.

"Oh, and by the way . . ." she caught my arm as I turned away, "I'm taking all the children now I've got the room. They're all coming with me. I rang the Child Support Agency. They'll be in touch with Barry soon."

I turned away again but she pulled me back once more. "Best of luck my love."

I don't know why I did it. For some mad reason I went to kiss her; at the very least to brush her cheek. But she had her hands up in an instant, and quickly pushed me away.

"Not in here. What do you think you're doing?" She wiped her lapels. "Not in here. People know us. Anyway, you'll mark my fucking suit."

She is treating me like Barry. Perhaps she treats everyone like Barry. Being Barry. We are all Barry now.

That night I took Laura back to the hospital for her operation. Back to the place she dreads. We got out of the taxi and stood at the entrance beneath a flickering neon light. Children were milling round the electric doors, making them open and close. Youths in baseball caps stood outside. Occasionally they walked in and out.

We picked our way along the green arrow and back to the same old counter with a different, but equally harassed, receptionist behind.

I gave Laura's name and address and she brought her details up on the screen. "Oh yes. You're in C1." She passed over some forms for me to sign. Liability for costs arising from the use of operating theatre and hire of surgical equipment; for anaesthetic, medicines, bandages and gauze. I couldn't read it all. For 'hotel' accommodation. For use of wheelchairs, trolleys, and ambulances, and yes, for incidental expenses arising out of any Post Mortem, and consequent use of the morgue.

"C1 is almost ready. Please take a seat in the meantime. We shouldn't be keeping you long."

We sat as far away from the entrance as possible and I found a magazine for Laura to read. Something for women about fashion and next season's coming trends. At this time of day there weren't too many people about, but the atmosphere must have got to them – they sat and stared at their feet.

For something to do I went over to the drinks dispenser and managed to get Laura a cappuccino which was almost too hot to hold.

"No thanks," she held up her hand as I juggled the paper cup, "nothing to eat or drink."

She looked around at the posters, the photographs of smiling administrators, children's paintings – the depressing cheerfulness of it all – and settled down to wait.

Two hours later I left her in the ward of the flashing alarms under the care of the same team who had obviously remembered me from the time before. It doesn't do to complain.

Everything was as dilapidated and as depressing as we remembered it. Only the patients had changed.

Had they died? Or, by some lucky chance, recovered. Thrown off their bandages and drips and walked away free of this place forever? I doubt it. I could smell the breath of the tomb in the flat, heavy air.

Laura was frightened and held on to me to the last, her nails digging into my back. What strange yet repetitive forms passion can take. She clung to me in the same way as I remembered a different urge had impelled her many years before, her huge eyes begging me to stay.

But I had to go. There was no ulterior motive. She had to rest to stand a better chance.

"Best of luck, I love you," was all I could think of to say. My great contribution to the cause. Her operation was scheduled for 7.30 in the morning. Why her not me? Why anybody? Would she survive, pull through, get better? Is it written? Who decided what to write?

I looked one last time at her huge luminous eyes following me out of the ward, I heard her catch her breath and I knew she would start to cry and gaze around her at the beds and drips and paraphernalia surrounding her fellow patients and watch and wait alone.

Next morning I watched and waited alone. I paced up and down our kitchen and eventually gave in and opened a bottle. I fiddled about, went to the shops for a paper, did the pots. There was nothing else to do. What could I do? She was in the hands of others. What stage had they got to? Were her ribs cut and upturned to the ceiling whilst the surgeon delved inside. How was it going? Had they hit a snag? A sudden crisis perhaps, blood pressure falling, a flat line on the screen. Laura's body convulsing; and white coats gathered around. Or were things going swimmingly? Easy access, nothing much to find, a little mopping-up, and the closing sutures applied. How did I know? How could I know? I opened another bottle, I'd either lost or drank the first.

What did I think I was doing with Pauline yesterday? Ringing her up. Arranging to meet her in the Stag at Bay. I remembered how she fended me off. What was the point? And did it matter now?

I thought of Laura and wondered for the thousandth time how it was going and whether to give the hospital a call. And back to Pauline. Back to happier times. Those carefree days at Waterfront Mews, Antonio's, at Pat's Place when Laura was well and Pauline was keen.

Did it betray Laura to think of someone else? Somehow diminish her chances? Making plans before she was dead.

But she wasn't dead and she wouldn't die. I thought of the children. They didn't even know she was ill. Not that ill. She told them the tumour was benign. Just to explain the baldness. The baldness. I always came back to that. And the drips and the flashing buzzers and the nurses who couldn't care less.

The phone suddenly rang. The only call I'd had all morning. I knew before I answered it, it was Mr Mitchell ringing as he promised to give me the good news or the bad news, as soon as he'd finished, either way.

"How did it go?" I didn't even ask his name. "How is she? Is everything all right?"

"She's resting in Intensive Care. It'll be a while before she comes round. Not to worry. It went well. A little malignant tissue – not much – just as well I went in. The odd enlarged lymph node. Nothing much. But there is one complication. Afraid I nicked the spleen. Often happens. Had to take it out."

Take it out? What does that mean? How important is the spleen? I didn't even know what it was or what it was supposed to do. Was it like the appendix? A fellow traveller. More trouble than it was worth. Better out than in.

"I don't understand. Is it important?" I had to ask. "Does it mean she'll die?"

"No. No. Nothing really, easily do without it. Just have to take antibiotics for the rest of her life."

For the rest of her life? However long that might be.

"Don't worry," he reassured me. "Laura's doing fine."

A shortened oesophagus, half a stomach and now no fucking spleen. Lucky Laura.

"Thank you for all you've done," I told him and I meant it. I wonder how many times he'd heard that.

"Just remember when you go and see her. She's had major surgery. Major surgery. Above all she needs rest. Stay five minutes. Remember. Five minutes, no longer. Henry, I really must insist. You mustn't stay too long."

Chapter 33

The technology was amazing. Machines, wires, monitors everywhere. Beautifully cared for – shining and immaculate as if just polished; gleaming enamel, twinkling metal, sheets brilliant white.

All I had done was walk up a short flight of stairs and travelled from Stone Age to Space Age in a matter of yards.

From Ward C1 to Intensive Care.

I took a chair beside Laura's bed and settled down to wait.

A tube was taped to her mouth. There was another in her arm, and electrodes attached to her chest. I looked round at the screens recording what I imagined to be her every bodily function. Her heart beat, temperature, respiration; the chemical contents of her blood.

God knows what else. Perhaps they recorded her thoughts.

So far as I could tell (and what did I know), everything seemed normal. Lines were moving up and down on the screens, a needle was scratching a chart – I leaned over her bandaged face and caught the hint of a breath.

She seemed so tired and peaceful I began to stroke her cheek. She could come round anytime, they told me, and I wanted to be there when she did.

I held her hand and waited for however long it might take – and as I did I shuffled my chair closer and intensely studied her face. Her eyes were closed but her eyelids had grown translucent, and in that light, I thought she was looking at me. Perhaps I imagined it, but I felt she was waiting for me to say something, to comfort her, to talk to her, so I leant further over and did.

I whispered the operation was finished and I had spoken to Mr Mitchell and he was sure it was a success.

He had removed the cancer. All of it. Cleaned out, cleared up, stitched up and done. Nothing left. Not a trace. Nothing. It was over and all she had to do was rest.

I wondered if she could hear me as I stared into her eyes. What was going on inside her?

A nurse glided up and looked at the monitors.

"Don't worry, she's doing fine."

So I told her that as well, and how she'd be going home and walking round her garden and eventually lifting a spade. And how she'd soon be cooking, and walking, and shopping, and opening a bottle of wine. And how life would go on for us together, and how we'd look back on this and maybe laugh or maybe not, and go away on holiday and spend our time together and be grateful for the chance.

I must have bored her back to life.

As I watched she dragged herself up from that deep warm well towards consciousness until finally with a sigh that seemed to shake her body she opened those large eyes, and with an effort, focused and tried to smile.

"I know," she said. "I know."

How did she know? How could she? Did she know everything? I reached across and kissed her cheek and whispered to her once again all that had happened. What Mr Mitchell had said – or most of it – and what we must now do to get her better, to get her home, to get her out of this, to get her back to her bed.

And her eyes never left me. They smiled assent. She knew what she had done and what remained to be done and everything that lay ahead. Her eyes signalled encouragement. They signalled love.

"Not too much longer Mr Wallace," I didn't hear the nurse come up behind me. "What she needs is rest." Laura's eyes clouded over. She stared at me intently. I could feel her hand tighten around mine, and she flashed another sign. A sign that I should stay. She wanted to hear it. She wanted to hear it again.

I don't know what made me do it. What came over me. A moment of madness or selfishness. Perhaps I wanted to clear the air. Start again with a clean slate absolved by a confession. Somehow I wanted to get if off my chest. I began to tell her about Pauline. Hesitantly I heard myself begin.

"There's something I have to . . . ."

But the nurse was back. Perhaps she'd never left. "Sorry Mr Wallace. That's it. Doctor's orders. Tell her that you love her and give her one last kiss." She leant past me and talked directly to Laura. "He'll be back in the morning. Just you get some rest."

I thought about what I had nearly confessed as I walked home through the park. I could hear an owl distantly hooting somewhere in the willows on the other side of the lake. It made me turn cold. I stopped by the bandstand and looked at clouds drifting over the moon.

Why had I nearly told her? Why had I done it? What was I thinking of? But of course I wasn't thinking – not the vestige of a thought in my head. I was just reacting to the moment – moved perhaps by relief. Instinctively responding to the drama – being my usual self-indulgent self. But she knew my weakness.

She loved me – not in spite of – but because of my failings. She gave me love as a gift.

Chapter 34

It was a joy to get Laura home again. The animals went mad. It was all I could do to stop the dogs in their excitement jumping up at her and knocking her to the kitchen floor. She sat down in her usual chair. Tenderly, slowly, but firmly none-theless. She rested her feet on the central stretcher of the table and looked around.

"Who's been cleaning up my kitchen?" she demanded. "Why have you moved all the pans from the side? Where have you put everything?"

She looked up at the ceiling. "Who's cleaned my cobwebs off? I told you not to do anything." She turned to me furiously. "You have to go buggering about messing things up. You know I like a bit of dirt."

It was a strange thing about Laura but she couldn't stand for things to be too clean. She didn't like bleach, never cleaned the surfaces, hated hoovering the carpets and never, but never, dusted anything at all. She loved flowers. Was brilliant with flowers and a genius at arranging them, but for some reason, some unknown reason, would leave them dead in their vases dotted all over the house for months and months on end.

"There is something beautiful in a dead rose, don't you think?" she would say. Not that I could see it, I have to admit. But this eccentric quirk never changed and throughout our years I had never been able to persuade her to remove the cobwebs that grew from our bedroom ceiling, nor clear away dead flowers that slowly dried in a bedside vase.

"And where's my butter churn gone?" she wanted to know. "Who the fuck's had that? I can't leave you for a week without you fuck the whole job up."

I must say I was feeling a little miffed about her reaction. What did she want the bloody butter churn for? It's not as if she ever made butter.

"It's in the garage out of the way" I told her.

"Well go and get it back," she ordered. "You know it belongs on top of the fridge. And where's Sandy's dog basket? And his bones?"

This was not the reception I had expected.

"Who's had his bloody bones?"

I tried to be patient. I tried to reason with her. "Laura, my love, relax. Take it easy. Have a drink. The dog basket was years old. Falling apart. Bits of bloody wicker everywhere. Sandy didn't like it anymore. He's getting to quite like sleeping outside."

"Sleeping outside! . . . Sleeping outside! My Sandy. Have you gone fucking mad? Sandy never sleeps outside. He sleeps under my bed."

If only this were true. If only it was under the bed. How many times have I woken up with Sandy between us, his tongue licking Laura's face, his wagging tail in mine?

"And he never sleeps in his basket. You know that. He never sleeps in his basket. He uses his basket for keeping his bones in. So what have you done with his bones?" She was unremitting. "You'd better not say you've thrown them away. He's had them for ages."

"Laura," I pleaded, "Laura, I'll get him some new ones. Some nice new bones for a nice new basket."

But she was not to be mollified. I was delighted she was looking so well.

"I can't believe you have done this to Sandy," she cried. "What have you done to the rest of the house?"

So I decided to come clean. Better get it over with all at once.

"You remember the bathroom carpet?" I told her. "Well it was going rotten in the corner. Where Sandy buried a rat. I thought it would be nice when you came home to set your feet on a new one."

"A new one!" Laura was astounded. "Why a new one? Do you know my mother bought us that for our wedding? Why do you do these things? Sometimes I simply cannot understand you." A thought occurred to her. "You'd better not have touched the garden. I hope to God you've kept your hands off that."

I thought it might be wise to keep out of the way for a bit. Possibly for a few hours whilst Laura completed her inspection and grew accustomed to the improvements I had made; and so pretending the arrival of a new important brief that required my urgent attention I drove over to chambers to find Giles in a mood of black despair.

"You'll never believe what those bastards have charged us," he said bitterly. "After all the work we've done for them." He threw the bill down on the counter of the Stag at Bay. "£165,000," he said, "how the fuck does it come to that?"

"Sounds like we should be taking lessons," I told him. "They think we're made of money."

"Not any more. Not any more old boy," he complained. "That's just our solicitor's bill. Add another £220,000 on for Jackson's. We're going to have to pay that as well. Well, all I can say is that chambers is going to have to brace itself. We are just going to have to look cheerful and pay up. It's only money after all."

"Do you have any idea . . ." I politely enquired, "what this is going to do to our contributions? After all, as I remember it, and I hesitate to remind you, the whole purpose of this exercise was to reduce how much we have to pay."

"Don't ask me," he told me, "don't even think about it. Our man in the silver suit is in charge. Ask bloody Horace. He thinks we are going bankrupt. And of course . . . Absolutely bloody of course . . . we are still paying Jackson his 10%, and worse . . . Oh yes . . . much worse . . . now he has got it in writing!"

I went out with Jackson later. We thought it expedient to go to a different place. We didn't want to bump into Giles drowning his sorrows. But I was surprised that Jackson was not in a celebratory mood. He seemed philosophical. Quiet and thoughtful. Sober. Maybe sad.

I knew he'd been visiting Laura in hospital. They had always been very close. He'd told me how shocked he was when he first saw her. The tubes, the drips, the smell. He'd leant forward to kiss her hollow cheek to tell her how well she looked.

"God, I couldn't believe it. So thin, so wasted, so spent." He dabbed at his eyes with his spotted handkerchief.

When one of us is stricken, worries of mortality intrude upon the rest.

"She asked me how old I was. Wouldn't believe it when I told her." He sighed and looked about at our novel surroundings. "Thought I was older than that."

He looked down at his liver-spotted hands, "I'm going bald, getting fatter, my legs are wasting away. Anyway, she pulled herself up on my shoulder. I can see her now. Harrowed face. Those huge and blazing eyes. What do you think she said?"

I said nothing. Perhaps I was fearing the worst.

"She asked me a question. How many people on their deathbed say, 'I wish I'd worked harder'. As they lay dying. How many people say that John?"

I looked across at him. "Good question. What did you say?"

He sat thinking, looking into his glass. "What can you say? I went home and talked it over with the wife. Up half the night. She's always been on at me to pack it in early. Lots of things she'd like to do. Me too. This latest thing with chambers. It's been the last bloody straw. Nobody does the job right. Nobody plays the bloody game. I've made my mind up. Got better things to do."

It had never occurred to me that Jackson must have been worried for his part. That litigation takes its toll on both sides.

"I've had enough of it. Laura's brought it home to me. The wife agrees. I'm leaving bloody chambers." He fumbled in his jacket pocket and handed me an envelope addressed to Giles. "Give this to fucking Baring. Put them out of their misery. Forget the contract. I'm leaving tonight."

I watched him walk slowly away, slightly stooped against the weather, pausing at the kerb before slipping through the traffic and across the road to where his car was parked for the last time in chambers' car park. He didn't bother to put up his umbrella and I followed the silhouette of his raincoat as he picked his way around the puddles and caught one last glimpse of his tired face in the interior light, before he started the engine and drove away.

The end of an era. One of the last of the 10% men. Famous in his lifetime as the best clerk on circuit. The man who had started chambers, walking away with nothing. If we had been more noble spirited and generous, we could have given him £250,000 to retire, and saved ourselves money on the deal. We could have avoided all the acrimony and bitterness. John would have still remained in touch, ready to help out in emergencies. Ready to go 'looking for work'.

We could have held an annual dinner to celebrate his forty odd years, and he would have attended with his wife, made a speech, and received a present, and gone home happy.

And I could have rung him from time to time to ask for his advice, or for his intervention with a difficult problem or just to have a chat. Perhaps I still could. Just to give him the gossip and keep him in touch.

But none of this could ever happen now. Giles and our man in the silver suit had seen to that. Chambers would never forgive him. Never forget the humiliation of losing to their own clerk, and certainly for years to come never be able to forget the huge bill for costs that would have to be paid by an annual increase in our contributions that would be a constant irritant, and a constant reminder of defeat.

I wondered what he would do in his retirement. Play a little golf perhaps. Take up shooting or bridge. Live in a bungalow in the country and become a character in the local pub.

It was chambers that kept him alive. The pressures, the stress; they kept the adrenalin going and the blood vessels open. It got him out of the house. It kept him from doing the dishes and plugging in the hoover. It got him out and away from under his wife's feet and gave him something interesting, or funny, to tell her about when he got home at night. Now, thrown together twenty-four hours a day, they would get on each others nerves, become irritable, snap back at an ill-considered remark — long hours of reproachful silence in separate parts of the house.

Maybe Laura was right. Maybe Laura was wrong. I know she meant well. Maybe John and his wife did enjoy ambitions of all they might do. Plans for the future. Evenings out together in the company of congenial friends. Travels to exotic places. Taking up fresh hobbies. But what is the reality? Locked together in a pitiless rural retreat, and I daresay John dead within three years of disillusion, boredom, and the dawning reality that retirement had nothing more to offer other than the excitement of walking into the village and taking all day to pay the gas bill and do his bit of shopping in the only village shop.

Laura, with his best interests at heart, had condemned him to death in the company of those who loved him, but in the end, perhaps like us, were glad to see him go.

Chapter 35

Richard Grantham was found dead in his cell. The Post Mortem recorded death by misadventure. An overdose of heroin. Apparently he injected himself overnight. On more than one occasion. In the morning his two cell mates had found him rigid and cold beneath his prison blanket and had banged on the cell door and shouted through the grill at the guards to put down their bacon sandwiches, if only for a moment, and help.

He had been dead for hours.

It could not be established either way whether he overdosed deliberately or accidentally. In other words, whether his death was suicide or not. It was impossible to say.

The Coroner, however, had some unpleasant things to say about the prison service.

"In these days, in order to stop dangerous drugs being smuggled into prisons where, might I say, there is an undoubted (and possibly growing) problem of drugs being freely available to every inmate with the means to pay for them, the prison authorities have installed every possible security device. There are security cameras at every entrance and exit. There are security cameras, obviously, in the visiting areas. Video footage is taken and scrutinised twenty four hours a day. One-way mirrors are installed. Suspicious persons are kept under constant surveillance. There are ways of trapping material flushed down toilets. Trained sniffer dogs circle every visitor. It is therefore beyond me, beyond all reason, how dangerous drugs continue to find their way into our prisons and into the hands of prisoners. How is it being done? Who is responsible? Am I driven to assume that prison staff are actively complicitous or are they turning a blind eye? Possibly for reward. Or are they simply negligent? What is going wrong? I suggest, I strongly suggest a public inquiry."

The fact is, drugs get into prisons by many different routes.

Male visitors secrete them in polythene bags hidden in the anus, to be removed at the earliest opportunity in the privacy of the lavatory. There are no cameras in there. Women visitors carry them in their rectum or vagina. The vagina being the route of choice during menstruation to better confuse the dogs. Either sex can swallow a bag of heroin and "sick it up" in the toilet. Perhaps the simplest route is best. Push it under the tongue and slide it into the mouth with a kiss.

However it gets in − it's certainly not in short supply. There's more inside than out. Never a problem to get 'sorted' by a mate. Many prisoners complain they first became addicted when in jail.

It breeds a hierarchy and a chain of command. It leads to violence and intimidation. Together with phone cards and tobacco, it has become a currency. It provides a recreation. It is instructive in business skills. It is a constant source of conversation. Occasionally it leads to death.

Richard Grantham had left a note. More accurately, he had left a letter half-written to his wife.

"Dear Michelle, I love you," he began. "I love you to bits, I can't live without you. I don't want to live without you. What is this I hear about Freddy Platten? If you are fucking carrying on I will kill you. I have heard he is round our house all the time. What is going on? I can't stand it. Some mates have told me he sleeps the night. In our bed. That fucking Freddy Platten. He was supposed to be my solicitor. Now I see why I got five and a half years. It's fucking obvious. Those bastards wanted me out of the way. You never come to see me anymore. I am going mad in here. What is happening with my appeal? Nobody tells me anything. I keep writing to Mr Tomkinson but he never writes back. Nobody lets me know what is going on. All I hear about is you and that fucking Platten . . ."

And there he stopped. To deliberately take an overdose? To deliberately kill himself?

Or had his pen slipped from a dying hand poisoned acci-dentally some time before? More likely, he couldn't care less.

I thought about it. After all, I knew him well.

Locked daily in his cell going mad with jealousy and unable to make his feelings felt. To speak with his wife. Reason with her. Try and talk her round. Anything just to see her. To hear her tell him to his face. To lie to him, or tell the truth. To see her he would know. But the not knowing was driving him mad. The constant rumours; the whispering in his darkened cell at night. And she never came to see him. Never brought the kids, and hardly ever wrote.

He'd even tried writing directly to Freddy Platten. The accredited representative of Cranmer Carter & Co. His solicitor. But Freddy had just rolled the letters into balls and laughed, flicking them at the wastepaper basket in the corner, to be shredded by the cleaner later on.

"He won't be out for years," he told Pauline when she warned him of the dangers.

"Fuck him. The white-coated Spiderman eh? He'll be in Armley for years. Let him try and climb out of there!"

The Coroner had also had some unpleasant things to say about Cranmer Carter & Co. in general, and about Freddy Platten and Mr Tomkinson in particular. "I do not know the truth or not of the rumours that so patently drove this unfortunate prisoner to the end of his tether. I am particularly concerned that there may be a breach of the fiduciary duty a firm of solicitors owes to their client. Can it be said they have acted in his interests? I think not. Apparently the deceased had written many letters to them. Prison officers have testified to this effect. I accept their evidence. Yet there is nothing on his file at Cranmer Carter & Co. Nothing. What has happened to this correspondence? Has it been lost? Has it been destroyed? Have this firm been negligent?

It seems to me that once a man is incarcerated this firm wash their hands of him. Is it because there is no more money in it for them? I hope not. Their duty clearly extends to advising him upon appeal. It has always been my practice to expect a little welfare and support after sentence and a little guidance (I do not say a lot) during the course of sentence so as to best help him serve that sentence and prepare for eventual release. This firm seem to have done nothing.

Worse, if these accusations are true then their accredited representative, one Freddy Platten has acted execrably. And unprofessionally. He has taken advantage of his client's wife. I hope this isn't true. It is lamentable conduct if true. Once again, prison officers (whom I believe) have told me of the prevailing rumour within prison and the affect it had upon the deceased.

What have Cranmer Carter & Co. and their senior partner done to investigate these allegations? Nothing. They have not lifted a finger.

I consider it to have been beholden upon them to have made every enquiry. They have made none. I note from the deceased's last letter he expressed concern at a sentence he thought unduly severe. I can make no comment on that. It is beyond my remit. But certainly it is apparent that the unfortunate Mr Grantham was suspicious. He harboured a sense of grievance. He thought he had been used. I am afraid that his counsel Mr Wallace could not give evidence before me. I understand he has very good personal reasons for that. Nevertheless, he was kind enough to write. He does consider the sentence in his words to be 'manifestly excessive' and has enclosed copies of his Advice on Appeal and Grounds of Appeal.

Apparently they were sent to a Mrs Dawson who passed them on to Freddy Platten. They appear to have gone no further. Certainly the Court of Appeal have not received them. So what has happened to this appeal? Why have his papers gone missing? Mr Tomkinson in evidence was pitiful. He could not give any answer. He knew, and I have to say this, precious little about the case. Mr Platten was even worse. Whilst acknowledging he had a distant memory of receiving these papers from Mrs Dawson, he cannot remember what, if anything, he did with them. He has speculated that he put them in the file. He hints that he left them on Mr Tomkinson's desk, along with other papers of an urgent nature. As I have said, Mr Tomkinson does not appear to have found the time to read them. That is if they were ever there at all.

This is negligence. There is no other word for it.

It is a negligence that is rendered more suspicious by the ugly rumours that circulate around this case, and the suspicion that Mr Platten was conducting some sort of affair with the deceased's wife. She has refused to answer any questions about this alleged relationship. I find this suspicious in itself. If innocent, she would have been the first to say so. She has remained mute. Why? Has she been got at? I do not know. I have no way of knowing. But what I do know, and I can say, is the behaviour of this firm has been reprehensible. It falls far below the standards expected of a competent and diligent firm.

I shall be referring my papers not only to the Law Society but to the police."

I received a frantic call from Pauline. "Can you come across? This is an emergency. We know the problems. How is Laura by the way? It's the Grantham case. You know. The fucking Spiderman. It was your case. Yes. Not for long. Mr Tomkinson would be enormously grateful."

He didn't seem that grateful when I was shown into his office. Didn't even offer me a drink. Pauline and Freddy standing up. The great man behind his desk. I took a seat behind Pauline. This was going to be good.

Tomkinson seemed unhappy with the front page of the local newspaper.

"SPIDERMAN DRIVEN TO SUICIDE BY LOCAL SOLICITORS?" screamed the headline. He threw the paper at the wall. A nice start.

And underneath a photograph of Richard Grantham, a full report of the Coroner's remarks. The article ending as bleakly as it had begun.

"We approached Cranmer Carter & Co. many times. No one was available for comment."

But Tomkinson had plenty to say now.

"Thank you team. An excellent piece of work. I'm either going to get struck off or prosecuted. Not only has our dear departed friend got five and half years – and I blame you Wallace for that – but whilst he is languishing in jail we have lost his appeal papers, ignored his correspondence, and started shagging his wife. Not only are we all over the evening papers, but I can look forward to seeing my photograph in the nationals tomorrow. First you Freddy. Have you been shagging his wife? Yes or no. What is it? – don't even think of fucking me about."

Freddy looked at the floor. Pauline said nothing. Tomkinson sat waiting. I knew the answer. I remember the way he looked at her in court.

"All right" he said, "I'll tell you straight. You've got to know. Yes I have. For the last six months. But nothing serious."

"Very well," Tomkinson stayed calm. "Very well. So long as we know. I shall issue a press statement. I shall say . . . this firm does not interfere in the private life of its employees. It is our understanding that our Mr Platten and the unfortunate Mrs Grantham are in a relationship. A loving relationship." He looked up at Freddy. "I assume it is a loving relationship?" Seeing Freddy hesitate he pressed on. "Don't tell me. Don't tell me. It is to be hoped that the untimely death of Mr Grantham and the unfortunate and hysterical publicity in the press will not impair that relationship. Indeed, it is our understanding that once a suitable time for mourning and the healing of wounds has passed, that this troubled pair propose to sanctify their liaison in marriage . . ."

"Fucking hell," cried Freddy, "he's not even buried yet! I can't marry her. She's got kids, hundreds of them for all I know. She's a fucking druggie. She's a fucking slag. She's on the fucking game for Christ's sake!" He looked round at me for support.

"Our Mr Platten has the highest regard and deepest affection for this lady . . ." Tomkinson didn't miss a beat, "and wishes to do the right thing by her. Through our good offices he makes this simple request. The unhappy couple wish to be left alone, to re-build their lives together, to salvage what little happiness is left to them in the peace and privacy of a respectable caring family life." Mr Tomkinson looked up.

"And Freddy. Before you say anything, anything else, you don't have to do it. You just have to say you will."

And of course Freddy assented. He could see it made sense. I could see he was grateful. Sincerely grateful for the first time in his life. Tomkinson could so easily have sacked him. Publicly washed his hands of him. Told the press that the miscreant Platten had failed miserably to meet the high standards imposed by a firm of the calibre and reputation of Cranmers. He could have been hung out to dry. Out of a job and his career in ruins. Not a partner in the firm would have lifted a finger to save him. "Thank you Sir," he mumbled, "I shan't forget it."

"As for the fucking appeal and the mysteriously disappearing correspondence," Tomkinson pressed on. "First of all, I don't blame you Pauline. As ever, your conduct has been exemplary. I shall simply say that this firm has conducted a thorough investigation. We have consulted the barrister concerned." I was beginning to wonder why I was there. "No stone has been left unturned. It is possible, and we candidly admit it, that there may have been a small break down in communications – but we have tightened up procedures and completed a full review of the excellent service we have hitherto given to the public and are confident that this temporary and unfortunate lapse has been corrected, cannot recur, and our large and growing client base can continue to place their full confidence in our renowned expertise and skill."

He looked up and smiled. "What do you think boys and girls? All is well. Job sorted! No comments to the press apart from me. Remember that. And I am talking to you Freddy. No talking to the press. Loads of publicity. Cranmers vindicated. And Freddy. Congratulations. You're getting married to a wonderful girl!"

"Yeah," said Pauline, "great. Everybody's happy. Cranmers exonerated, Freddy's off the hook, Mrs Grantham's getting shagged, looking forward to a happy marriage. Pity Grantham can't be there."

Tomkinson looked directly at me. He could barely repress a sneer.

"Thanks for nipping over. I assume you did draft an appeal?"

"Ask Pauline. Ask Freddy. Why not look on your desk?"

I'd had enough of all of them. I'd got better things to do.

"It might be if you had actually found it Grantham might

be alive and you wouldn't be in this fucking mess. Chambers will send you another copy in the morning. Try and keep it in the file."

I walked stiffly to the door.

"Are you coming Pauline?" I enquired.

"Sorry," she was already getting up, "got a prior engagement."

"Yes," said Tomkinson, "she's having a drink with me."

Chapter 36

Examination of some of the material removed from Laura's body produced the expected laboratory report. Oesophageal carcinoma. Particularly malignant; intrusive to use their delicate phrase.

Dr Hussein suggested (I suspect at Laura's persistent instigation) that she have one last course of chemotherapy. A final 'mopping-up' to eliminate any clusters of cancerous cells that may have evaded the surgeon's knife.

Laura was more than willing to submit. She was anxious to get started again, knowing – as she must have known – of the sickness and vomiting that awaited her and the daily collection from her pillow of the new soft hair that was just beginning to grow.

So the Hickman line went back in her neck and we began again the daily routine of carrying the pressurised phial, dripping in her prescription, cleaning her tubes and the inevitable nausea, cramps and pain.

Laura accepted this – welcomed it in fact – like many suffers of this terrible disease in an attempt to survive and live her life, enjoy her family, stroke her pets, drink her wine and wake up one morning without that dragging ache in the pit of her stomach. Was it too much to ask? To be able to look out of her window into the park and feel well and happy again.

She was prepared to pay any price, undergo any pain, endure the embarrassments of an illness that made her dependant upon me to nurse her, clean the sheets, and somehow or other get her on and off the toilet and in and out of the bath.

She wanted to live, had the will to live, and the courage to try. But the pain came back. Slowly at first; tiny pangs sufficiently small to overlook; eventually growing into the insistent dull ache that cannot be ignored. She had finished her last course of chemotherapy bed-ridden and exhausted but had rallied herself over the next few months. Eating as much as she could and exercising as much as she dare, she had got herself downstairs and triumphantly outside and once again into her garden where she was busy with her secateurs hacking away at the jungle that my tiredness and ignorance had left.

I saw her stop and catch her breath. She was holding her stomach again – ironically almost in the same spot near the garden seat where I remembered watching her a year before.

She had to rationalise. She had to stay sane. She began to speculate that it was her ribs that were causing the problem. Several had been severed during the operation and her bones had always been difficult to mend. Broken ribs are notoriously painful aren't they? And she would brighten up, "Anyway I feel loads better today," and exultantly, defiantly, punch the air.

I told Pauline that I was worried that Laura's recovery was unnaturally slow. Actually, I told her what I really thought – that something was wrong, seriously wrong and that Laura's pain was coming back and that she was slowly turning yellow and walking (if walking is the right word) with an almost permanent stoop to her back.

She gave me good advice. "Henry, take her away. Forget the work. Forget the money. What does money matter? Take Laura away somewhere. Somewhere where she's never been but always wanted to go. Not too far. Somewhere where there are street cafés and flowers. Somewhere warm."

Oddly enough Pauline's attitude irritated me. She was too smart, too confident. All right, I admit it, I resented her independence – but, I had the sense to take her advice.

Laura and I travelled to Verona for ten days or so in late September when the heat had subsided and the crowds diminished. It is a beautiful town, and small enough for us to walk from our hotel and be within the central piazza almost at once.

We visited the cathedral and the castle and the many lovely churches. We walked along the river arm in arm. I took her shopping along a surprisingly modern and fashionable street and she bought the girls some clothes, but nothing for herself.

We took the tiny tourist train and admired the cathedral and ancient tombs. We visited Juliet's balcony and Laura for once enjoyed the crush. Her eyes darted from under her white hat hungry to see the sights, to drink in the beauty of this world. The light caught by the floating water of the fountains, the market stalls; the buildings and the statues; the noise of the passing crowd.

One day we tried to climb the steps of the huge coliseum that bestrides the Central Square, but Laura could only manage a few steps in the unseasonable heat of that day, and so I went on alone to the top and looked back down at her tiny figure sitting alone far below and returned her cheerful wave.

She was trying hard to eat. Probably for the first time in her life she wanted to put weight on. I would tempt her with any delicacy I could find. Little pastries and tarts. Sweets. Chocolates. Anything unusual or interesting or what I thought might be nutritious, advertised on the menus outside any restaurant we passed. But she was drinking. She had become very partial to Bellinis, a sort of cocktail concocted from peach liqueur and champagne, a taste she enjoyed and whose name she liked. We would start at lunchtime and spend a few hours sitting in the square watching the crowd stroll by, and when, a few Bellinis later and after picking at a salad, Laura grew tired I would slowly walk her back to our hotel and sit on the balcony smoking whilst she lay fitfully asleep on the bed and the flies droned round the chandelier above her head.

By evening she would regain her strength, and arm in arm we would walk slowly back into the cooling square, amongst the tiny lamps and candles adorning the kerbside tables arranged in rows before the spreading shadows of the coliseum, and Laura would order her first Bellini and sip and savour it, her large green eyes reflecting the candlelight and hungrily watching everything that passed.

And slowly, as we meandered through the night and several Bellinis later, something featured on a menu displayed outside a lantern-lit café would catch her fancy (or was it just to please me?) and I would hold her chair and ease her down, and at some small table outside on the pavement, she would place her order and fiddle with her meal, and then suddenly and silently stand and make her way through the tables to the lavatory inside or in the yard at the back and, as I realise now, be sick.

But we had a lovely time. Slow and peaceful. Tender and close, as we dropped into our languid daily routine chatting together as old couples do about the family, about the gossip, about her little businesses and of course about her plans for the future and how she would travel and visit all those places she had always wanted to see.

"Know your planet," she would advise me. And then wistfully, squinting into the reflected light from the marble walls of an ancient church. "Know your planet . . . whilst there's time."

I brushed a wasp away from her unfinished plate. I tried to sound sincere. "There's lots of time my love," I told her, "lots of time. We can go anywhere you want."

But I had a sense of foreboding. I was worried by the careful way she held herself, her painful loss of appetite, her diminishing strength and the cloudy faraway look that occupied her eyes.

She turned almost abstractedly to look at my earnest face. "Anyway," she said, "whatever happens – promise me you'll go."

On our return I telephoned Dr Mitchell (I couldn't bring myself to call him anything else) to arrange another appointment. "She doesn't seem to be getting any better," I explained. "It's been months since the operation," and gently oiling the wheels, "which was of course a great success, but I had hoped she might be a little better by now."

And eventually at my insistence he agreed to arrange another scan. "Purely precautionary," he stressed, "no need to worry the patient."

But Laura was worried. Furious would be a better word. She didn't want to go. Refused to go. "Why do you always have to interfere?" she cried. "Why are we tempting fate? I am doing fine. I feel fine. I don't want them looking inside me. And they're not fucking going to."

I remember the day well. Every detail. It was Laura's birthday, just fifty eight, and we were sitting side by side in the clean and fresh private hospital waiting to see Mr Mitchell who had asked us to come together to discuss the results of Laura's scan.

The scan she feared to have. The scan she had persistently and angrily refused to take until eventually her resistance worn away, she had given in to my wishes, to put my mind at rest. But it wasn't just for me. She had to know. Perhaps she knew already. A confirmation of what she feared.

We sat silently waiting, Laura gathering herself, steeling herself to face whatever came.

Mr Mitchell didn't waste time after we were shown into his tiny private consulting room and Laura safely lowered into a huge reclining chair – he told us straight. Perhaps experience had taught him it was the kinder way.

"I'm sorry Laura, terribly sorry, but the cancer has come back. It's in the stomach and very probably the liver. Inoperable. There's nothing left I can do. I'm terribly, terribly sorry. Enjoy what's left of your life."

Even sensing what was coming – no, it was stronger than that – knowing what was coming, I was stunned and sat there looking straight ahead without a word and, truth to say, without a single thought within my head, my mind a spinning blank.

Laura smiled. Not a tear. Not a sob. Not even a pause for breath.

"Oh well!" she said, "It's another happy birthday then. Thank you for all you've done. Thank you for trying." She held out her hand and they both shook hands. Laura shaking the hand that had no doubt held the scalpel that in the end had failed her. "Best of luck," she whispered, "and thank you once again. I know you did everything that could be done. I know you did your best."

And as we trailed miserably away across the car park in the general direction of where I had left the car, she suddenly stopped and turning to me with that old intensity cried out, "We're not fucking finished yet, not by a long shot! Get hold of Dr Hussein. Do it today. I want more chemotherapy. The stronger the fucking better! And while you're at it, get hold of that faith healer everybody's talking about and that fucking horse doctor or whatever he is, you know, the one in Sleaford. Do it Henry . . ." She must have sensed my impending protest.

". . . Just do it. Do it for me, I will not give in. I will not let this beat me. I will have my fucking life. So do it. Do it just for me."

She was stabbing the air defiantly with her tiny hand and, as she cried out, she clutched her stomach in what had become that so familiar way and leaning against the nearest car had gasped.

"Why me Henry? Why me? What the fuck have I ever done to deserve this? What have my children, my lovely children . . ." she began to cry, "What have they ever done to deserve this? For God's sake, get me home. Take me home my love. Never leave me. Call the children. Get them home. Get everybody home. What have we, any of us, done to deserve a fucking thing like this?"

Chapter 37

Jas telephoned me again from prison. It was a bad time to call. Laura was feeling particularly ill and I was nursing her single-handedly and doing what I could to help her in my limited, amateurish, even clumsy, way, and I didn't need distractions that took me away from her and left me holding the line listening to someone else's problems far away.

He was exuberant. He didn't sense my mood of mounting desperation. His studies were going well and I could tell he had a firm grasp of contract, tort, equity – everything he was reading in fact – especially crime. He wanted to tell me every detail. How he had received such and such a mark for this subject and a distinction in that. How he was showing such promise that the prison authorities or the Home Office or Howard League for Penal Reform or some other similar worthy body was funding the regular attendance of a peripatetic tutor who came to see him once a week to review his progress and coach him in subjects where he needed help. And how gradually their time together had been extended, and what had started as the occasional hour in the afternoons after his tutor had travelled half way across England, now began in the mornings (after his tutor had stayed overnight in a nearby hotel) and lasted the rest of the day.

"I'm looking at distinctions," he told me, "distinctions all the way. My tutor expects me in the top ten in Bar Finals at the end of the month. Special arrangements have been made to allow me to sit the papers in a prepared room over-looking the exercise yard, where I daresay the invigilator can find some occasional distraction watching the other prisoners shuffling about below. Between you and me Henry, top ten isn't good enough. I am going to come first. Top of the whole fucking list. 1st Class Honours. Who can refuse me then? Think of the publicity. It'll be in all the papers. 'FRAUDSTER IS TOP BARRISTER!' the headlines will scream." He laughs excitedly. "Alternatively, 'BARRISTER IS TOP FRAUDSTER!'"

Either way I think. What's the difference? "All those who have supported me . . ." he goes on, I cannot stop him, "will come out of this smelling of roses. A pat on the back for the prison authorities. Me on the front page posing with the governor. Possibly a picture of the Home Secretary shaking my hand . . ." Surely he is getting carried away, but one never knows the limits to which a Home Secretary can stoop, "and I'm going to include you Henry. For all the help you've given me."

This is more like it. Perhaps I may be permitted to shake his hand too. Possibly on the same photograph as the Home Secretary, with the Lord Chancellor giving me a playful punch on the arm.

". . . and for all the help you are going to give me." This is more ominous. I feel a twinge of anxiety. Beneath his cheerful animated youthfulness there is always the hook waiting to be slipped into my unsuspecting back.

"What I want you to do Henry, as a friend, as a sponsor really, my guiding light and inspiration even . . ." I am waiting for it. I know it is coming. I know I am going to have to drag myself away from Laura and waste precious time running around trying to do him some favour or other for which, to be fair to him, I know he will be grateful and remember. And why not? Laura spends more and more time asleep these days lying sideways on our bed or propped up in an easy chair in the garden, her white hat pulled low over her eyes. It might pass some time. It will be something to make her laugh when she wakes up.

"I want you to persuade an Inn of Court to accept me as a student member. Nothing to it really. Tell them how good it will look. Enlightened and forgiving, they recognise that Jasbir Singh has repaid his debt to society. They have swept away the old class barriers, they embrace the notion that a man confined alone in his cell can, day after day, work towards a major academic qualification and that his efforts – eventually rewarded in a 1st – are recognised, saluted even, by one of the great liberal institutions of our time."

I am beginning to wonder who he is talking about. Whether any of it makes any sense.

I think I can hear Laura stirring above my head.

"You belong to the Middle Temple, don't you Henry? . . ." He forgets nothing. "Get me in there!"

I hate to disillusion him. I am not a man with influence. I do not move in high circles, I am not a member of a London club, or the confidant of Cabinet Ministers, nor do I receive dinner invitations from society ladies. A vision of Pauline momentarily floats before me. She makes a face.

"Tell him to fuck off," she mouths.

"Jas," I say hesitantly, "I'm not sure about this. Do you think I'm the right person?"

"You're all I've got." He is emphatic, but it can't be true. I know this man. His energy is boundless. He will have written to his MP and his relatives' MPs in constituencies up and down England. He will be in contact with the Imam of his local mosque, having recently rediscovered his Muslim roots or Sikh destiny or whatever religion he currently (and transitorily) embraces. I daresay he will have approached the Lord Chief Justice and the Master of the Rolls. He may have telephoned Prince Charles.

"Jas," I say warily, "what exactly do you want me to do? Tell me. I promise you I will do my best."

"Get me into the Middle Temple. It's in London," he tells me. I know where it is, but let it go. "That's all there is to it. I take the vocational course and then there is nothing – nothing at all that can prevent me practising at the Bar. And threaten them with this. No. Hint at it. Hint that I have powerful men behind me not unfamiliar with the European Convention of Human rights. Tell them that. And if they refuse – trickle in how unfortunate it might turn out if I were forced to go to the European Court."

He seems to have forgotten the Exhaustion of Local Remedies Rule that he is studying so hard, and must first appeal to the Visitors. Why should I tell him? It takes too long. I've neither the patience nor the time.

"All right Jas. Leave it to me," I assured him. "Isn't this

phone call going on a long time?" I enquire. "It must be costing you a fortune." I was trying to get him off the line.

"Don't worry," he laughed. "Normally it would but I've found a way of doing it for nowt."

And he is gone, and as I drag my weary feet back up to our bedroom I know that this means problems, and that big trouble lies around the bend crouching in some formless menacing shape that I am too stupid or tired to decipher. I sense that Jas is going down again and that in some way, not yet immediately clear, that unless I have the energy to extricate myself from his persuasive coils, I will be joining him and we will be going down together.

Laura has insisted the chemotherapy re-start. No question. No discussion. She wants it now. Full strength.

How she can even contemplate it in her condition is beyond me, knowing as she does the terrible effect it is bound to have upon her already crippled body.

I watch her turning fitfully upon our brass Victorian bed and I pull her cotton nightie down to cover her sticks of legs where her constant turning has caused it to ride up and crease around her tiny thighs. She is taking morphine capsules now and is drifting in and out of her drug-induced, almost hallucinatory, sleep.

That it should come to this.

She can barely eat and her constant efforts have loosened her teeth so badly that the slightest touch causes her gums to trickle blood, which she quickly swallows in the hope I have not seen. It is there on the pillow in the morning though – together with a little vomit and foul black sputum that seems to come from the back of her throat and makes it so hard for her to breathe.

Behind her head the walls are covered with family photographs taken in happier times.

Laura holding our first-born with her long dark hair hanging down her back on a visit to Lincoln Cathedral.

Laura on holiday looking at me directly behind the camera with mounting irritation as, fiddling with the controls, I advance and retreat trying to capture the perfect shot as she grips the impatient tiny child on either side of her and soothes the youngest crying in her arms. Laura and three little children stood in front of the Sphinx; Laura at Karnak in Brittany leaning against an ancient stone her hands in the old familiar place – before her stomach cradling an unborn child.

Laura in a photograph she hated, drunk in some Spanish bar with her blouse carelessly open to reveal rather more than she deemed proper that it should. It always made me laugh.

Laura showing even more, in our large bath, with our five children now lying down beneath the suds, fragments of foam in their hair, and on their goggles, the remnants of some splashing fight that Laura always lost and that I had crept in to capture before she locked the door.

And now this. Laura under morphine on her bed. I will not take a photograph of this, I don't need to, it will stay with me forever.

I had told Pauline over the telephone in one of our intermittent calls how things were going, and how Laura was now reduced to eating baby food and soup.

"She is fond of custard though," I tell her. "I have learned to make it properly and she can often keep it down."

Pauline's kitchen I know carries the hallmark of one who cannot cook. It is spotless. "Good idea," she tells me. "It's always best to use the powder."

"No. No." I correct her. "One vanilla pod, two egg yolks, a little cream. First take your bain-marie . . ."

"No bloody wonder she's always sick."

I have also spoken at great length to Dr Hussein. He knows the treatment Laura is demanding might kill her and cannot do her good. Yet she remains insistent. She will not be diverted. The delay is causing her distress. "Bring her in tonight. To my clinic directly. There is no question of a Hickman Line. She must understand that. I will inject into the back of her hand. Don't tell her, but I am telling you. The only good it can do is ease her mind."

And so eventually we make our way to the same car park that only a few short days ago we had stumbled across numbed by Mr Mitchell's news.

But Laura cannot get out of the car.

For some reason she cannot move her left leg. She cannot swing it sideways from where it sticks to the rubber mat covering the footwell and the effort and frustration makes her cry. We learn later that this was her first stroke. The first of many. But she will not give in and I am compelled by the force of her will to lift her out and help her stand so that we walk with her hands on my shoulders, edging backwards, very slowly towards the clinic door to be met by anxious nurses, who have noticed our macabre progress and have brought a wheelchair out to help.

Laura waves it away.

"I am fucking walking. Fucking walking. Keep going Henry. Don't stop," she orders, "don't put me in that fucking chair."

Through the door and backwards, inch by inch, down the corridor I go. The nurses run before us opening doors and moving chairs and trolleys out of the way, until finally I am able to lower her against a bed and turn to face the kind and horrified face of the white-coated Dr Hussein hovering in his room.

"In God's name, why have you brought her out like this?" he whispers. "Don't you understand how ill she is?"

How can I explain? She walked to the car. Slowly of course. I helped her get in. I made her comfortable. She was walking when we left. Something happened on the way.

"What do you want me to do?" I whisper back. "She was all right when we started. For God's sake, what do you want me to do?"

What can we do? What is there left to do? Something rational, decent, and sane. Where else can we go?

Laura is getting impatient.

"Come on boys," she shouts, "let's get started."

And so Dr Hussein, shooting sidelong glances at me, fills his syringe and gently inserts the needle into the back of Laura's hand, and fills her veins with what she craves. Laura's eyes are closed. She sighs.

"Thank you. Thank you. Give me some more tomorrow.

I'll be back. Henry take me home, and – don't even think about it – I'm not going in that fucking chair."

I walk backwards down the same corridor, Laura with her hands now locked behind my neck followed by the anxious doctor, to the door where the nurses, having gone before, help me manoeuvre her down the steps. We creep across the car park, Laura tiring now. Dr Hussein is still by our side and as we finally reach the passenger door (why did I park so far away?) he takes the keys from my jacket pocket and helps me settle her safely inside.

"What have you given her?" I ask.

He looks up at me with those kindly brown eyes and sighs, and then, spreading his hands in mute apology, whispers one chilling word. So softly spoken it is almost impossible to hear.

"Water," is all he says.

Chapter 38

Laura lays on our bed propped against a detachable frame; a syringe driver tucked under the covers whirrs intermittently, passing morphine by the minute directly into a vein in her chest. The tube is coiled and stuck to her prominent ribs with pink tape.

She cannot walk now. Cannot swallow. She is blind.

She squeezes my hand – the hand I never leave – bound to her forever by the touch of our interlocked fingers through which somehow or other she conveys, and I can understand, her every wish.

She wants to talk.

I crane my neck forward and place my ear against her dry and cracking lips. "Henry," she whispers and squeezes my hand, "is there someone else?"

"Don't be silly," I tell her, "there never has been and never will. I love you forever."

Her lips move slightly in a smile. She squeezes my hand again. Urgently. "There better fucking not be," she says and relapses into her morphine sleep, quiet, smiling and at rest.

She died at 3:35 in the early hours of Wednesday morning, her children stood around the bed, two dogs and three cats curled up at her feet, their heads turned silently towards her, as she slowly slipped away and her body finally lay cold and still.

Her boat had come home, crossed the turbulent reef, floated across the lagoon and drifted gently into the silver sand where she would lie forever.

Chapter 39

Had she gone forever? No. I think not. I felt her spirit in her house, at her table, on her bed. I brushed my hands against her jacket hanging neatly on the screen. I kissed the banister that she held so tightly struggling by herself to reach the lavatory from her bed. I touched the picture of St. Theresa, to whom she'd prayed for help. I stroked her pets. I squeezed a dead rose between my drunken fingers. I smoothed her pillow straight.

She was everywhere.

Until we meet again.

Thank God for my children. The girls took over everything. The pots were cleaned, the floors were scrubbed. I heard the constant sound of distant hoovering. I saw Laura's clothes washed (I don't know why) and neatly stacked upon our bed; her make-up and perfume set out on the dresser; her jewellery hidden away. All those invitations, documents of long dead pets, birthday cards and Christmas cards, invoices for holiday destinations, photographs, school reports, letters and bills arranged in cardboard boxes and put away somewhere.

I was a mute witness to the careful reconstruction of her life by the ordering of her things, and when consulted as to some newspaper clipping or other, or this letter, or that flyer advertising the auction where we bought our house, nodded in numb assent.

It all passed over me as I sat at our kitchen table and drank my way to sleep.

I must have looked a sorry useless figure to the funeral director when he called.

"Try to pull yourself together dad," my children told me. "Try to concentrate. This is very important." Finally, I sensed their desperation. "Come on dad. Get a grip."

I looked up at our visitor towering above me. He looked

the part. And my God, he acted the part. A tall, gaunt middle-aged man with long black straggly hair at his collar and one of those natural flashes of white hair starting from his forehead. He held his forms and brochure in his bony fingers and, moving my bottles and glass, spread them before me on our table.

"These are the caskets," he told me. "They come in chipboard, pine or elm. You can have mock brass, real brass or gunmetal. Whichever you prefer. You will find the price in small type beneath. Do not feel constrained to buy the best. Order what you like and what you feel you can afford."

A bony finger discreetly indicates a 'casket'. "This has been one of our most popular models. Understated. It has dignity. We find it 'carries well'."

What does it really matter? They are all destined to decay. But in my drunken obstinacy I want the best. Or I want the most expensive, which I presume will be the best.

"No dad. That will not do. Mother would not want that. Pick something more discreet."

I leave it to the girls. It is all too much for me.

"The church is not available for some days." The funeral director must get on. He has a job to do. "Would you like Laura to be embalmed? It is not disfiguring – we find it helps. We need to dress her. Could you select the clothes? May we have a wig and possibly a little make-up? Will she be wearing jewellery?" I cannot seem to concentrate on this.

"Will you be placing mementoes beside her? Will there be a wake? Have you decided whether or not you want a full procession or do you prefer our more modest 'limited' or even 'budget' service? Tell me what you'd like."

So many bloody questions. I can't decide. I don't want to decide.

I sit there looking at my empty glass waiting out of pride for him to leave as the girls, exchanging glances, make decisions over my head.

"And the flowers," he asks, "what do you want to do about flowers?"

Flowers? Flowers? I've seen flowers. Our house was full

218

of flowers – living lovely flowers arranged by Laura's living hands.

I've seen dying flowers, dead flowers – they're still here – huge vases full, fixed, transfixed, by a hand of delicacy and taste now dead.

The stand on tables, shelves, on top of cabinets, in corners on the floor.

Flowers? I know about flowers. Something about flowers seems to rouse me.

I want flowers. I know it's wrong. Of course it is. I should raise a forbidding hand; adopt a pious voice. 'No. No flowers thank you. Donations to charity instead. The British Heart Foundation. More accurately Cancer Research. Don't send flowers, send your donations – your hopefully generous donations – to them.'

Well I can't. What have they done for her? Drugs, drips, a knife, and death. After all that. What has it done for her? Nothing. So they can all fuck off. Don't tell me I'm selfish or self-indulgent, bitter, or daft. I don't care. I want flowers. Something to her memory; something she loved. Something to remind me of how she used to be. If you can't be selfish now when can you be? It's what I want that counts.

Or does it? What would Laura say? 'Flowers cost a fortune, drape a coffin, litter a church and die. Swept away with the garbage and the confetti. Money to cancer could save some-body's life. Somebody like me. Somebody's wife. Mother of children. Someone with a life, with grandchildren, doting on an irascible old fool, laughing, drinking, travelling, enjoying their tired old age. Why flowers? Don't waste the money. Give it to them instead.'

But I can't. And I won't. Why should I? Let someone else know what it's like. Left by yourself looking at some boring repetitive 'view' through a dusty window. No one to talk to but yourself. Nothing to touch but a cat. What do I care? They can all die for me. Probably will anyway. What's a few flowers going to cost? Is some old lunatic going to ring me up to complain? My extravagance cost him his wife. Anyway, I couldn't care less. Let the bastards die. Let someone else feel what I feel. I'm going to have them. It's what I want that counts."

I look up at his expectant face. "No. I don't think so," I stared across at my daughters. "Flowers, if nobody minds."

"Very well," he nods without debate, writing in his pad, "and have you yet decided – take your time of course – whether Laura will be cremated or interred."

The truth is, I don't know what to say again – or rather I hesitate to say it, it was Laura's wish – one she had emphatically stressed over and over again – that I was to take her ashes to India and float them down the Ganges out to sea.

I look up at the enquiring faces staring down at me. I know they are not going to like this. They are not going to believe it. They may misconstrue her wishes as my joke. The girls distressed; the boys annoyed. The funeral director will not want to go to India. Or perhaps he will. I hadn't noticed a reference to it in his brochure.

I suppose I must have looked lost and indecisive. Actually, I was seriously weighing up the odds. I know this is what Laura really wanted. On the other hand, there would be nothing left, nothing around when I wanted to be close. Nothing to cling to, nothing to commemorate her life.

I knew the answer. I heard myself say what I had decided long ago.

"Laura will be buried in London, in the Brompton Road Cemetery. She loved London, and she will be nearer for my children, and possibly my children's children." Already we drift apart. "She will be buried in London where we can all visit her and where it will be convenient . . ." Is that the right word? Should convenience come into it? "Where she will be accessible to us all."

I went to see her many times over the next few days where she was laid out in her modest coffin in the 'Chapel of Rest'. I know they had done their best, but it had not been easy. It was a testimony to her determination that she had shrunk so far before giving in. Her tiny body; her poor wasted shrunken face; those brittle stick-like arms gently folded in frozen repose across her treacherous stomach; those full-blooded almost living curls of false hair cascading down upon her shrivelled neck. She lay there, eyes closed silently waiting – deaf to the miserable piped music and the low persistent throb of the refrigeration. Where was the shrinking strand of connection between Laura, animated, warm, in life, and this still, decorous thing?

She was almost a stranger. I leaned carefully over to kiss her, as I had done thousands, possibly millions, of times before. Her cheek was as hard and as cold as ice.

But she got her crowds. The old beautiful Norman church in the centre of town was overflowing. People I had not seen for years. People I saw yesterday. People crowding in the porch and standing down the side.

At the insistence of the girls, her flowers had been laid out on the stone floor before the Altar. They were everywhere and Laura was carried in to meet them, slowly borne on the shoulders of six attendants; the funeral director, hair hanging over his gaunt white face, striding slowly behind. And as she was gently lowered to the ground, the congregation rose to sing the first hymn so carefully selected by the girls.

The organist in the loft above our heads seemed oblivious to the audience beneath. He was playing to and for himself. He rattled along somewhere up there, all alone, racing away at a pace too fast and a pitch too high to accommodate any normal voice below. Perhaps the church had a tight schedule that day. Perhaps the organist had grown too used to catering for the high falsetto of a chorister on speed. It was difficult to recognise the tune, and the singing trailed away.

One of my girls had insisted on making a speech. We had tried to stop her. Begged her not to add to the pressure. We, all of us, feared disaster. A mawkish, amateur, hesitant demonstration of affection falteringly delivered and embarrassedly received. But she would not give way and ignored our protests. She would do what she felt she had to do.

And so, with her long legs shaking, and teetering forward in borrowed shoes, she made her laborious way to the lectern and stood there silently looking out over the congregation, her face set straight ahead holding her crumpled speech in the fist of her tiny right hand.

We told her not to do it. Had begged her not to embarrass us. I had stressed over and over again how difficult – how nerve-wracking – public speaking can be, especially at her age, especially when she was so upset and especially when she had never done it before.

She was magnificent. Confident and clear. Above all, direct and simple. She described her mother. She described what her mother had been like when she had been a child growing up with her brothers and sisters in our noisy house. She described her last desperate struggles. Her courage. Her determination and her refusal to submit.

"She never complained. Never," she said, her voice ringing out. "She never gave in. I will never forget it. I will never, not for one moment, forget her. I will love her forever." She stood there still tottering in her borrowed shoes, and received, yes it really happened, a ripple of applause which – tentatively begun – eventually rolled round the pillars and down the aisle and through the porch and back again as she made her way (picking a route through the flowers) back to the safety of her pew where I waited to squeeze her hand.

And then another hymn taken at the gallop with bewildered voices struggling far behind, before the vicar rose to deliver his sermon eulogising Laura and her life.

"We are gathered here today . . . those of us who knew and loved . . . er . . . Laura to rejoice in her life and in her salvation . . . and in her . . . . er . . . memory."

He told Laura's favourite joke. I had never heard it before. He told of Laura's most embarrassing moment. Laura was never embarrassed. He told of ambitions she never had and of decisions she never made.

"And so I commend our . . . er . . . . dear Laura to the Lord."

And back to the organist on his psychedelic perch racing away to lunchtime with a Jerusalem too fast and high to be approached by any ancient feet below.

The girls had arranged that Laura should leave the church

accompanied by her favourite song. I'd never heard of it. She never had a favourite song.

How little one knows of the person with whom you spend your life.

The church said they had the very latest facilities – some music system or other – that was in place, tested, and ready to go and so as Laura was borne away, her departing music struck up and jammed into one endlessly repeating chord, over and over again. It seemed to last forever and no one had the wit to free, or, at the very least, turn off.

I turned to the funeral director outside, thankfully returned to the world of sanity. "That was terrible," I protested, "terrible. That wasn't a rehearsal. It was a disaster. A fucking disgrace." Even in such a moment I was still selfishly mindful of keeping face.

"Don't worry," he assured me, "it happens every time. Oh and by the way, another envelope from the vicar. His bill for 'little extras'. You may not have noticed the choir, apparently they were in there somewhere. They very well might have been singing. Oh. And there's something for extra flowers and the use – if that's the right word – of the sound system and the standard charge for the bells."

What's the point of arguing? To bicker over trifles at a time like this?

I reached once more for the cheque book and made out a cheque to the Holy Anglican Church which had kindly despatched poor Laura in speed if not in style. The next funeral had already started as I turned away to follow Laura's coffin.

A mournful echo of the recent past. "We are gathered here today those of us who knew and loved er. . . ."

The conveyor belt clanked on before a smaller congregation – fewer perhaps to be offended – but I had heard enough. Laura was right. I should have taken her ashes to India and trusted the Ganges swirling tide instead.

She was buried in London three days later with a touching graveside ceremony conducted by a female Irish vicar who would take no money but suggested a charitable donation instead.

It is enough to quote her final words:

May the road rise to meet you
The wind be always at your back
The sunshine warm upon your face
The rainfall soft upon your path
And, until we meet again, may God hold you in the palm of his hand.

Chapter 40

Chambers could no longer afford to hold its meetings in smart hotels. Gone are those happy days of coffee and fruit juice, sharpened pencils and clean notepads, followed by prawn and smoked salmon for lunch.

Members would compete to see how much they could eat. It seemed a pity to waste it. After all it was free. But it wasn't free. Not really. Not even then. Tax deductible perhaps. Now we don't pay enough tax.

Those carefree days have disappeared down the yawning chasm of litigation. Now we know how punters feel. And, of course, there was the additional expense (not thought of at the time) of securing Jackson's replacement. What he did then, it took two to do now.

No. Those days are over. Now we meet in straightened circumstances. In chambers itself in fact. To be precise – in the upstairs recreation room where early attenders grab a chair, most of the rest sit on the pool table, and latecomers squeeze down on the floor.

Giles has set up his stall next to the kitchen sink with his papers balanced on the draining board. He looks awful. His blazer needs cleaning, his shirt pressing. Wisps of toilet paper cling to his chin where he's cut himself shaving; holding his agenda with the same trembling hands.

"Item 1. Jackson."

Where have I heard that before?

"I don't want it getting round what happened. None of us do. It won't look good. He won. We lost. Now we're paying the costs. I wish I'd paid more attention to that new contract . . ." he looked up and frowned as McIntosh lit a cigar, ". . . I was too bloody relieved to get it over. I didn't notice what those local clowns who represent us had agreed. There's a clause in his written contact – yes his written contract – that he's entitled to some negotiable tax free sum now he's retired and I have no idea, before you ask, what that is likely to be. Something about former earnings. Anyway, that's for Horace to sort out."

"Is that wise?" McIntosh pauses to look for an ashtray but changing his mind flicks a column of ash into the centre pocket. "What sort of figure are we looking at? Give us a ball park sum."

"No. Definitely not. I have no idea. It all depends whether the litigation we began against our previous solicitors turns out a success."

"And what if it isn't?"

"It goes on our contributions. As usual. Why do you bother to ask?"

Soon there'll be nothing left. I look round at their bewildered faces. Browne-Smythe puts his hand in the air. "Can I take it Giles we will not be having a farewell presentation?"

Giles shakes his weary head.

"Item 2. Letter from the Lord Chancellor. I had it here somewhere . . ." He knocks his papers into the sink. "Christ. Oh fuck it. It doesn't matter. Anyway, happier news. After a full investigation the Lord Chancellor is satisfied that we are not a bunch of racists . . . Ah. I have it here. And that McIntosh in some misguided fashion was merely trying to be funny . . . but is nonetheless concerned to find we have no ethnic representation in our membership . . . apart from McIntosh that is . . . . but that issue aside . . . which he trusts we will address, is content to close this unfortunate matter on the understanding that we accept liability for the costs.

I have had enough. As we used to say in the dim and distant past, I am going 'looking for work'. I wonder. Perhaps Humphrey or McIntosh might join me. It's miserable drinking alone.

Giles must have seen me edging towards the door.

"Item 3. Don't go Henry. This concerns you."

Christ, not that again. I don't need reminding of that. The fucking saga of Waterside Mews. More litigation. More costs. Probably my own.

"On a far happier note. I have received this letter. Christ, where is it? I had it a moment ago . . ." and peeling a sheet from his sodden wad, ". . . Ah. Here it is. An application to become a pupil in these chambers. An excellent candidate. First class honours. Top of the list. And what's more, he's an Asian. Two birds with one stone. Apparently he knows you Henry and wants you to be his pupil master. Says in his letter – I can't for the life of me understand why – he's learnt all he knows from you."

Well I knew it was coming. Sooner or later. Apparently now it was here.

Do I tell them that he's a fraudster? About how I represented him, or misrepresented him, at St. Albans and how he's served a prison sentence, still serving it in fact, and how, according to his last message from prison, he was applying for parole.

"Did he say when he might be available to start? I've got a feeling he might be otherwise engaged."

"Yes . . ." Giles squints at the letter. "Says he's got an overriding previous commitment. Reckons about another six months."

"Come on Henry," Giles persists. "You seem to know him better than anybody. What do you think? Is he a suitable candidate for membership of Whitebait Chambers? Will he fit in?"

What can I say? Have I the heart to tell them? Well actually boys and girls, he's far too smart for you. Afraid he'll leave you standing. And yes, he could fit in anywhere. That's not the problem. He's got an unfortunate flair for accounts.

I daren't tell them he's doing time for dishonesty, they'll dismiss him out of hand. But will they? You never know, they might find this rather glamorous and attractive in an odd sort of way. There's no telling with people. Particularly when in a committee. They might take him as an act of defiance; as a gesture of how sophisticated and liberal they are. Look at us! Whitebait Chambers! Taking a convict! More accurately, an ex-convict. Not for us the usual stuffy reaction. We move with the times. A little unconventional? Sure. Perverse? Possibly. But who knows. We stand for the unusual, the exciting, the bigger picture, the wider view. We stand above all things for talent. 1st in Bar Finals, you don't get much better than that. Oh yes, this is Whitebait Chambers. We only take the best.

"Will he bring in any work?" Horace Pickles and Brown-Smythe jump up together. Ah well, back on safer ground. The universal question uppermost in every barrister's mind – "Will he bring us any work? What's in it for me?"

Not, please note, is he clever or is he a good advocate, hard working, loyal and true. No. None of these. Is he conscientious? A good team player? A man with a wide range of knowledge, or possibly an expert in a novel subject that would extend the range of the service we offer. Somebody good (not too good of course – we don't want too much competition) but somebody who knows what he's about, somebody who gets on with the job.

No. When the call came Whitebait Chambers found wanting again.

"Will he bring us any work?" The question enjoys unqualified support.

I say nothing. Giles looks up expectantly. "I suppose that's what it comes down to. Come on Henry. From what you know of him. Will he bring us any work?"

Jackson was right. There comes a point in any chambers when the incompetent gain the ascendancy. Thereafter they recruit others like themselves. Whitebait Chambers had reached that turning point to extinction. Only this time they were in for a big surprise.

I savour the moment. The whole pool table awaiting my verdict. "Let me see. Let me see. Yes," a thoughtful pursing of the lips, "yes, I am sure of it. This man one way or another will bring us lots of work." I held my hand up as if to ward away a torrent of applause. "I cannot say in precisely what category of course. He is a man of many talents . . ." He most certainly is. He could be playing any role. But one way or another they could depend on it. "Yes . . ." I told them, ". . . he'll bring in lots of work."

"Excellent. Excellent," Giles reaches across his dripping papers to clap me on the back. "Just the chap we're looking for. I think we all agree." He looks around the room. Not one dissenting voice. "Carried then. At last a unanimous vote. Wonderful. Wonderful. Thank you Henry. Thank you for that comprehensive recommendation. I'm sure we're all enormously grateful to you." Applause all round. A sea of smiling faces. "Thank you Henry and well done. The right decision at last."

I looked round for the last time at their happy expectant faces. Unanimously bound at the prospect of fees.

I remembered when they voted against Jackson. Those identical cheerful smiles.

Chapter 41

Pauline had taken a few days off work, so I went to see her at her new house. She had described it over and over again. The hall, the kitchen, the lounge, the three bedrooms (one en-suite), the patio, the garden, the plants. The lovely area, the nice neighbours, the nearby shops. It took some time to find it. All these developments look the same. When I got there she was lying face down on her sunbed wearing the bottom half of a small yellow bikini.

"Glad you could call," she said, "pour yourself a glass." I sat there perched on the edge of one of those white plastic garden chairs looking down at her back. "What do you think?" she asked, not turning round. "Pretty good for a start." I thought it better not to argue, and squinting against the sun drifting behind the fence a few short feet of grass away, peered around at her choice of potted plants.

"Those flowers you described as having round leaves are called geraniums," I remarked, "and that's a cordyline not a fern."

"Who cares?" She was sipping at her gin and tonic through a straw from where it rested beneath her on the tiles. "It's all the same to me. Mr Tomkinson was as good as his word for the deposit. Let's hope he won't want it back."

I poured myself another drink and studied the groove running down the middle of her back; the way her shoulder blades awkwardly stood out at an odd angle to each other. The skin I used to touch.

"He's not too bad when you get to know him. Been very helpful of late." She got up with a snort of irritation and marched away over the grass.

"Why do they do it? Why can't they put them somewhere else?" She bent over and picked up an empty bottle that must have caught her eye resting under the fence.

"I can't lay looking at that all day." I watched her walk

back towards me, breasts swinging full and low. The sun was hurting my eyes. "Here, take it," she handed it over, "put it in your pocket with the rest."

She leant back, yawned, and stretched her arms.

Why does she do it? Is it some sort of signal? Am I misreading the signs?

"That prisoner's getting difficult." She settled face up on her sunbed. "The very important client you know? Always ringing up or writing. Driving me bloody mad. Mr Tomkinson told me not to bother. There's nothing in it for us. What do you think? Do you think I should see him one last time?"

I looked down at her body and could make out the lines at her neck, the small criss-cross furrows at the corner of her eyes. What makes her do it? All this laying out baking in the sun. A tan for days – wrinkles for life.

"Yes, I'm sure you're right," I told her. "A complete waste of time. I wouldn't bother myself."

I went to see her again the next day. She was propped up in bed with a tube in her nose. Her cold eyes glittered at me over the bandage.

"Jesus Christ, what happened?"

I could sense rather than hear her sigh.

"Pauline. For Christ's sake, what happened?"

"He beat me up. Then he raped me. Then he sodomised me. Then they pulled him off."

"For God's sake, when, how?"

She said nothing. I watched her breast rise and fall beneath the surgical gown.

"Why?"

She was talking with her eyes. An almost imperceptible shake of her head.

"How could it fucking happen?"

She breathed slowly out, another shake of her head. "Pauline, can you hear me, how could it fucking happen?"

"Ask them. Ask the Prison Officers. They were supposed to be guarding me."

"But didn't you press the button? Didn't you hit the alarm?"

"Of course I fucking did. He was fast but not that fast . . ." She paused.

I knew I hadn't got much time. They had warned me. A couple of minutes at most.

". . . and those warders were there. I know they were there . . ."

I watched her eyes. Cold as stone, not a trace of a tear.

". . . you can always tell. In their fucking fish tank. I could sense them behind the glass . . ." She paused again as the drip softly gurgled, ". . . I know. Whatever they fucking say. I know those bastards were there."

"But why?"

She said nothing.

"Pauline, why?"

She turned her head away and looked at the wall.

"Pauline. Listen to me. Why would he do it?"

She closed her eyes.

"Pauline. I don't understand. You were in prison. In a prison with fucking guards. In a secure room. Top Security. A room with a fucking alarm."

She turned her head slowly back to me. The slightest movement seemed to cause pain.

"Pauline. Why did he do it?"

She shrugged her shoulders and turned away again.

"Pauline." I was getting nowhere. "My love, how do you feel?" Perhaps I should have asked her earlier. Perhaps I shouldn't have asked at all.

"Does it hurt? Are you damaged?" The sentence trailed away. "Will you get better?" I couldn't seem to stop. "Will you be all right?"

She turned back to me.

"Will I be all right? Oh yes." That old spark of defiance. She seemed to mimic my voice. "Yes I'll be all right."

"My God. My love." I reached out to kiss her; squeeze her shoulders; put my cheek to hers. Anything. Just to comfort her. Just to comfort myself.

"Don't fucking touch me."

The nurse came in as she said it.

"I'm sorry. The doctor says it's time to go."

I left still looking at her but she wasn't looking at me. Somehow she'd turned her head and was gazing once more at the wall.

I rang Tomkinson as soon as I got back to chambers. "Why did you fucking do it? Why did you tell her to go?"

"Look I'm sorry. It's her job. It's what she fucking does."

"What? Visit dangerous prisoners. Get herself attacked." I couldn't bear to say the detail.

"Don't you think I care?" Why were we shouting at each other? "Of course I fucking do. Probably more than you. She was in a top security prison. Dogs, guards, the bloody lot. What do you want me to do?"

"I don't know. I don't know." I didn't want him to do anything. Not really. Just to leave us alone. "She's got some idea the warders were watching, I don't know if it's true."

"Yes, I know, she told me." He was talking normally again. As normal as we'd get.

"It's bollocks though. Got to be."

"She pressed the alarm." Perhaps she hadn't told him that. Only me. "She told me the alarm bell was ringing and nobody came."

"I know. I've spoken to the governor. Apparently there was some trouble in the canteen and the warders were called away. It was an emergency. That's when it happened. Would you fucking believe it? When no one was bloody there."

"Nobody." I was incredulous. "You mean they all went? Every bloody one?"

"Apparently. That's what he told me. There'll be a report. An overriding duty to protect other officers. Imperative for safety. Good for morale."

"It's bollocks. How can you leave a woman alone with someone like that?" Already we were beginning to believe them. Turning Pauline's suspicions aside.

"God knows. Staff shortages. Recruitment difficulties. Disruptive prisoners. This is not me talking, remember – it's what he told me."

"It's what they always say."

"Yeah. It's what they'll say in the report."

"Anyway, she's having another operation. Maybe one more on her face."

I knew he was going; winding up a troublesome call.

"We'll keep in touch," he continued. "I'll let you know how it goes."

When he put the phone down I thought about it. Envisaged the damage. Raped. Sodomised. Jesus Christ. Operations. Bandages to her face. And all the time the alarm bell ringing and Pauline, my poor Pauline, writhing about on the floor.

There would have to be charges. Police statements. Photographs. I winced. Medical reports. Never a fucking trial though. There could be no defence to this.

And what of Pauline? God, I loved her. How would it affect her? Her way, her life, her style. And what about her looks? I didn't want to think it, but what about her body? What about her head?

Why hadn't she let me kiss her? Why had she pushed me away? I could remember her shudder clearly. Why, for God's sake, couldn't she love me?

For a moment I hated her. I nearly thought it but I didn't. If I did it wasn't for long. Just a tiny flash; an incredible millisecond of resentment somehow bound up with love. Did I really think it? Did it pass involuntarily through a primitive part of my mind? I doubt it. Not really. How could it?

That tiny aperture opening momentarily on evil.

I wished I'd done it myself.

I went back again a few days later. I was getting used to hospitals. You don't stand in a queue. You don't hang around waiting for permission. Forget visiting hours, just walk straight through – there's no one there to say no.

Tomkinson must have had the same idea. We arrived at her door together before going in and taking up our positions at each side of her bed.

I thought she looked brighter, some of her old confidence coming back.

"Listen to this you two." She was propped up on her pillows.

"Listen to this and tell me what you think." She adjusted her glasses on the end of her nose. "Dear Miss Dawson, I have been asked by the Secretary of State to convey his sympathy and condolences concerning your recent unfortunate accident. Might I assure you that he intends to conduct the most detailed inquiry. No stone will be left unturned. The governor has already individually interviewed the particular officers on duty that day. Their trade union representative has assured the governor that at the time of this unfortunate incident officers had been called away to an overriding emergency in the canteen where knives are available and where prisoners had been threatening staff.

In spite of being temporarily undermanned, it seems that any trouble had already been successfully contained and that your officers were able to rapidly return to you.

It is a tribute to their professionalism that their swift intervention brought your unfortunate incident quickly to an end.

I am sure you would like me to extend your thanks to them.

As for the prisoner. I can assure you that the police are conducting a thorough enquiry and I expect appropriate charges to follow soon.

In the meantime, I hope that your recovery continues to progress and look forward to welcoming you back to our establishments in the very near future, with my assurance that your safety will always command our most rigorous concern. With best wishes and kind regards. The Director of Prison Services on behalf of the Secretary of State.

Pauline folded her glasses on her lap. "So what do you think?"

We sat in silence. Tomkinson was the first to speak. "Sounds like it's all your fault." He reached over and squeezed her hand. "Well, I'm not going to wait. Forget any inquiry. We know now what they're going to say. Understaffing. An overriding emergency somewhere else. You were a regular visitor who knew the procedure and signed the forms. Seemed to get on well with the prisoner. They'll hint you got too close.

Forget it. Why wait for whitewash? Sue them now. All of them. The governor, the prison authority, every single bloody officer." He was getting angry. "It's a fucking disgrace and I'll make them fucking pay."

He put his hand on her shoulder. "Don't worry, I'll get counsel's advice." He looked across at me. "Competent counsel. I'll go to London for the best. Fractured cheek, fractured jaw, internal injuries." I wondered if he knew it all. "Post traumatic stress disorder."

I doubt it. Pauline's as tough as you get. She looked at him and smiled before briefly turning to me. "Just let go of my hand a little Henry. I want to hear what Charles is trying to say."

"The trauma of surgery. Possible residual scarring. Sleep disturbance at night." He droned on and on.

So we sat there, the three of us. A happy tableau. All we needed was Barry. I kept looking at the door. For some reason I expected him to join us. Great. Just perfect. We could hold a reunion party. At our age a rubber of bridge.

"Don't concern yourself about the detail. Just leave everything to me." He reassuringly patted her hand. I'd had enough of this. It was time to slide in the stiletto.

"Bumped into Freddy yesterday. Said you act for the rapist as well." Tomkinson dropped her hand, his dark eyes glittering. "Something about a very important client. Went to his interview with the police in prison. Told him to go 'no comment' all the way."

"How dare you?" Tomkinson was incensed. "How can you? Cranmer Carter & Co. has more than one client charged with wounding – not that any of them will concern you – more than one client involved with 'sex'."

"Oh yes, I know how busy you are." I let slip the killer question. "But how many are charged with wounding Pauline? How many charged with her rape?" We both got to our feet and stood facing each other over the bed. I could see his hands working; he was finding it difficult to speak. "We don't represent him. We did represent him but after this," he gestured towards Pauline, "I'd never represent him now."

"But you do, and you know you do. You'd represent anybody whatever they've done. Whoever they've done it to. You do it for the money. It's what you bloody do."

He looked down and shook his head dumbly at Pauline. "I didn't know. I swear I didn't know."

She turned to me and back to Charles again, easing her body carefully on the bed. "Henry, he didn't know," she told me, "you know he didn't know."

Was she right? I knew now all right. I could tell by the look on his face. But it was more than that. I knew before I accused him. At the back of my mind all along. Of course I did. Some fool takes a call in the office – the police are ready to interview, the defendant's asking for you – and off goes a runner, Freddy as it happens, only doing what he's paid to do.

Of course I bloody knew. I was hoping Pauline wouldn't. That's all. It wasn't much to ask.

"Go on now. Both of you." She closed her eyes. "I don't want to hear anymore."

We left together saying nothing, but once outside stood toe to toe in the hall.

"Christ, Wallace, in front of Pauline, how could you?" He didn't seem to realise that he'd won. "You absolute cunt, you absolute fucking . . ."

I seized his arm and stopped him. It must have been my expression; the colour draining from my face.

"Charles. Charles." I clung to him. Why had I never thought of it before? Why was I calling him Charles?

"It's just hit me. Stop. Think about it. What if he's given her Aids?"

Chapter 42

Pauline had agreed to counselling. I was surprised when she told me that. Perhaps it was part of her claim. Anyway, it couldn't do much harm. She'd do all the talking.

But she wouldn't talk to me. It was impossible to be alone with her for more than a few seconds at a time. Every day I would visit – as soon as I could get out of court – but whenever I arrived, either the screens were round with the doctors and nurses privately fussing behind, or her family were listlessly sitting around fiddling with their flowers and fruit, or Tomkinson was already there leaning over and whispering in a conversation I could neither catch nor interrupt however hard I tried.

In fact Tomkinson was always there. He seemed to have deserted Cranmer Carter & Co. Perhaps as the senior partner he could pick and choose his own hours, and as a solicitor of course he didn't have to go to court to get paid.

I got the impression, as I dolefully looked on, that he was bringing his work to her bedside. And of course, quite apart from the everyday cases of a criminal firm, they now had Pauline's claim to draft; Tomkinson's response to both the police and the Law Society in the Grantham affair to consider; and other matters that seemed so intimate I got the impression that my presence was somehow resented and I was becoming a luxury they could no longer afford.

I grudgingly came to admire Tomkinson. He was a better man than I thought. He had stood by Freddy in his troubles. Now he was showing the same loyalty to Pauline and was forever by her side, even on one occasion, as I resentfully noticed, being allowed to be present with the doctor behind the screen whilst I was kept waiting and hanging around outside.

If only he'd leave us both alone, even just for a while, there's so much I would like to say. Not to criticise of course; anyone can make mistakes. I'm sure she was only doing her duty and trying in her conscientious way to do her best for a difficult client that in his blind quest for publicity Tomkinson had deemed to be, and eventually entitled, 'very important' and deserving of her best.

She ought to sue the bloody firm of Cranmer Carter & Co. They gave her the case, probably pushed her into it even, demanded constant visiting and let her go alone. Why not sue those bastards, at least we know they're insured.

If only she'd listened to me. Well she couldn't really, come to think of it, because I didn't know. I was too busy in St. Albans and too shattered by my appalling loss. If only she'd told me, I know I could have seen the warning signs, and put her on her guard and advised her about getting too close to punters, particularly when she knew, or should have been told, they were dangerously criminally insane.

If only she had taken me into her confidence instead of relying upon her own instincts and the selfish counsel of her firm.

If only she had rang me up, asked my advice, told me the whole story, I know I could have seen where this was going, where in effect it could only go – I don't pretend I could have predicted an event as calamitous as this – but I would have sensed the general direction, I know, of letting a beautiful woman get too close to a man like that. A psychopath. In and out of solitary. No medical treatment. No visitors. No hope of parole. And as I learned later, Pauline comes tripping in from the outside world, bright and breezy, to give him some really bad news.

No, your appeal is not going well. In fact, it's been turned down. I thought they wrote to you. I thought you already knew. And no. Not really. Your MP is not very bothered. I suppose he can't see too many votes. Yes, I have tried other counsel. Afraid they want paying up front.

European Court of Justice? Sorry. No. Made enquiries. No possible chance of success.

If only she hadn't left me – it would never have come to this.

It was while Giles and I were sharing a drink together, the only customers in the Stag at Bay after a particularly wearying and fruitless day, that the idea came to me.

"Given that Pauline's beauty was now impaired, given that her enthusiastic participation in the act of love (with me at least) was non-existent, given that she may be forever psychologically damaged, given that her marvellous skipping run was very likely a thing of the past – I ran through each item with the silent Giles – given, most importantly of all, that she very likely now had Aids . . ." I put down my glass.

"Giles," I cried. "I will marry her. I will provide for her. I will care for her. I can nurse her back to health. I can give her the confidence to get better . . ." I took a long drink. I was proud of myself. "What a gesture. What a fantastic gesture. It shows that whatever has happened in the past, and what terrible ordeals may lie ahead . . ." I was becoming excited, exhilarated even. "Whether or not she has Aids – I don't care – I will stick by her, and show the depth of my love and my disregard – my total absolute and complete disregard – for all injuries and diseases, I will marry her! Yes marry her! What do you think?"

I clapped him on the shoulder. "What do you bloody well think?" Giles looked at me as if I were mad.

"Oh yes. Oh yes," he repeated sadly and took a long pull at his Chardonnay. "Oh yes Henry old boy. That is if she'll marry you."

It was my turn to look at Giles. He must have taken leave of his senses. Since Jackson had gone, his work was trickling back and I had had to give up one of my pigeonholes, but the worry of having to look after Whitebait Chambers and the multiplicity of problems, not to mention law suits (actual and pending) must have slowly driven him mad.

"Don't be a fool Giles," I told him sternly. "Sometimes you talk absolute bloody rubbish. Best to get off home and have a good night's rest."

And I was off. Out of the Stag at Bay with a song in my heart, and as I raced away, my feet flying over the wet cobbles in the general direction of the hospital where Pauline lay waiting and totally unsuspecting of the amazing proposal I would make, I resolved to do it now – to do it tonight and propose at her bedside; what a romantic selfless thing to propose across the drips and bandages to the woman I loved regardless of her injuries, regardless of her troubled past.

Talk about in sickness and in health.

I shot through the front door of the hospital and up the stairs two at a time, bursting through the door of her room I was disappointed, but upon reflection not surprised, to see Tomkinson already there.

As ever, he was leaning over the prostate figure of Pauline, whispering. Always bloody whispering.

But I had great news. I would bloody well show him. I strode purposefully to the bed and stood at the other side looking at Pauline and waved Tomkinson away before he could interrupt.

"Pauline," I announced, "I've got something to tell you my dear. It simply can't wait. What I want to say, my love . . ." but my words trailed away. Pauline held up her hand. I could not miss the glittering ring on her finger.

"Henry. You are the first to know. Charles has just proposed."

She turned her hand to show me the diamonds. "We're going to be married as soon as I'm well."

Chapter 43

What do you do? What do you say? Where do you go?

I am now completely alone. Well, not quite alone. The barmaid is polishing some glasses. She looks over the bar at where I am seated at my usual table next to the fire in the back room of the only place that is still warm and carries some memories of happier times.

Laura has gone. Pauline has gone. So has Jackson. Chambers is moving beyond me.

I look through the bottom of my empty glass at the grain of the old oak table.

Enjoy what you have whilst you have it. Nothing lasts forever. Order another drink. Remember the good times. Don't try and look over the horizon. There is nothing left to see but the bad.

I remember, was it only yesterday, the time when the roof finally fell in. When my little fantasy world finally imploded. What do you do? What do you say? What can you say?

"Congratulations," was all I could think of.

Recommended Reading

If you enjoyed reading *Pleading Guilty* there are other books on our list, which should appeal to you. If you like books with anarchic humour and that satirise political correctness we recommend:

Androids from Milk – Eugen Egner
When the Whistle Blows – Jack Allen
The Black Cauldron – William Heinesen
The Lost Musicians – William Heinesen
The Staff Room – Markus Orths
Letters Back from Ancient China – Herbert Rosendorfer

If you enjoyed the emotional intensity and the gritty realism of raw emotions that characterise parts of *Pleading Guilty* we recommend the novels of Sylvie Germain and Yuri Buida, in particular:

The Zero Train – Yuri Buida
The Book of Nights – Sylvie Germain
Days of Anger – Sylvie Germain
Night of Amber – Sylvie Germain
The Medusa Child – Sylvie Germain

These can be bought from your local bookshop or online from amazon.co.uk or direct from Dedalus, either online or by post. Please write to **Cash Sales, Dedalus Limited, 24–26, St Judith's Lane, Sawtry, Cambs, PE28 5XE**. For further details of the Dedalus list please go to our website www.dedalusbooks.com or write to us for a catalogue

Contemporary English Language Fiction from Dedalus

Dedalus first list on 30 November 1983 consisted of three first novels and we remain committed to finding new authors and developing our contemporary English Language fiction list.

Titles available include:

When the Whistle Blows – Allen £8.99
The Double Life of Daniel Glick – Caldera £7.99
D'Alembert's Principle – Crumey £7.99
Music, in a Foreign Language – Crumey £7.99
Pfitz – Crumey £7.99
The Acts of the Apostates – Farrington £6.99
The Revenants – Farrington £7.99
Pleading Guilty – Genney £9.99
The Cat – Gray £6.99
The Political Map of the Heart – Gray £7.99
False Ambassadors – Harris £8.99
Memoirs of a Byzantine Eunuch – Harris £8.99
Theodore – Harris £8.99
The Dream Maker – Haugaard £7.99
Gabriel's Bureau – Haugaard £7.99
The Arabian Nightmare – Irwin £6.99
Exquisite Corpse – Irwin £6.99
The Limits of Vision – Irwin £5.99
The Mysteries of Algiers – Irwin £6.99
Prayer-Cushions of the Flesh – Irwin £6.99
Satan Wants Me – Irwin £7.99
Primordial Soup – Leunens £7.99
Faster Than Light – Lucas £8.99
A Box of Dreams – Madsen £8.99
Memoirs of a Gnostic Dwarf – Madsen £8.99
The Confessions of a Flesh-Eater – Madsen £7.99
A Bit Of A Marriage – Mellinger £9.99
Defying Reality – Mellinger £9.99
Citizen One – Oakes £9.99
Dragon's Eye – Oakes £9.99
Zaire – Smart £8.99
Bad to the Bone – Waddington £7.99

Contemporary European Fiction from Dedalus

Dedalus began its European Classics List in 1984 with the D. H. Lawrence's translations of 2 books by Giovanni Verga. In 1992 to celebrate the Single Market of the European Union as a cultural event Dedalus began translating contemporary European fiction.

Titles available include:

The Land of Darkness – Arsand £8.99
Helena – Ayesta £6.99
The Experience of the Night – Béalu £8.99
The Prussian Bride – Buida £9.99
The Zero Train – Buida £6.99
An Afternoon with Rock Hudson – Deambrosis £6.99
Milagrosa – Deambrosis £8.99
Androids from Milk – Egner £7.99
Alfanhui – Ferlosio £8.99
The River – Ferlosio £9.99
The Man in Flames – Filippini £10.99
The Book of Nights – Germain £8.99
The Book of Tobias – Germain £7.99
Infinite Possibilities – Germain £8.99
Invitation to a Journey – Germain £7.99
Magnus – Germain £9.99
The Medusa Child – Germain £8.99
Night of Amber – Germain £8.99
The Song of False Lovers – Germain £8.99
The Black Cauldron – Heinesen £8.99
The Lost Musicians – Heinesen £9.99
Alice, the Sausage – Jabès £6.99
The Great Bagarozy – Krausser £7.99
Lobster – Lecasble £6.99
Portrait of Englishman in his Chateau – Mandiargues £7.99
Mr Dick or The Tenth Book – Ohl £9.99
The Staff Room – Orths £6.99
On the Run – Prinz £6.99
Enigma – Rezvani £8.99
Letters Back to Ancient China – Rosendorfer £6.99

When the Whistle Blows – Jack **Allen**

"Caleb Duck, a burnt-out inner city comprehensive teacher of 'integrated studies', marks off the days by sticking bogeys to the classroom radiator. At war against the national curriculum and his officious Head, Duck watches as the school descends into an anarchy of sex, drugs and cannibalism. Allen's bitter black comedy will strike a chord with disaffected pedagogues everywhere."

Andrew Crumey in Scotland on Sunday

"He is often crisply funny in the style of Tom Sharpe and has created a smattering of excellent characters such as Errol. The missives, forms and questionnaires which appear throughout the book add a touch of authenticity, and there are some majestic scenes such as the one in which the inspectors arrive to find 'garlands of flowers placed around their necks by scantily dressed maidens.' Although the tone is surreal, it is clear that events in the book are rooted in real crises in school. . . . If you need an uplifting read to relieve the pressure of the job, then this tale should come with a health warning. If, however, you're in the mood for a journey inside the warped mind of a burnt-out teacher-soldier, and enjoy acerbic humour and caustic observation, then this comes highly recommended."

Jonny Zucker in The Times Educational Supplement

"Fictional teachers tend to be on the saintly side. So it's refreshing to get one who doesn't give a toss."

The Big Issue

£8.99   ISBN 978 1 87392 79 1   265p   B. Format

The Zero Train – Yuri Buida

"It's a brutally powerful book, set in a landscape of railway track and sidings that could have been postulated by Beckett, but shot through with grotesque, surreal lyricism. 'All the women he'd ever known had smelt of cabbage. Boiled cabbage. Every single one.' Except Fira. He saw her naked once, washing, 'her heart and its bird-like beat, the gauzy foam of her lungs and her smoky liver, the silver bell of her bladder and the fragile bluish bones floating in the pink jelly of her flesh.' A sensational novel, moving, unforgettable."
> *Brian Case in Time Out*

"*The Zero Train* is the most remarkable book I've read this year. It has been hugely successful in Russia, and was short-listed for the Russian Booker prize. This chilling, brilliant and deeply moving novel goes to the heart of what Stalinism did to individual lives."
> *Helen Dunmore in The Observer Books of the Year*

"*The Zero Train* is a beautiful moving novel, charting the unfortunate life of Ivan Ardabyev whose sole purpose of his existence is to ensure the spooky Zero Train runs smoothly and on time through the station each day. Others around him lose their minds such is the isolation and fear of exactly what the high security trains really contain. Some are convinced that they hear screams, the darkest moment being when one girl throws herself under the oncoming train thinking she can hear her missing mother's cries. Ivan, on the other hand, fears what will become of him if the train stops one day. He rejects leaving the station for a better place, stupidly hanging on to this empty existence. Being an unwanted orphan and a nomad in his life, it appears the Zero Train is the only constant reliable presence Ivan has ever experienced. When eventually the train does stop, Ivan's mind begins to unravel as his entire world comes to an abrupt end at his own weak hands. A shortlisted entry for the Russian Booker Prize and a powerful read."
> *JP in The Crack*

£6.99   ISBN 978 1 903517 52 9   137p   B. Format

The Book of Nights – **Sylvie Germain**

The winner of 5 literary prizes in France and The TLS Scott Moncrieff French Translation Prize in the UK.

"A big, somewhat unusual novel, which certainly possesses striking qualities – qualities not easy to visualise coming from the pen of an English-speaking author. Christine Donougher has given us a translation possessing remarkable consistency and smoothness of tone, while her pages reflect in English much of the ampleur, the ripeness, the overflowing lyricism, of the text by Sylvie Germain, with its scenes of elemental passions and unexpected atavisms."
The TLS Scott Moncrieff Translation Prize Jury

"*The Book of Nights* is a masterpiece. Germain is endowed with extraordinary narrative and descriptive abilities . . . She excels in portraits of emotional intensity and the gritty realism of raw emotions gives the novel its unique power."
Ziauddin Sardar in The Independent

"The novel tells the story of the Peniel family in the desolate wetlands of Flanders, across which the German invaders pour three times – 1870, 1914 and 1940 – in less than a century. It is hard to avoid thinking of *A Hundred Years of Solitude* but the comparison does no disservice to Germain's novel, so powerful is it. A brilliant book, excellently translated."
Mike Petty in The Literary Review

"This is a lyrical attempt to blend magic realism with la France profonde, the desolate peasant regions that remain mired in myth and folklore. Nothing is too grotesque for Germain's eldritch imagination: batrachian women, loving werewolves, necklaces of tears and corpses that meta-morphose into dolls all combine to produce a visionary fusion of the pagan and the mystical."
Elizabeth Young in The New Statesman's Books of the Year

£8.99   **ISBN 978 1 873982 00 6**   278p   **B. Format**

Night of Amber – **Sylvie Germain**

"There is little that can be said that would do justice to the controlled brilliance of Sylvie Germain's writings – *Night of Amber* is a fantastic book, a wildly inventive novel about childhood, death, war and much else. It creates a rich fantasy world, yet it is also very moving, and deals with the emotions of grief and love with an understanding and insight which few writers can match."

Edward Platt in The Sunday Times

"Germain's sequel to her prize-winning first novel, *The Book of Nights*, follows her anti-hero Charles-Victor Peniel on his hate-filled journey through life. It sings with a strange poetry, pitting politics (the Algerian war and May '68) against the vagaries of individual minds."

Ian Critchley in The Daily Telegraph

"*The Book of Nights* and *Night of Amber* cover a century in the life of a peasant family, the Penniels. Germain describes, with great compassion, the suffering of rural people subject to wartime invasion, and twists this together with fairytale components such as wolves and angels. Dead wives turn into dolls. The hero wears a necklace of shed tears. There is nothing twee or fanciful about all this, the tone is elegiac, sombre. The beautiful images are not decorative but express psychological truths."

Michele Roberts in Mslexia

£8.99   **ISBN 978 1 873982 95 2**   339p   **B. Format**

Days of Anger – **Sylvie Germain**

Winner of the Prix Femina

"It reads like Thomas Hardy rewritten by some hectic surrealist and it plants in its rural glades a medieval vitality."
Robert Winder in The Independent

"A murdered woman, lying buried in the forests of the Morvan, is the still beating heart of *Days of Anger*. A rich, eventful saga of blood, angels, obsession and revenge, this marvellous novel is a compulsive, magical read, passionate and spell binding."
James Friel in Time Out

"Fans of Angela Carter will relish the latest Gothic romance from her French near equivalent, Sylvie Germain."
Boyd Tonkin in The New Statesman

"Germain's creations are strong such as Hubert Cordebugler, the despised village knicker-thief who recycles lingerie in his secret love-chamber, and Fat Ginnie, a voluptuous, towering sherry trifle of a woman who gives birth to a strapping son every Feast of Assumption. An icon for women of substance everywhere."
Geraldine Brennan in The Observer

£8.99   **ISBN 978 1 873982 65 5**   238p   **B. Format**

The Medusa Child – Sylvie Germain

"Sylvie Germain's *The Medusa Child* beautifully translated from the French by Liz Nash, tells a heartbreaking and violent story about sin and redemption in fantastical language; a myth from la France profonde."

Books of the Year in The Independent on Sunday

"The ascetic sex scenes between the eight year old and the 'blond ogre', and omnipresent sense of sin and salvation, show what a good writer Germain can be."

Carole Morin in The New Statesman

"Germain's language is redolent with decay, rich with religious torment and ecstasy, and filled with the decadence so loved by this publisher."

Time Out

"*The Medusa Child* is her most accessible novel, and my favourite. A coherent pattern of metaphor depicts an enchanted country childhood. Lucie explores the marshes around her home and studies the stars. But when she is given a room of her own, an ogre starts to pay her nocturnal visits. Helpless and alone, Lucie decides to fight back by turning herself into a monster. This is a superb and compassionate study of damage and resistance."

Michele Roberts in Mslexia

£8.99   ISBN 978 1 873982 31 0   247p   B. Format